KT-167-714

00401211290

THE
PHOTOGRAPHER

THE
PHOTOGRAPHER

MARY DIXIE CARTER

HODDER &
STOUGHTON

First published in Great Britain in 2021 by Hodder & Stoughton
An Hachette UK company

1

Copyright © Mary Dixie Carter 2021

A CIP catalogue record for this title is available from the British Library

Hardback ISBN 978 1 529 35091 3
Trade Paperback ISBN 978 1 529 35092 0
eBook ISBN 978 1 529 35093 7

Typeset in Minion Pro

Printed and bound in Great Britain by Clays Ltd, Elcograf S.p.A.

Hodder & Stoughton policy is to use papers that are natural, renewable
and recyclable products and made from wood grown in sustainable forests.
The logging and manufacturing processes are expected to conform to the
environmental regulations of the country of origin.

Hodder & Stoughton Ltd
Carmelite House
50 Victoria Embankment

For Steve

THE
PHOTOGRAPHER

CHAPTER ONE

I caught a glimpse of Amelia Straub through the front entry glass. Then the door swung open, and I stepped inside.

"Delta, darling!" Her large brown eyes landed on me with commitment. "I'm so grateful you made it here in this"—she gestured dramatically in the direction of the storm outside—"this tempest."

We'd only just met, but the warmth in her voice was that of a close friend. She assumed the best about me. If she had a test, I'd passed it.

Behind her, a floating sculptural staircase, seemingly lit from above, with glass balustrades and bronze railings, ascended dramatically from the stair hall. A wide passage extended the length of the house so that even from the front door, I could see a sparkling kitchen in the back, and three sets of floor-to-ceiling glass-and-steel bifold doors that opened up to a deck and backyard. I'd found before-and-after pictures of the house online—a Greek Revival brownstone in Boerum Hill with an understated façade and an interior that Amelia and her husband, Fritz, had designed and transformed. But the photos hardly did it justice. Casting my eyes about the house was like viewing a series of paintings, one more striking than the next. In and of itself, the staircase was a work of art, and seen in the context of the home as a whole, it surpassed itself.

Amelia hung my coat in a pristine hall closet next to a sleek purple down Moncler. (I knew the price of that coat: more than two thousand.) Her long, slender arms danced gracefully around her body while she told me, in the most effusive terms, how much she admired my work.

She led me to the rear of the house, where a group of well-dressed tween girls sat at a long farmhouse table, in front of more than a dozen plastic containers of beads and chains. I recognized eleven-year-old Natalie Straub in that group because she vaguely resembled her mother. The planes of her face, skin tone, posture, hair texture and quality. These are the things that I notice. When photographing anyone who has a weakness in one of these areas, I compensate with lighting and angles. Natalie did not have a weakness, per se, but neither did she have a particular strength.

She was a tall girl who held her arms tightly to her sides, as if she didn't feel comfortable taking up too much space. In an otherwise bland appearance, I was relieved to see she had sharp gray eyes. Try photographing a moron. It's next to impossible. What I'm always looking for is the sparkle in the eyes. The curiosity. If the subject of my photograph is not thinking or doing anything, the photograph comes out blank.

A small girl on Natalie's right repeatedly swung her red hair over her shoulder, one way and then the other. I overheard bits of the girls' conversation, mostly having to do with their recent Thanksgiving break. "Montauk," one girl said. "Insane traffic."

Natalie had an oval face, fair almost translucent skin, and nondescript dirty-blond hair. I could predict that her mother would take her to a colorist when she turned thirteen, or maybe even sooner. Most of the mothers I met touted their daughters' academic success, sports, music, art, what have you. They didn't think it seemly to brag on their daughters' looks. Not to say that it didn't matter to them. They were hardwired to want pretty daughters. They really couldn't help it.

I'd been working as a family photographer for almost a decade. I'd started off assisting on weddings, but my talent and skill in capturing children was impossible to ignore. People want me to photograph their children because in one photograph, I'm able to give them the life they want to believe they already have. In most cases, they don't and they won't. But my photographs tell them the story they long for.

In the kitchen, white gleaming marble countertops and a white backsplash contrasted with the dark wood accents on the cabinetry and a suspended glass cabinet hung from the high ceiling. A handsome man, whom I presumed to be Fritz Straub, opened the fridge and took out two beers. He offered the second beer to a younger man with dark hair, perhaps a junior colleague, based on their body language.

I pulled my camera out and shot a few photos of Fritz. In order to take good photos of anyone, I need to believe in that person's beauty. If I can't see it, then the camera won't see it. And no one else will be able to see it either. My subjects are always beautiful in my eyes. If they don't start out that way, I force my brain into contortions in order to see it that way. In Fritz's case, I didn't have to talk myself into believing he was handsome. He had sandy hair, a strong jaw, and green eyes so intense that they blazed through his glasses.

At one moment, he appeared to be sharing some sensitive information. He lowered his voice and turned his body away from the room. He looked over his shoulder, repeatedly, to make sure no one was within earshot. I probably could have stood close enough to hear the conversation. For many people, I'm invisible, the same way a servant is. I'm performing a function, and they don't take in the degree to which I see and hear what they say and do. That inconspicuousness usually benefits me. Years ago I felt slighted in these instances, but over time I've grown to appreciate them.

Several minutes later, when Fritz became aware of my presence, I turned and walked from the dramatically high-ceilinged great room, which extended the width of the house in back, through the media room and entered the library at the front of the house, where Amelia was seated in front of a roaring fire, holding court amid a group of four girls. She shone down on them like the sun. In my experience, eleven-year-old children are rarely drawn to the adults in the room. They are usually drawn to each other. But Amelia had such a powerful presence that the standard rules didn't apply to her. It was practically impossible not to pay attention to her performance, partly because she seemed to expect that everyone would.

"Ingrid, we're so proud of you." Amelia spoke in a lilting voice. "Natalie told us about your tennis championship."

Ingrid's face colored and she giggled.

Amelia placed her fingers lightly on the child's face and brushed the hair away from her eyes. "The semifinals? What an accomplishment."

Objectively speaking, I was more attractive than Amelia was. I had larger breasts, a smaller waist, and fewer lines in my face. I was certainly younger, by ten years at least. Amelia had chiseled cheekbones and deep-set eyes. Overall, her features were a little sharp, but striking nonetheless, and she had remarkable magnetism—the kind of person to whom men and women alike gravitate.

A wall of bookshelves at one end of the library stood in contrast to the pristine furniture, glistening glass everywhere—a room that didn't suggest the presence of a child. Natalie appeared to have self-control and restraint beyond her years, so I gathered that she didn't pose a threat to the breakable objects in the room, nor did they pose a threat to her, at least not now. Perhaps she had learned the hard way.

I wouldn't have been able to blend into the crowd so well if it weren't for my affluent high school boyfriend, son of an Orlando lawyer, whom I'd dated for three years. I had the luxury of time in which to study his parents, his sister, and him, individually and collectively. Even at fifteen, it was obvious to me that you need to immerse yourself in the lifestyle if you want to fit in, if you want people to believe that you belong to their world. It's a matter of osmosis. It turned out my boyfriend was a prick. He pulled a knife on me once. When I explained the nuances of the situation to his parents, they got me a full ride to the University of West Florida. It was the least they could do. If they wanted gratitude, they should have gotten me into Yale.

My talent as a photographer is multidimensional. I'm a documentarian when called upon to be that. Of course, I can disappear into the woodwork and capture the interactions that naturally occur at a gathering among family and friends, but that sort of photography often leaves me unsatisfied. I like to *create* the moments. I see myself as a director.

I reappeared in the dining area with my camera out several minutes later, followed by Itzhak, the Straubs' aged bloodhound, who wandered in and among the girls, eventually sidling up to Natalie. Absentmindedly, she scratched him behind his ears.

I began with discretion, as the documentarian. From twenty feet away I snapped photos of the girls. Natalie held herself in reserve much of the time. The others were presumably her friends, but she didn't seem to trust their friendship. Amelia might have misjudged how long they would spend on jewelry-making, because most of them finished their projects relatively quickly and soon looked bored. Natalie appeared self-conscious, as if she felt responsible for entertaining the girls.

Over the years I'd learned that the children needed to be in a good mood, or the photos would fail. I'd come up with ways to save unsuccessful parties and had become particularly adept at party tricks, such as balloon animals and face painting. I always came equipped with a dual-action hand pump, balloons, face paint, brushes, stencils. Once in a while I chose to pull out some of my supplies. Only when I sensed a party going off the rails. Surprisingly, even so-called sophisticated children, as old as thirteen, found such things delightful. Balloons especially. They usually elicited gestures and facial expressions that suggested innocence and joy. In New York City, many children lost that early on. Jaded children made very poor photo subjects. Balloons gave me the best chance of capturing something that looked like happiness.

Natalie said yes to the balloon animals. Responding to her friends' requests, I made a unicorn, a giraffe, a cougar, a castle, a yacht, and a helicopter.

The balloons worked. I got the shots of Natalie and her friends that I needed—faces illuminated, energized, in medias res. Even the most constrained and constraining parents craved images of their children diving headfirst into the world without fear or inhibitions, living, experiencing. What they, themselves, had wanted to do but couldn't. Most of the time my raw material turned out well. And if all else failed, of course I could photoshop.

•   •   •

Toward the end of the party, Fritz gathered the girls around the dining table and Amelia brought out a large birthday cake, shaped and decorated like a cello and bow. Eyes on her daughter, Amelia beamed as she placed the cake in front of Natalie and knelt on the floor next to her daughter's chair. Amelia's posture, her tilted head, her soft smile, were intended to convey extreme devotion to her daughter. Not that I considered her disingenuous. But I gathered that loving her daughter in front of witnesses helped cement a necessary self-image.

The assembled girls sang to Natalie, crowding in to get a better look at the cake. And then Natalie blew out the candles. These are the most important shots: the cake, the song, blowing out the candles. If you miss them, there is no way to make up for it. They aren't going to happen twice. No other moments of the party come close to those in magnitude and weight.

Ideally, I need to capture both parents with their child when the cake is presented. The parents rarely acknowledge it, but they want to see themselves as much as they want to see their children.

They want to see themselves being good parents. They want proof. That is what I provide.

Fritz sliced the cake and handed it out to the little she-wolves. Then, like clockwork, the parents showed up and most of the children disappeared within ten minutes, except for a few stragglers.

I packed my camera case, found my coat, and was getting ready to follow, but Natalie stood in the front doorway and blocked me. "Delta! You said you'd make a balloon *elephant*! That's my favorite animal!"

"Sorry, Natalie." If I were to stay later than we'd agreed, I'd be devaluing myself and my time. And I'd also risk being viewed as intrusive. In the past, I'd occasionally made the mistake of allowing myself to become friendly with a client, and it hadn't always ended well. But something about this family and this house was difficult to resist. The edifice itself, the rooms, the people. Every aspect of it beckoned to me.

"Please!" Natalie's wide eyes locked with mine.

I yielded and returned to the dining area to make an elephant and a few more balloon shapes for Natalie and her remaining friends. In my peripheral vision, I could see Amelia and Fritz continuing to socialize. Fritz shook hands with the man he had been speaking to earlier and clapped him on the shoulder affectionately. "See ya, Ian."

One by one, Natalie's guests left, except for a precocious-looking girl named Piper, who disappeared upstairs with Natalie following her. Though it was Natalie's house, Piper looked to be calling the shots.

When Amelia and Fritz noticed me, they appeared pleased and asked me to stay for a glass of wine. The invitation was precisely what I'd been hoping for.

In the front library, Fritz placed his glass of pinot noir on the sharp-cornered glass coffee table. "You've got a natural facility with kids. It's impressive." His green eyes—distractingly green—flashed at me through square tortoiseshell glasses. "Do you ever get tired?"

"It's peaceful, really, spending time with them." I noticed my nails on my wineglass and regretted my failure to get a manicure earlier that week. I imagined that a manicurist showed up at the Straub home weekly, and Amelia made business calls while an underpaid Filipino girl filed her nails.

"Do you have any of your own?" Amelia was seated next to Fritz on one of two cream-colored midcentury sofas. She leaned her back against the sofa's arm and hugged her knees to her chest. The casual pose—faintly at odds with her feline comportment—was evidently designed to cast herself as a down-to-earth mom chatting with a girlfriend.

Itzhak whimpered at the sound of the wind outside and placed his wet muzzle on the sofa next to Amelia. Occasionally I could hear Piper's voice from upstairs, but couldn't make out any words.

My fingers made slight indentations in the arms of a buttery leather chair. "One son."

"How old?" she asked, as if the answer meant a great deal to her.

"Five," I said. "Jasper's in California with his father. In Malibu. We recently divorced."

"I'm so sorry to hear that." Amelia placed her hand on her heart in a gesture of sympathy.

"For the last two years of our marriage, Robert was having an affair."

"So sorry," Fritz said, but he didn't appear terribly disturbed by the idea of an extramarital affair.

I took my cell phone out of my purse and opened my Favorites folder.

"This is Jasper." I held up the phone so they could see the picture. "And here I am with Robert."

"Why is Jasper in California?" Amelia's desire for information was part and parcel of her sense of entitlement. It didn't occur to her that any of her questions might be rude.

"His father got a job there. Robert hasn't spent much time with Jasper recently because of his long hours. His new job gives him some flexibility. He asked if he could take Jasper for two months, and I said yes, but now I'm regretting it." My voice sounded thin and reedy in my ears, as though it were disconnected from my diaphragm and my body. "Last week I flew there to visit him."

"You must miss him." Amelia frowned, and I became aware of the lines in her forehead and between her eyebrows.

The long smooth finish of the 2002 pinot noir lingered in my mouth, quite different from the malbec that I'd been drinking the night before. "Of course I do."

Fritz leaned his body in my direction, his knee barely grazing mine, perhaps intentionally so. Amelia scratched Itzhak's head. Neither one of them spoke. I felt obligated to fill the silence.

"In my line of work, I spend a lot of time with children. But I miss the quiet times. Reading bedtime stories. Doing puzzles together. I miss those simple activities that are so important."

Amelia's cell phone registered a new text. "Lauren canceled for tonight," she said to Fritz. "She has a fever."

"I'm sure it's not a date or an audition." Fritz spoke with thinly veiled sarcasm.

"And Avery's out of town." Amelia turned to me. "We have a client dinner tonight and our babysitter canceled." She checked the time on her phone and laughed sharply. "We're never going to find someone else."

"Oh God." I felt a wave of disappointment, disproportionate to the situation, an aching sensation in my chest when I recognized that I would probably be leaving the house shortly, but accompanying that, I saw a glimmer of possibility. "Can I help in some way?" I said.

"We're supposed to leave in half an hour." Amelia was pacing the room, looking through the contacts on her phone.

"Look, Amelia," I said, "if it's really important, I can stay."

Amelia folded her hands in front of her face in a prayerlike pose. "Oh, Delta, you would?"

I saw Fritz's frozen face, his jaw slack, and gathered that he didn't like the idea.

"If it's an emergency," I said. "I mean . . . I don't usually babysit."

Fritz appeared to recover from his shock. He raised his eyebrows and smiled broadly, as if he now thought this was a perfect solution. "It would be really great for us. We're in a bind."

"We can't cancel the dinner," Amelia said.

Every muscle in my feet, calves, thighs, shoulders, jaw, scalp, and brow all contracted and then simultaneously released. "Yes, then. Yes."

CHAPTER TWO

━━━━━━━━━━━━━━━━━━━━━━━━

I'm usually a voyeur, not a participant. Amelia and Fritz were embracing me and including me—turning to me in a time of need, as a trusted friend.

Amelia and Fritz went upstairs to freshen up. Natalie said a perfunctory goodbye to her friend Piper at the door. Alone, without her friends around her, I found it easier to study Natalie's character and appearance. Her features were lacking in definition, except for her silver eyes, surrounded by black eyelashes.

She pointed to something resembling a braid in her relatively short hair. "Piper started it, but I really wanted a Dutch braid. Do you know how to do one?"

I examined the mass of Natalie's tangled hair. "Let's try."

Natalie led me up to the small, but impeccable, second-floor bathroom. A subtle striped wallpaper surrounded us. She picked up a thin purple hair ribbon, one of many ribbons and clips that were resting on the marble vanity. "I'd like for you to weave this in."

Dutch braids were in my repertoire, but Natalie's fine, layered hair posed a challenge. She watched me in the oversize mirror as I untangled Piper's braid, if you could call it that. Once Natalie's hair was tangle free, I started by braiding the shortest hair near the crown of her head and then I pulled a little more hair into each section each time. Most of the shorter hair tucked into the Dutch braid neatly. Where it didn't, I used a bobby pin. Apparently, it was good enough for her.

"Mom!" She ran out of the bathroom and down the hall into what I guessed was the master suite and then disappeared inside. "Look!"

"Lovely, sweetheart." I heard Amelia's voice from behind a closed door. I imagined Amelia seated at her dressing table in front of a Hollywood-style vanity mirror. Next to her on the chaise longue lay the outfit she'd chosen for the evening. "Make yourself at home, Delta," she called out. "Help yourself to anything you see."

Another tide of warmth flooded my body, similar to earlier when Amelia had asked me to babysit. What exactly was she referring to when she said "anything"? Food, wine, clothing, cosmetics, linens?

Natalie came running back out of the master bedroom toward the bathroom again. "I've got an idea! I can do *your* hair!"

I didn't love the idea of anyone braiding my hair, not even a child. "But you also . . . you might want to learn to do the hairstyle on *yourself*," I said. "It's different from doing it on someone else." I realized too late that this could not be achieved. She was young and impatient. And she didn't have the advantage of being able to see her work while she was braiding. With each new attempt, she was growing more frustrated.

Ten minutes into the lesson, Amelia and Fritz appeared in the bathroom doorway. Amelia had changed out of her jeans and into a silky purple wrap dress and low pumps. She wore red lipstick and gold hoop earrings.

"Looks like you guys are having fun." Fritz, who had also changed, adjusted his tie and the collar of his sports jacket.

"We have leftover lasagna in the fridge," Amelia said to me, then turned to Natalie. "Lights out at nine thirty, sweetheart."

Amelia and Fritz both kissed Natalie on the forehead.

Natalie stopped mid-braid, and her small amount of progress was lost. "I don't want you to go," she said to them. "It's my birthday!"

"*Tomorrow*'s your birthday." Amelia's voice was like music, the words rising and falling in pitch. "Today was your birthday party." She clicked her tongue to indicate excitement, perhaps.

Fritz high-fived Natalie. "Awesome party, dude." Seeing the disappointment in Natalie's face, he hesitated. "So . . . are we on for chocolate chip pancakes in the morning? Or should we have spinach pancakes for the birthday breakfast?"

He didn't wait for an answer. He and Amelia disappeared down the stairs and out the front door.

"You have my cell if you need anything!" Amelia called out. I heard the heavy front door close behind them.

Natalie's frustration with her braids escalated after her parents' departure. "I suck at this!"

I needed a new activity to distract her. "You know what I realized? I haven't seen your room."

She sighed loudly, like she wasn't interested in showing it to me.

"I'd love to see it," I said.

"Fine." Natalie led me to the third floor and stopped outside a closed door. "The theme of my room is unicorns. Did you know I collect unicorns?"

"No, I didn't." I wondered if the concept of a themed bedroom was prevalent and I'd somehow missed it.

I stepped inside. Numerous objects in the room reflected light, so it was hard to identify any primary light source. Indeed, I saw unicorns everywhere I looked. Little statues of unicorns lined three shelves. Several pictures of unicorns were hung on the walls, with one mural painted directly on the wall, apparently by a child.

She showed me around, explaining the provenance of each unicorn. As she did so, her mood improved. I paused in front of a rainbow unicorn on a bookshelf, because I recognized it as a

Disney souvenir. My parents had worked as janitors at Disney in Orlando, and I'd lived there for most of my childhood.

I envied her bedroom. Or maybe I envied the life that seemed to go with the bedroom. I'd seen my share of wealthy children's bedrooms—rooms that were decorated so as to appear "magical," with a few items purchased for that reason. But Amelia and Fritz were working on a much deeper level. A great deal of the magic in Natalie's room came from the lighting. It was clear that the materials and colors of the drapes, rug, furniture, walls, ceiling were all chosen to work with the lighting—to reflect it or absorb it, depending on the desired effect—and create a true feeling of otherworldliness. This child's room might as well have been an art installation, it was executed so well. To a layperson, it appeared personal, authentic, and unstudied. That was what made it so effective.

·   ·   ·

Turning the brass knobs on the Straubs' extravagant oven, grasping the substantial pulls on the smooth sliding drawers, handling the kitchen faucet, all of these actions were gratifying to my senses.

Natalie sat at the counter and watched me. I found the lasagna in the fridge. "It looks delicious. Did your mom make it?"

"My mom?" Natalie laughed sarcastically. "No."

I could tell Natalie enjoyed pointing out something her mother didn't do well.

"Does your dad cook?" The kitchen tools were all coordinated, as were their dishes and their copper pots and pans. The items hadn't been acquired over many years. It was clear that they'd been purchased all at once, and all other items had been disposed of. Amelia was obviously purposeful in deciding what she wanted to include in her life and what she wanted to exclude. I felt honored that I was being included at this time.

"Sometimes. We get some meals delivered."

The Straubs probably catered to liberal, sensitive, and socially aware clients, the kind who named family as their priority and considered the kitchen the center of the home, whether anyone cooked or not. And, naturally, their own home would reflect that sensibility. I tried to envision a typical evening in their house and felt a tinge of irritation when I thought about the kitchen sitting unused.

Natalie swiveled back and forth on the kitchen stool.

"Piper seems nice," I said.

She shrugged. "Yeah."

"But she's no hairstylist."

I was relieved to see Natalie laugh. She appeared to relax a bit.

"Did you have fun with her?" I said.

I noticed a temporary tattoo on Natalie's hand that was already disintegrating. It said, *She Inspires.*

I served her a plate of lasagna and sat on the stool next to her.

"Piper likes to tell me how much fun she has with her other friends."

"I see."

She took a bite of lasagna. "She doesn't want me to think I'm an important friend."

"Maybe she's worried *she's* not important."

Natalie paused as if considering the idea. "Maybe."

She was quiet and pensive while she ate. After dinner, I served us each a piece of cake. I rarely ate dessert, because I wanted to maintain my figure. But I needed Natalie to feel as though I was celebrating her birthday with a full heart. She ate all the icing off the outside of the cake, then the cake itself. Then she served herself a second piece of cake.

"Your mom said you're a really good cello player." I was looking for a subject that would put her in a good mood.

"She wishes I was."

I searched for a lighthearted response. "No, she really thinks you're amazing. Do you like playing the cello?"

She smiled on one side of her mouth. "I don't know what I like doing."

"Play something for me."

Natalie inhaled quickly. "Yeah . . . OK."

When she finished her cake, she found her cello in the media room and played a piece from memory. She was actually quite good.

I clapped. "Stunning!"

She held back a smile, but I could tell she was pleased by my reaction. "That was Elgar's Cello Concerto I played for my recital last week." She modestly returned her cello to its case.

"I wish I'd seen the recital."

"My parents got a video from my teacher, since they couldn't make it. I can show it to you sometime."

Later, in her bedroom, she put on her unicorn nightgown, brushed her teeth, and climbed into bed under her unicorn sheets. I kissed her forehead, exactly like her parents did when they left for the evening.

•   •   •

I ran the dishwasher, using the Straubs' organic dishwasher detergent, and wiped down the counters, leaving the kitchen with a minty smell that made me queasy. Then I fed Itzhak his organic dog food. I was bitten by a rottweiler when I was eight and ended up in the hospital, once my third-grade teacher noticed the inflamed bite marks on my arm. Since then, I've never been entirely relaxed around dogs. Itzhak was too feeble to hurt anyone, but some fears are not rational.

The wind picked up outside and the windows shook loudly. Itzhak howled at the ceiling. "Shhh." He settled back down after a few minutes. I thought about how my life compared to Itzhak's life. He'd been raised with unconditional love by people who cared about his physical and mental well-being.

When finished in the kitchen, I had the rest of the evening to myself. I was free to peruse the house without anyone looking over my shoulder. Many of my clients had indoor security cameras, but I wasn't surprised that the Straubs didn't. Cameras would interfere with the exquisite lines of their design. I walked into the library and toward the far wall of bookshelves. I looked through each shelf methodically and stopped whenever I came to a book that had been read several times. Without stepping away, I would remove the book and read a few pages, then flip through to see if anyone had written something in it. I put it back in the exact same spot.

I'd expected to find a lot of books on architecture and art, which I did: exquisite large, heavy books with thick glossy pages and saturated photos. Many cost more than a hundred dollars. They were the kinds of books most people would display on a coffee table, but the Straubs had too many to display.

I moved to the side bookshelves and found a few how-to and self-help books on the bottom shelf close to the wall. Next to them was a stack of several books with the spines facing away from the room. I picked up the stack and turned it over. They were all books about fertility. I removed one from the shelf and flipped through it. In the chapter titled "Miscarriage," several pages in a row were dog-eared. Someone had written in the margins: *blood clotting disorder, ask Metzger*. Based on a few dates in the margins, I surmised that Amelia had had four miscarriages, all of which had happened after the birth of Natalie. It was helpful information. I sensed it would serve me to learn as much as possible about this family, in case a time came when they needed my support.

In the kitchen, I opened a utility closet and found a Miele vacuum, brooms, and more cleaning supplies, arranged in perfect rows. A second door led to an inviting space I had not yet seen, apparently a home office with one entire wall of glass doors. The office opened up to a shallow deck that wrapped around the back of the house, too, and a spiral staircase led down to the backyard.

In the middle of the office, two identical midcentury desks faced each other. I identified Amelia's desk because her burgundy silk scarf lay draped over the chair, then I examined each stack of papers and folders, which were clearly labeled and held together with rubber bands. She was almost as organized as I was. Only a few Post-its with handwritten notes marred the perfectly organized work space. On one such piece of paper were the words *cello teacher* and a phone number. I picked up another piece of paper, which read *Jenny Douglas,* then a phone number, then the words *due date July 10.* I wasn't able to remember even one time that I'd focused on a pregnant woman's due date to the degree that I would actually write it down. On a third piece of paper, the words *birth mothers* were followed by three names. Perhaps the Straubs were looking to adopt. My pulse quickened.

After returning each paper to its original location, I sat down at Fritz's desk. His labeling system wasn't as consistent as Amelia's, but his handwriting had more to offer than hers did. (I'd read several books about handwriting over the years and had tested my knowledge by comparing acquaintances' handwriting with their behavior, to see if the two were aligned.) Fritz's narrow *L* loops indicated tension, probably in his marriage. Perhaps he was disappointed in his wife's inability to carry another child. The loose placement of his *i* dots led me to believe he had an extraordinary imagination. Thoughts of Fritz made my body tingle.

At ten thirty, I went up to the third floor to check on Natalie, and brought my digital Canon EOS with me. The bathroom and closet lights shone into the room and I could easily make out her face, even though my eyes were adjusting. She was sound asleep, but her hand was still clutching her stuffed unicorn. I pulled her thin cotton blanket up over her and sat down on the edge of her bed to observe her. Holding my fingers inches from her nose and mouth, I felt her warm breath.

When I look at someone through the viewfinder of my camera, I can see what lies below the surface. I studied Natalie and captured several images of her sleeping—a gift for her parents at some point, maybe. Natalie's chest moved up and down, almost imperceptibly. Her face appeared thin and fragile, as did her body. She reminded me of myself at that age. She took refuge in her imagination. Children with hyperactive imaginations are usually running away from something, escaping from something. Some children don't have imaginations because they don't need them.

I used to play a game with myself, looking for the perfect parents. Living at Disney, I had a lot of people to choose from. In due course, I found a gorgeous mother and a debonair father and named them Isabel and Peter. Isabel looked like a ballet dancer, flawless ivory skin, long neck, turned-out feet. Peter had salt-and-pepper hair and large clear eyes. Their children would surely have had all the toys, dolls, stickers, dresses that I coveted. For the next several years, whenever I was feeling inferior or depressed, I envisioned myself as their daughter. Over time, I forgot exactly how Isabel and Peter looked and how they spoke. But I held on to the idea of them—the opposite of my own demoralized parents. By the time my mother was thirty, long hours in the Florida sun had coarsened her face. "Your skin's too smooth," she'd say to me. "Get away, I can't bear to look at you."

The memory of deprivations sometimes remains dormant and you might think you are past it. But it's actually just below the surface, ready to rear its head with the slightest provocation.

Meeting the Straubs reminded me of my game, because I'd always felt certain that Isabel and Peter were architects too.

The front door opened downstairs, and I heard footsteps. A minute later I met the Straubs in the stair hall, having deposited my camera in its case on the hall bench. I sensed that they wouldn't understand why I was still taking photos. Many people don't realize that I use my camera to interpret the world around me. It's another set of eyes.

Fritz had a beet-red face and smelled of alcohol. Amelia stumbled toward me and almost fell into my arms. It appeared that she'd recently applied lipstick and had done so poorly, as I could see lipstick outside the lines of her lips, like a clown, and on her teeth. The rest of her makeup had worn off.

"*Delta Dawn, what's that flower you have on?*" She belted out the first lines of the Tanya Tucker song. "*Could it be a faded rose from days gone by?*"

Faint bells sounded in the distance. How unlikely that Amelia would know that song well enough to sing it to me. It was a sign of our strong connection. My mother had given me the first name Delta to go with my last name, Dawn—her tribute to Tanya Tucker. I wasn't proud of the name, but I couldn't separate myself from it. And Amelia singing it to me, it was like she understood all that. She understood me. She recognized me.

"Amelia thinks she can sing," Fritz said. "Too bad she didn't grow up in Nashville instead of Pittsburgh." His comment was likely meant as a joke, but came out sounding slightly hostile. Amelia didn't appear to hear him. She reached into her purse and pulled out four crisp twenty-dollar bills.

It hadn't occurred to me that she would pay me. I'd viewed myself as doing the Straubs a favor. "No, I shouldn't . . ." A familiar ache pulsed behind my sternum until I looked into Amelia's eyes, where I saw real affection. She didn't look down on me.

"Delta!" she cried, pushing the bills into my hand. "La Divina!"

CHAPTER THREE

The ringing bells slowly faded on my train ride home to Crown Heights and disappeared entirely by the time I entered my apartment. My cat, Eliza, a champagne-colored Burmese, greeted me at the door. I'd found her at a shelter in Orlando ten years earlier, right before moving to New York. She had uncommon intelligence, sensitivity, and the ability to judge character. I considered her to be my closest friend. She circled the room, then leapt up to the back of the sofa, walked across it like a gymnast, and jumped back down. After hanging my coat and placing my camera equipment in its cubby, I filled Eliza's personalized ceramic bowl (*Eliza* in a cursive font) with dry cat food and placed the bowl on the floor of my kitchen. While she was eating, I used a Swiffer to dust the bookcase, the coffee table, the small dining table, the end tables, and the kitchen counter.

My apartment faced north, into an interior courtyard. From the living room windows, I could see a sliver of sky above. Concrete dominated the courtyard below, with a few plants and flowers dotted around the perimeter, the ratio of planted to unplanted square feet being extremely low. A committee had been formed in an effort to spruce up the courtyard, but none of the penny-pinching residents in the building were willing to spend any money on it.

The five lamps in my living room provided moderate cheer at night, but during the day, they called attention to the absence of natural light and had the opposite effect. When I first moved into the apartment six years earlier, I'd painted the walls pale lavender, but had used a cheap paint. A full-spectrum paint, at three times the cost, would have reflected a broader range of light and brightened the atmosphere. As it was, the flat, low light lent the walls a muddy cast. I found it ironic that I didn't have the money to realize my artistic vision, while so many ordinary people did.

I turned on the television, then crossed to the kitchen for a glass of wine. One of my clients had recently given me a brass-and-marble wine opener as a thank-you gift. My clients often give me high-end gifts that are not in keeping with my lifestyle. (I had little storage in my apartment, and no space for luxury items.) I had stopped drinking about a year earlier, but recently, because of the exquisite wine opener, I'd started drinking again. Just a glass or two once in a while.

I opened a new bottle of malbec. The weight of the wine opener in my hand gave me immense pleasure. I looked around the apartment for an appropriate display area for an in-home bar. The lowest shelf of the bookcase, which was also the top of the built-in cabinets, would most closely approximate counter height and was the only one that had clearance for a bar display. A second idea: I could use the peninsula of my kitchen counter for the bar. Finally I landed on the most sensible answer. In my office (the smaller section of my L-shaped living room), I'd been using a rattan table with a glass top for odds and ends. In its present capacity, it was underutilized, so I moved it to the living area relatively near the entry, so you would appreciate it when you walked through the door.

Other bar-related presents from clients included: an ice ball press kit, a handblown tortoise ice bucket with gold tongs, a brass squirrel bottle opener (you use the squirrel's tail to open the bottle). I arranged the ice bucket, the tongs, and the bottle opener next to the wine opener on the rattan table (along with my set of six wine-glasses and six double old-fashioned glasses). I'd never returned any of the gift items, because I believed that one day I would have parties and entertain. One day I'd be the host, not the guest. One day, friends would linger at my home until the wee hours of the morning, having meaningful conversations. The presents would all contribute to those future gatherings.

I craved a clearly defined role. I wanted to know where to place my body, where to step, where to sit down, where to lie down. I didn't have many personal connections. The ones I had were soft with no teeth.

After changing into my most comfortable lounge outfit, silky pants and a satin camisole, I poured a glass of wine and brought it with me to the office, which was furnished with an IKEA desk and chair. On my monitor, I saw an open folder with thumbnails displayed, including the ones of Jasper and Robert that I'd shown Amelia and Fritz earlier that evening.

The prior night, I'd worked until 3 A.M. in an attempt to salvage the photos of Jasper's disastrous birthday party. In several shots, he had been yelling, his mouth wide open. It hadn't been difficult to combine the images of his small white teeth with separate images of his mouth. My Content-Aware Move Tool was useful in shifting the shape of the mouth and turning the corners up into a cheerful grin. Then I pulled the corners of his eyes and cheeks up to make crinkly laughing eyes and a variety of heartwarming smiles. I wanted at least one picture of Jasper and his father embracing, but unfortunately, I hadn't witnessed a lot of affection. So I used Puppet Warp to move their limbs into the correct position. One shot with both of Jasper's arms around his father's neck. Another one with Jasper leaning his head on his father's shoulder. And finally one with me and Jasper, my hand on his face.

Later on, just for my enjoyment, I'd layered my own image onto a photo of Robert, and adjusted my head so it appeared that I was sitting next to him and leaning my head onto his shoulder. The photo of me and Jasper unwrapping the present had posed an even greater challenge, but it actually came out quite well. I'd successfully fabricated an expression of hopeful anticipation on his face.

Before closing the folders from the night before, I set to work on one more version of Jasper—placing him at the beach in California. I felt the need to give his life more dimension. I printed an 8 x 10 of Jasper surfing, and hung the photo in my living room alcove. It was exquisite. It's amazing what you can do with visualization. All you need to do is create memories. Memories are images that we play in our minds. If I purposefully played certain images in my mind, they would become memories. In fact, if I played them often enough, they might become stronger and more vivid than "real" memories.

I only edit photos when absolutely necessary. People remember events selectively. It's a matter of self-preservation, and I don't see anything wrong with it. Who's to say that the memory I create is any less "true" than the original one?

Finished with Jasper's folder, I uploaded the photos from Natalie's party. As I scrolled through them, I could feel the tension in my shoulders dissipate. The photos of the Straubs provided me with terrific comfort. I clicked through several of Natalie and her friends and several of Natalie alone. Then I landed on one of Fritz, leaning against the library wall, laughing, his intense green eyes looking straight into the camera. It was his kindness and intelligence that made him handsome. I'd sensed those qualities in him the instant we met. I felt a tug of longing in my gut—some combination of emptiness and desire.

I pulled up some shots of myself that I'd used for my website and superimposed my body, in profile, next to an image of Fritz in profile. I moved his face close to mine, so it looked as though we were confiding in each other, in a close conversation that others couldn't hear. And then, practically feeling his breath on my face, I closed the gap between the two mouths. His warm lips pressed against mine. Then his fingers were in my hair. A frisson of surprised delight surged through my body.

My first attempt wasn't perfect. Fritz's lips and mine were puckered in an awkward and artificial way. In my second attempt, I altered the shape of Fritz's mouth in profile and the muscles around it. I brought his arm up so that his hand was caressing my face. It was an arresting photograph. I hadn't kissed a handsome man for a few months, but the photo was almost as good as the real thing. It lifted me up. Previously, I hadn't taken my photos in quite so personal a direction. Perhaps some ill-defined scruples had held me back. Or perhaps Fritz elicited a feeling in me I wasn't able to ignore.

I imagined Amelia's reaction if she were to see this picture. She would roll her eyes in an amused manner. I would laugh and say, "So ridiculous, right?"

Returning to the folder of Natalie's birthday, I clicked through the photos until I landed on one of Amelia embracing the mother of one of Natalie's friends. It was clear from the nature of the embrace that the women were peers and that their relationship was one of mutual respect. I replaced that woman with a photo of myself. The woman's stance was a challenging one to replicate, because I didn't have a photo of myself from the same angle. After several failed attempts, I combined my face with the other woman's body. The final product was barely satisfactory.

I scrolled through more pictures until I reached the end of the party, when everyone was singing "Happy Birthday" to Natalie. Amelia was kneeling by her daughter, looking up at her with pride. I replaced that image of Amelia with one of myself. Now it was me looking up at Natalie as she blew out the candles on her cake.

Finally I landed on the one I'd been thinking about all night. Amelia and Fritz were sharing a piece of birthday cake. Amelia was holding out her fork so Fritz could have a bite, and he was leaning toward her with his mouth around the fork. I replaced Fritz's image with my own. I was eating cake off Amelia's fork, chocolate frosting around the outside of my mouth. We were laughing at a private joke. We were intimates. I contemplated the picture, and optimism bubbled up in me.

It was fascinating to me that an image of a relationship accomplished much of what I was looking for, so that the relationship itself wasn't altogether necessary. The efficiency of this pleased me.

I printed the picture of Fritz kissing me, and the one of Amelia feeding me cake. I placed each 8 x 10 in one of my large supply of clear acrylic frames and hung them side by side in the alcove next to the photo of Jasper and me.

It was already two in the morning, and I had a lot of work the following day. I labeled one folder Straub Family and one folder Straub, Alternates, the latter being photoshopped images for my personal use. Then, I closed down my computer, knowing that I could return to the project as often as I needed to, as an ongoing source of comfort.

•   •   •

The following morning I received a text from Amelia: *Natalie adores you. You made such an impression!*

When I saw the text, I realized that I'd almost been holding my breath. Had I not received her note, I might have attempted to reestablish contact myself.

I wrote back. *Natalie's a special girl. I'd love to babysit anytime. Do you mean it?? How about Friday?*

They wanted me to return. They wanted my involvement in their family. I had proof of that now. Oddly, I dreaded Friday as much as I longed for it. I dreaded the moment when I would no longer have the evening to look forward to, because I already knew how deflated I would feel when it was over.

I stayed up late Sunday night, looking at photos of the Straubs' work online, beginning with their own website. I'd glanced at it before Natalie's party, but now I studied it with renewed interest. I later found an illuminating interview in *Architectural Digest* from ten years earlier in which the Straubs were discussing the success of their partnership. "'Fritz is big picture and I follow up on all the details,' Amelia Straub says with a self-deprecating laugh. 'He's the most talented architect I've ever met. That's why I married him!' Fritz Straub interrupts: 'Yeah, right, we all know who's running the show.'"

A recent interview in *Metropolis* had a strikingly different tone. "'Fritz has his projects and I have mine,' Amelia Straub explains, 'and we don't actually have much overlap.'" Fritz was not quoted at all.

Before going to sleep, I ordered a copy of *Defining Light: Twenty-First-Century Architecture from the Straub Group* for sixty-five dollars on Amazon.

For the next couple of days, I was occupied with photo shoots, while my evenings were devoted to editing and album layouts. On Wednesday, when I arrived home and saw a package from Amazon, I felt like it was Christmas. I stayed up late, studying the Straubs' book from cover to cover. The graphic design was exquisite. The images were strong and forceful. I found fault with very few of the photos.

I took my time with each page, analyzing each picture and reading every word. I was growing to understand how much I had in common with the Straubs. Quantity and quality of light drove the majority of their architectural choices. The same was true for my photographic choices. The Straubs used natural light to create the spaces in their homes, as much or more than they used structures and walls.

The first five chapters of their book focused on country houses in Long Island, Nantucket, Martha's Vineyard, the Hudson Valley, and Connecticut, respectively. The next five were dedicated to urban residences, culminating in the Straubs' own Brooklyn residence, the pièce de résistance. The book had a more comprehensive selection of photos than those I'd found online. Included were three spreads of the Straubs' parlor floor, showcasing the sculptural staircase, the library, the majestic great room, the glass-and-steel bifold doors leading to the expansive deck outdoors.

The next two spreads revealed the master suite seen from several angles, including two shots of an otherworldly bathroom with a rain showerhead and a Spoon bathtub. An intense desire to immerse myself in the master suite radiated through my body. Just studying the photos and imagining myself there afforded me some visceral pleasure, but I wanted more. I felt compelled to penetrate their space, as if it ought to belong to me.

The very last photo spread in their book surprised me the most: pictures of a one-bedroom apartment on the garden floor of their building—as captivating as the rest of the house, with the same aesthetic and flawless execution.

I hadn't known such an apartment existed.

· · ·

Friday arrived. I had a nervous stomach and couldn't eat breakfast or lunch. At 4 P.M., I allowed myself to begin preparations for the evening. My outfit for babysitting Natalie had a specific set of demands, distinct from what was required as a photographer. My clothing needed to say "responsible, mature, ebullient, and charm-ing." These parents were leaving their child alone in my care. I was required to be a reliable adult, but one that connected to children, an adult with a sense of fun and vivacity. I chose a pair of dark jeans, my leather boots, a thin sweater, and a sparkly necklace—one I felt certain that Natalie would like.

I maintained a decent wardrobe because I'd always considered my clothing a business expense. I recognized that my appearance mattered, especially when photographing at the home of an afflu-ent family. I didn't want to attract too much attention. However, I needed to look like I belonged in the home and was comfortable in the setting. In a service role, yes. But a level above the people who were preparing and serving the food. Two levels above the people who were cleaning and washing dishes. The parents liked to view me as an almost peer. Most of them would never choose to socialize with me. Nevertheless, if we ended up in conversation, I could hold my own, and they would find the conversation pleasant enough.

My clients probably assumed that my education and breeding were not up to theirs. And was that true? It depends on how such things are defined. Yes, I attended college, but a mediocre one. Not to say that I wasn't educated. An autodidact, I read incessantly and processed images incessantly. In one image, I could extract more information than many people could extract from an entire book. I could look at a photograph of a group of people and, with surpris-ing accuracy, detail the relationships among the various parties.

I had always been aware of my deficits and had worked hard to shore them up. To be frank, I resembled the proverbial English butler who learns all the rules, who lives and breathes the rules, without necessarily internalizing what is underneath them. I learned the rules for the sole purpose of serving the ruling class, making them comfortable, and fitting in. (The idea of a "ruling class" had never bothered me. It was only if you acknowledged the existing hierarchy that you could use it to your advantage.) I paid attention to every intonation in people's sentences. How they tied their shoes or didn't tie them. I paid attention to the minutiae until it became second nature. I didn't want to appear to be striving for something that I wasn't inherently given at birth. Yes, I'd been born into white trash. But I, myself, had a drastically superior mind and sensibilities.

My clients felt relaxed enough to discuss their finances in front of me. They couldn't talk about money with someone who was poor. They could only talk about money with someone who understood money. I considered that my job—to convey to them that I understood their world. And that I understood their children's worlds. And because I understood their children's worlds so well, I was the artist who could translate all of that into a photograph.

•　　•　　•

As I approached the entrance to the Straubs' home, I took a slight detour to glance down the exterior stone steps that led to the garden apartment. The shades were down. The lights were out. It appeared no one was there.

I returned to the main steps of the front entrance, noting the lanterns on either side, which looked to be original nineteenth century. Amelia greeted me at the door in slacks and bare feet with a fresh pedicure. Her glossy brown hair was pulled up loosely in a clip. She wore gold Aztec coin earrings and a matching necklace. It was expensive jewelry, but unconventional and effortless. If you didn't know anything about jewelry, it might seem understated.

She shone her smile on me, and I experienced the same sensation of warmth and light that I'd experienced upon meeting her. It was as though she saw something extraordinary in me.

"Natalie thinks she's too old to have a babysitter." Amelia spoke in a hushed, conspiratorial tone. "But she feels like you're her *friend*." She led me into the kitchen and offered me a blue reactive-glaze mug filled with hot lemon water. She sank down onto one of the counter stools, and as she did, her smile faded. "All our evenings out. It's the nature of our work. Relationships.

"Most of our clients are lovely people," she said, "but once in a while we end up in a relationship with someone who can't be pleased. And then we've got to work through the project and get to the other side. I'm probably preaching to the choir, right?" She took a sip of her lemon water.

I felt flattered that she was comparing her work to mine. I hesitated, however, not wanting to criticize a client. "Are you struggling with a particular person right now?"

She blossomed when the attention was on her. "Not exactly. But it's been a hard year."

"Yes?"

"Just . . . a lot of disappointments." She frowned. "I count my blessings, though." Her face had a worn appearance, but regardless, I found her arresting. Even the prior week, when she'd come home drunk and messy, she'd still glowed like a beacon. She lit the room up when she walked in.

"If you ever want to discuss it . . ."

"I wouldn't want to burden you." Her fingers trailed down her neck.

I sensed that she did want to talk about it. "I admire you, Amelia. Your family, your professional success. If you only knew how impressive you are—to an outsider."

"You're not an outsider, Delta!"

"I'm honored to be included in your life."

"When will you see your son again?" she asked.

"I try to FaceTime every day."

"It must be hard," she said.

My hand was too hot. I set the cup down.

"Where did you grow up?" she asked, as if the idea had only just occurred to her. I was sorry that it had. My *roots*—that wasn't a subject I enjoyed and I usually chose to deflect the conversation away from that territory.

"Florida."

"Where in Florida? My parents live in Florida."

Amelia felt it was her prerogative to have the information she wanted, and ignored the social cues that might have led someone else to drop a subject. She wasn't oblivious to the cues. She simply disregarded them. I was usually adept at pivoting away from my own story after providing only the most rudimentary information, but not in this case.

"Orlando."

"And your family?" she asked.

"I have an older sister." I'd always wanted an older sister. "My parents both died a few years ago. Several months apart. They were very close." My mother had died in a car accident right after I'd graduated from high school, and my father might be dead. I hadn't seen him for fifteen years and had no desire to. So he was dead, in a sense. "I love Brooklyn. I have a family of friends. We celebrate Thanksgiving, Christmas, New Year's. Now that I'm divorced."

Amelia nodded sympathetically. "Two of our employees have stuck around for a long time. Ian Walker, he's an associate at the firm and holds the place together. Maybe you saw him at Natalie's birthday?" Amelia's eyes shone when she spoke of Ian. "He's like a member of the family, which is great since it's just the three of us and Natalie doesn't have any siblings. So far."

I found myself envious of Ian. "So far?" I asked. "Is there a sibling on the way?"

Amelia looked down at her lap and shook her head. "I want another baby more than I can tell you." Her eyes filled with tears. I took her hand and held it in mine. As I did so, I feared I'd overstepped, but she pulled my hand firmly toward her, as if she was drawing comfort from me. Her skin was extremely soft. A circle of diamonds sparkled on her ring finger. All her fingers were long and slender. I wondered if she played the piano.

"I can't stay pregnant. It's devastating." Amelia's shoulders collapsed. "It's biological, I guess, the intense need for another baby. Maybe a desire to be young again?" She laughed awkwardly. "And the miscarriages destroyed me." She wiped several tears from her cheeks and smudged black streaks of mascara across her face in the process. "I've got to keep up this appearance. Maybe it's for Fritz's sake. I think he needs me to be the strong one."

I heard Natalie's footsteps on the stairs. Amelia pulled a tissue from the box on the counter and wiped away her smeared mascara. Natalie walked into the kitchen, wearing shorts and a torn T-shirt, her gangly arms and legs exposed. Did she know about her mother's longing for a baby, the miscarriages? Amelia didn't seem the type to play it close to the vest.

"Hi, Delta." Natalie turned to her mother. "I need help with my math assignment." She put a few stapled pages down on the white marble top of the kitchen island.

"My daughter's in the most advanced sixth-grade math class that ever existed." Amelia handed the papers back to Natalie. "She doesn't actually *need* help."

"I do."

"Homework's not my job!" Amelia closed her eyes tightly,

turned her head away, and held her hands out to indicate that she wasn't going to look at the homework. She reminded me of a child who was refusing to eat her vegetables.

I'd always been good at math and felt reasonably confident that I would understand Natalie's math, even if it was advanced. Still, it was a risk. "Can I try to help?"

"Fine," Amelia said. "But, Natalie, don't get used to it."

Natalie and I sat down at the farmhouse table. In lieu of flowers, a wrought-iron menorah served as the centerpiece. Itzhak crawled between her feet. I'd noticed that the dog liked being close to her. Natalie's homework included several pages of word problems with fractions and decimals, but not beyond my ability, and not beyond Natalie's, either. She probably wanted attention more than she wanted or needed help. She wanted someone to care about her homework, to care about her.

Amelia slipped upstairs and returned half an hour later in a cream-colored pantsuit and kitten heels. Hovering over Natalie, she stroked her hair. "All of our dinners are client dinners." I detected self-righteousness in her tone. "We never leave Natalie for a social event."

Perhaps Amelia thought I was judging her, and wanted to convince me she was a devoted mother.

"Of course," I said.

Amelia kissed Natalie on her forehead. "Delta, feel free to watch TV or borrow a book after Natalie's in bed." Amelia headed to the door. "We'll be home by midnight."

When Natalie and I finished her math, we turned to a diorama she was working on for a school contest—a three-dimensional model of an ideal public park. I attended an unexceptional public school, not a fancy private school like Natalie. I don't remember ever having had an assignment like hers—empowering and harnessing my ingenuity. She took it for granted.

Natalie wanted to start with a carousel. "I used to go to the one in Prospect Park with my dad," she said, "and also the one near the bridge, with glass around it."

I know a lot about carousels. More than the average person. I'd probably spent hundreds of hours on the bench in front of Cinderella's Golden Carousel. I can still picture each horse in detail. I can still hear the music.

Natalie and I cut out each component of the carousel and each individual horse, then mounted them on cardboard. We cut out and mounted the children also. Each cardboard child had distinct features and unique clothing. Natalie must have thought about the personalities and the inner lives of each child as she was drawing him or her, and the result was a group of diverse children. I found such a holistic approach extremely unusual for a child. Many adults who considered themselves artists didn't think that way.

"You remember in *Mary Poppins*," she said, "when the children jump into the sidewalk chalk drawing of an English countryside. They land *inside* the drawing, and the whole world comes to life. And then they ride the carousel, and the horses jump off and just keep running, away from the merry-go-round, through the fields, anywhere they want to go?"

I nodded, not sure if I'd ever seen *Mary Poppins* at all.

"They're attached to the carousel, going round and round, and they're stuck there. But then, all of a sudden, they realize they can ride their horses anywhere. It's like they could do that all along but didn't know it." She demonstrated with one of the cardboard horses, moving it through the air in leaping arcs around the room. "Every time I ride a carousel, I tell my horse to jump off and run away." She laughed. "None of the horses listen to me."

She finally glued the last horse into place.

We moved on to trees, a garden, rock formations, and a playground.

Natalie studied the completed diorama. "One day I want to build this park for real," she said to me conspiratorially.

"Are you going to be an architect when you grow up, like your parents?" A sharp burn of envy pierced through me, but it was mitigated by the unassuming expression in Natalie's eyes.

"If I'm good enough." Her quiet tone of voice indicated she didn't believe she would be. It was as if she thought there was only so much talent handed out to one family: Her mother had most of it. Her father had what was left over.

"You'll be good enough."

"I hope I win the contest," she whispered, though we were the only two people in the house.

I felt myself becoming concerned for Natalie. She was a very sensitive girl. As much as I admired Amelia and Fritz, I sensed that they were not fulfilling their daughter's needs. She didn't have enough of their attention. I understood exactly how she felt.

After dinner, Natalie got in bed and read for half an hour. I returned to her room to say good night. She turned back one of the pages of *The Giver* by Lois Lowry to mark her place and then positioned the book on her nightstand.

I picked it up and looked at the jacket copy. "How's the book?"

"It's about a community where everyone's assigned their life work," she said. "No one gets to decide anything or choose anything."

I studied the image of the man's face on the cover.

"I'd like to have some choices," she said.

"You'll create your own choices," I said, "like I do."

CHAPTER FOUR

In the Straubs' home office, I turned on the overhead lights and sat down at Amelia's walnut desk, where I found two new Post-its. One read *travel*, and underneath were written several dates. Another read *couples counselor* and a phone number. Amelia's inability to carry another child had obviously put a strain on the Straubs' marriage. Of course, I felt deep concern for both of them, but I also had the exhilarating realization that the Straubs and I had crossed paths now for a reason. Perhaps, I was in a position to help them.

Next to Amelia's keyboard, I noticed an exquisite pot of lip gloss. I opened the small gold jar to discover that it was fire-engine red. Amelia was a little old for such a bright color; it would make her look harsh. It was actually a better color for me. I applied a dab to my lips and returned the jar to its original spot. Next to her desk on the floor, a Post-it was stuck on top of an Asics shoebox with the word *return* scribbled on it. I looked inside and saw a pair of expensive running shoes. Before leaving the office, I examined the scene to make certain everything was returned to its original location. Then I turned out the lights.

I'd been dreaming about the Straubs' master suite for two days, anticipating my opportunity for exploration. The moment I walked in, I felt a thrill. It was the intimacy of being in their bedroom, deep inside their lives. Swimming in the pool of their merged identities—woven into their larger family identity. The bedroom looked out over a patio and the backyard. Underneath grand casement windows trimmed with brass hardware, a built-in window seat extended the width of the room. Crisp white molding set off the ivory walls. The duvet resembled a watercolor, as did the silk rug. In Amelia's closet and dressing room, the quality of the custom millwork equaled that of their kitchen cabinetry. Many thousands of dollars in clothing resided there.

It was the master bath that captivated me above all else. The photos I'd seen did not allow the eye to appreciate how each layer informed the other layers. It was a stunning vision of glazed silver floors, a polished stone vanity, large dramatic sconces, a spacious marble-lined shower with a rain showerhead, mosaic tile flooring, and an overscaled egg-shaped resin tub.

I approached the vanity and the built-in magnifying mirror

attached to the wall in order to study my reflection: golden hair framing a youthful complexion and shiny red lips. It was not until last year, when I turned thirty-five, that I noticed a few fine lines in my forehead and, even then, only if I looked closely. In one of the top drawers of the vanity, I found several beautifully packaged skin creams, along with a thirty-dollar mascara, a seventy-dollar concealer, and a pair of tweezers that I used to remove several stray eyebrow hairs.

When finished at the mirror, I turned to take in the magnificence of the bathtub. I'd never bathed in such a tub. I considered how much time I had. It was 10 P.M. The Straubs definitely wouldn't return home before eleven, and Amelia had indicated it would be later. If I were to take a bath, I'd have at least an hour before I'd have to worry about their arrival.

I pulled my shirt over my head, removed my bra, and examined my torso in the full-length mirror. I still had a flat stomach and a slender waist. I thought about conceiving and bearing a child. Childbirth can alter a woman's body, sometimes permanently. I sat down on an Indonesian stool and pulled off my socks, my jeans, and my underwear, then stood naked in the lavish bathroom and stared at myself in the mirror, savoring a sense of connection and intimacy with the Straubs. And also the power associated with claiming what I needed.

I considered the logistics of my bath. I ought not to use a towel for my bath, because I might not have time to wash and dry it. They would likely notice a damp towel or a damp tub. Maybe I needed to wait for my next visit and bring my own towel. The thought of postponing the bath brought my spirits down. I spied a damp towel draped over the towel bar and contemplated using that one. I leaned over to smell it and detected Amelia's musky scent.

Still undecided, I returned to the bedroom to study the Straubs' bed. A dozen pillows of various sizes and fabrics, and in various shades of blue, covered the upholstered headboard. I wanted to lie naked under their organic cotton sheets. Thoughts of Amelia and Fritz having sex entered my mind. Maybe they'd stopped having sex after all the miscarriages. Maybe it was too traumatic for them now.

Natalie's face appeared in the doorway. Her body lurched back at the sight of me.

"Hi, Natalie." I spoke in a calm tone, though a wave of panic ran through me. I spotted a throw draped over a nearby chair. "The craziest thing . . ." I wrapped the blanket tightly around my body. "Just a few minutes ago . . . Itzhak vomited. I was downstairs and lifting him off the porch. Awful for him. Really." I avoided her eye contact. "So all my clothes . . . I had to clean everything. It was quite a mess, and I'm . . . I'm going to wash my clothes in the machine. I'll just find a towel until they're dry."

"Poor Itzhak." Natalie crossed toward me in the direction of the bathroom. I feared she was going to examine my clothing to see if I was telling the truth about the vomit. But she stopped in front of one of her parents' nightstands to check the time. She turned around and walked back toward the bedroom door.

Fortunately, Natalie returned to bed rather quickly after a glass of milk. I was mildly concerned about how she would relate what she saw. She appeared to believe me when I explained about Itzhak. But I couldn't be certain.

Still wrapped in the blanket, I went back to the master bathroom, where I'd left my clothes, and sent Amelia a text: *can I use the laundry machine to wash my clothes? unfortunately, Itzhak's been ill.*

no! did he ruin ur clothes?

i'm fine

please use my bathroom to rinse off. The response allayed all my fears and filled me with the same sense of euphoria that I'd had earlier.

I placed my clean clothes in the laundry machine with detergent. Then, when I entered the master bathroom again, it was not as a trespasser, but as an invited guest. I sank down into a tub of steamy hot water. The water jets massaged my body, and I imagined it was someone touching me. Thoughts of Fritz consumed my imagination. Followed by thoughts of Amelia. I stared at the magical light fixture on the ceiling, a million drops of crystal held together by some invisible force. A feeling of deep contentment and optimism pervaded my soul. I stepped out of the bath, invigorated. Once I'd dried off, I returned to the laundry room to place my clothes in the dryer.

When Amelia and Fritz came home, they both apologized repeatedly. They felt awful for leaving Itzhak in my care, a dog with chronic gastrointestinal issues. In this situation, they could only see themselves as the guilty parties.

•   •   •

The next day, I woke up late with a headache, as if I were hungover, though I'd had very little to drink the night before. I checked my phone. The first time I'd babysat for Natalie, Amelia had written to me early the following morning, but I found no message this time. I checked again twenty minutes later. And again after that. I was hoping for some acknowledgment of our growing relationship. I feared sliding back. I drank a cup of coffee, showered, dressed, checked my phone again, then collected my equipment for the job I had that afternoon in Tribeca.

I arrived and stepped out of the elevator directly into a corner duplex penthouse: twenty-foot ceilings, white oak floors, a landscaped terrace, and sweeping views. Having photographed more than eight hundred parties given by wealthy New Yorkers, I was no longer impressed by the size of a home, nor was I impressed by costly art, furniture, or finishes. A majority of rich people have bad taste and derivative homes. Some of them have an impressive art collection dictated by an art consultant. It's possible to hire people who will tell you what art to buy, what dishes to buy, what sheets to buy, what color to paint your walls. But the final product does not reflect any one person's point of view, personality, taste, or sensibility. Just like any generic idea of what's good, it's actually *not* good.

The Straubs' home was different. Amelia and Fritz did not design their home with the goal of trying to re-create something that they'd seen before. They, themselves, were the artists. They, themselves, had the vision.

Since I'd arrived early at my clients' home, seven-year-old Boris was alone in the living room playing video games on an iPad. I approached the sturdy-looking child and handed him a box wrapped in green paper and silver ribbon. "Happy birthday," I said. He took the package and placed it on the floor next to his feet. Then he jumped, landing with all his weight on top of the birthday present. He picked up the crushed package and handed it back to me, with a snide look on his face.

"I don't want the party," he said. "I don't like anyone who's coming."

I turned the package over in my hands, noticing for the first time that my green blouse matched the wrapping paper. "Not even me?" I smiled at him.

He studied the camera around my neck and wrinkled his nose. "Especially not you."

I stepped away from Boris, determined to try again in a few minutes.

Across the room, in the kitchen, I recognized Chef Simone, preparing pigs in blankets and goat cheese canapés. "Hi, Delta," she said to me as I approached, and then quietly, with a nod toward Boris: "Little brat."

Over the years, I'd perfected an inscrutable expression on my face that was neither agreement nor disagreement. And that was the expression I offered Simone. I refused to be seen gossiping. Quite frankly, she was underestimating our clients. That energy gets out there and I know for a fact that the clients can smell it. Many of my clients were vulgar, shallow, arrogant, and/or insolent. But they were not stupid. They expected the people in their employ to feign respect, whether or not it was genuinely felt. I'd learned that lesson early on from socialite-turned–event planner Emily Miller when I was assisting on her weddings. If a client had the vaguest notion that you didn't think highly of her, you'd never get hired again.

Boris's friends arrived, followed by Mack the Magician. I'd known Mack for years, since I'd started shooting Emily's clients and their kids. He laid claim to performing at large venues and implied he did parties on rare occasions as a special favor to the parents. But we all knew that wasn't true. He had the identical act every time and the same tired jokes. He didn't even bother to rotate his show.

Most of the children crowded Mack during the knife-juggling segment of his show, causing my stomach to drop more than once, though I'd seen his show at least twenty times, and no one had ever died. Boris's parents, who were sipping Veuve Clicquot in the kitchen, didn't notice the knives.

Boris was the only child who derived no pleasure from the performance, or any other aspect of the party. I stayed for three hours, hoping that his frame of mind would shift, but nothing, not even the Avengers cupcakes, could shake him out of his mood.

Since the raw material from the party was unusable in its present form, I resigned myself to creating photos out of whole cloth.

I made it a rule not to drink while working, and not unless the hosts specifically offered me a drink. But on my way out, when the hosts were otherwise occupied, I drank half a glass of champagne. My nerves were on fire and I needed it.

·   ·   ·

As I was waiting for my car, Amelia's name came up on my phone. I felt a rush of exhilaration until I read the entire text. She explained that they were leaving town for two weeks. It was Natalie's winter break. She'd forgotten to mention it.

A heaviness settled into my arms and legs.

I spent several minutes composing a response in my mind. I didn't want to appear too eager, but I needed to hold on to the Straubs. My body craved our connection.

Finally I landed on a solution and wrote: *I could look after itzhak and water ur plants. it wouldn't be trouble. Let me know!*

OMG delta ur the best. itzhak is at a doggie hotel, but please water the plants! So amazing if you would.

Her message was an enormous consolation. There was terrific value for me in spending time in their home.

Another text from Amelia: *remember I told you about ian walker? he's a doll. i gave him your number!*

I resented Amelia pawning me off on Ian. It was mildly disrespectful. How did she even know whether I was single? After mulling it over, I decided that I'd go out with him anyway. I saw it as an opportunity to garner information on the Straubs.

Back at my apartment, I settled in and turned on my computer. Boris's party was going to require many hours of editing. Essentially, I would have to create a birthday party that had never happened, in order to showcase a delightful and affectionate child who did not exist. When I needed a break, I turned to the pictures from Natalie's birthday. In each and every image from her party, I saw opportunities to photoshop—ways for me to spend time with the Straubs. My interactions with them, even if only in photos, were a balm to my spirits.

• • •

Two days later Ian and I had dinner at a loud and crowded Italian restaurant in the West Village. When I arrived, I spotted him across the room. I recognized him as the man talking to Fritz at Natalie's party—early forties, dark brown hair, heavy eyebrows. No one would have called him out for being good-looking or bad-looking. He was wearing a tie, unlike the rest of the men in the restaurant. His hair was extremely short, as if he'd had a haircut earlier that day, and it appeared he'd cut his chin shaving.

Ian seemed surprised by me. Or maybe taken aback by my appearance. I gathered he wasn't used to dating women who were as pretty as I was.

I started by asking him questions about himself. I always preferred to do the asking. The person asking has more power.

The person answering is more vulnerable. Among other things, I learned that he grew up in New Jersey and attended Rice University for his master's. He spoke of his father, who'd passed away the previous year, and his mother's subsequent loneliness. I was bored by the subject of other people's loneliness, but Ian would have had no way of knowing that.

He'd just come from helping his mother clean her apartment, in preparation for trying to sell it, because she had bad arthritis in her hips and it wasn't easy for her to get around. She was so stingy, he said, she'd photographed the apartment herself, refusing to spend the money on a professional interiors photographer.

Some people consider themselves photographers because they've taken a few decent pictures on their iPhones. An infinite number of monkeys with an infinite number of typewriters and an infinite amount of time could write *The Complete Works of Shakespeare*. That's called the infinite monkey theorem, and it applies to cameras and photographs too. I didn't tell Ian about the infinite monkey theorem.

"The photos can make a big difference," I said.

"I know." He shook his head in disgust. "Her lousy photos are probably costing her forty percent of the sale price."

After a couple of martinis, Ian loosened up a bit. "Delta Dawn. Isn't that a song?"

I smiled. "Mm-hmm."

"It's a beautiful name."

"I've never liked it," I said.

"That's too bad."

"It tells people I don't belong."

"Don't belong . . . where?"

"Anywhere, actually." The words fell out of my mouth.

I could see that Ian found the comment troubling.

"I'm kidding!" I laughed.

He smiled awkwardly and ordered another martini.

Once the topic of conversation shifted to the Straubs, the evening flew, because it was a subject we both thoroughly enjoyed. He told me stories about residential and commercial projects they'd worked on together over the years. He'd been with the firm for ten years and had been promoted to associate three years earlier. One day he planned to start his own firm, but he said it was too challenging in the current climate.

Ian provided more direct information about the Straubs than I would ever be able to glean from perusing their house. For example, I grew to understand aspects of Amelia and Fritz's relationship— both personal and business. Fritz had been a wunderkind who'd started his own firm in his late twenties. Early on he offered Amelia a job at his firm, and eventually made her his business partner. Somewhere along the way, they got married. Meanwhile, though Ian didn't say it directly, I gathered that Amelia had risen quickly in terms of the demand for her work, and at this point she was the breadwinner, responsible for bringing most of the clients in. A reversal of power.

Ian was a veritable fount of information, and also mildly charming.

"I'm grateful for Amelia's friendship," I said. I'd finished a third glass of wine and a plate of spaghetti Bolognese. "She's inspiring." I had to raise my voice because the small restaurant had grown more crowded over the last hour.

I brought up the subject of babysitting Natalie and told him about the diorama contest for her school.

"Natalie's a sweet girl," he said. "But I worry about her. Sort of lonely."

The comment sounded vaguely disloyal to Amelia and Fritz. Fortunately, our waiter delivered our cappuccinos and I didn't have to agree or disagree with the notion that Natalie was lonely. Ian sipped his coffee.

"Maybe there'll be another little Straub on the scene soon," I suggested.

He cleared his throat. "Maybe."

"It seems like something Amelia really wants. Don't you think so?"

He shifted in his chair. "Well, they're not secretive about it, but they've been trying to have a baby for a few years."

"I had no idea." I wanted Ian to believe that I was a trustworthy friend. Not someone who was fishing for information.

We didn't order dessert, but our waiter forced a platter of petit fours on us.

I sipped my cappuccino in silence. "I wish I could help Amelia," I said. "I wish I could do something for her."

He studied the plate of petit fours and then took one of them. Apparently, his mind had wandered away from the subject of Amelia's infertility. He inched the plate in my direction and pointed to one of the mini tarts. "This one's really good."

I took the mini tart to satisfy him, though I didn't want it.

He cleared his throat again. "Amelia said you have a son." He smiled at me, like he wanted to make sure I knew he was pleased.

"Yes. Jasper." I pulled out my phone and looked up the picture of Jasper on the beach, playing in the ocean with a surfboard. I showed it to Ian. The photo was one of my best creations. "He's in California with his dad."

He smiled. "Beautiful picture. Is your ex-husband a photographer too?"

"No." I tried to laugh. "Not professional, anyway. Jasper's started surfing. Isn't that crazy? He's only five."

"Adorable," he said.

I put the phone away, and Ian paid for dinner.

Afterward, I wanted to walk a fine line in how I parted with him. Friends for now, but give him hope for the future.

We made our way to the coat check at the front of the restaurant, squeezing between tables and past waiters. "Listen, Ian," I said, while we were waiting in line, "if you want me to photograph your mother's apartment before she puts it on the market, I'd do it for free." He clearly wanted to say yes but was too polite to show it.

He looked down. "I don't want to take advantage of your time."

I handed my tag to the scrawny coat-check woman behind the counter. "I could add your mom's apartment to my portfolio."

"I don't want to impose." He blushed but appeared pleased by the offer.

"When would be a good time?"

He paused. "Actually, she was going to put it on the market on Monday, but—"

"So, how about tomorrow morning?" I had a job the following day, but since it wasn't a party, I was pretty certain I could push it back a couple of hours. I might not have another opportunity to ingratiate myself with Ian.

"It's really kind of you." Ian helped me with my heavy down coat. And then his own. Outside on the sidewalk, he leaned in toward me to say goodbye, but I shifted my weight and turned, as though I wasn't aware of his intention.

"So I'll see you tomorrow?" I said.

He smiled, and I noticed dimples in his cheeks. "Thank you, Delta."

•   •   •

Ian's mother's apartment had large windows and good light. I used my wide-angle lens. In the darker rooms, such as the master bedroom, which looked out on a brick wall, I compensated with Elinchrom strobes. In the living room, I ruthlessly cleared out all personal belongings if they didn't materially contribute to the beauty of the image—removing 90 percent of the vases, trays, boxes, plates, baskets, and other knickknacks from the frame. Clutter inhibits lines and light. Years ago I'd learned not to ask permission in situations like this. As long as I was doing a "favor," I intended to produce photos that would sell the apartment.

Once you see a photograph of an apartment, that image becomes the reality—like the pictures of my clients' children. It's actually more important than the reality of what you see when you walk in the door. Viewing an apartment in person is similar to looking at your own reflection in the mirror. The information your brain takes in is malleable. Whereas pictures are fixed. They don't shift as easily, because it's one point of view. One moment in time. We tend to trust pictures.

Ian and his mother, Paula, followed me around, observing my work. Occasionally I allowed them to look through the viewfinder. Paula asked me questions as we went along. I explained how to create more space, higher ceilings, a sense of grandeur. It's about the angle and the light. I was shooting from a kneeling position, corner to corner. And almost every shot included one of the mirrors hanging on the walls. "If you shoot a mirror from the right angle," I said, "you can create another window, or a painting, or a room that looks twice as large."

That evening, I sent Ian and Paula a few of the best shots. I had taken an attractive but drab apartment and turned it into a showpiece. My photographs could have appeared in any shelter magazine, and I say that with no hyperbole. With my lighting, that apartment transcended its limitations in terms of its size, scale, and design. I had created art. I had created an illusion.

•   •   •

On Friday evening I descended the exterior steps of the Straubs' brownstone. Amelia had given me the combination to a small lock-box, which was mounted behind a hedge near the entrance to the garden apartment. Their front door key happened to be on a key chain with two other unmarked keys. I surmised one of the extra keys might unlock the garden apartment. I paused to see if I could detect any activity through the windows, but the lights were out and the shades were down. I had yet to ask the Straubs if anyone was living there.

I walked up the main steps and unlocked the Straubs' front door. "Hello!" I called out. I was carrying two bags of groceries, which I brought to the kitchen and unpacked. I planned to make chicken Parmesan. The most mundane tasks, when performed in the Straubs' kitchen, took on a magical quality.

Since the Straubs were out of town for two weeks, I'd planned four visits to their house, thinking I could safely spend a few hours each time. More than that might raise questions. I felt certain that Amelia and Fritz would be pleased for me to spend any amount of time in the house, but even so, it would be best to steer clear of gossip.

I noticed an open bottle of pinot grigio in the door of the re-frigerator that had barely been touched. Since I knew it would spoil by the time the Straubs returned home, I poured a glass for myself and drank it. With my second glass of wine, I walked from one room to the next. Up the stairs and back down, absorbing every detail. Each and every vantage point built upon the last, so that the cumulative effect was a transcendent experience. The transitions between spaces, like the sculptural staircase, were isolated but spiritual, and the spaces themselves were earthbound and communal. An interplay between isolation and community.

I set my glass of wine down on a brass end table in the great room. I had yet to pay close enough attention to the silk rugs they'd chosen. I'd seen them in a magazine, listed at thirty grand each. They began as watercolors, painted by Brooklyn artists, and then were woven in Nepal. The Straubs owned four of them. I sat on the floor next to the most beautiful one and ran my hand across the smooth gray surface. It was softer than most sheets and pillowcases were. I put my cheek down on the rug, just to feel the silk against my face. It would be easy to fall asleep here.

I took off all my clothes, including my bra and underwear, and lay facedown on the rug. I felt myself to be fully inhabiting the home of Amelia and Fritz, in the deep recesses of their life. In spite of the many hours I'd spent in clients' homes, I always hit walls blocking me from entering all the way. I couldn't see the walls; I could only feel them when I came too close. I was forever hovering on the edge of something.

Early on in my career, I'd sometimes made mistakes, such as resting on the sofa in a client's study or snacking from their refrigerator. When a client saw me, their reaction was clear. I'd invaded, crossed a line, trespassed, taken liberties.

With my body spread naked on the rug, I felt a sensation of entitlement and power. I had penetrated the walls. I had pierced the barrier. I was claiming the territory as mine. The opposite of the deference and the hesitation that restricted me so often. No one could stop me.

I stood up. Still naked, I found Amelia's watering can in the kitchen and filled it up. I watered the ficus in the great room and the rubber tree in the front library. My nudity made me feel close to the Straubs—at the very core and center of their lives. I passed by the full-length hall mirror and stopped to observe myself. I posed my figure facing forward, and then in profile. My image, watering can in hand, resembled that of a Greek goddess.

After I dressed, I poured another glass of wine and set to work on the chicken Parmesan—pounded the chicken breasts, coated them with flour, eggs, and bread crumbs, before adding tomato sauce and cheese. The woman who cooked in this kitchen was a remarkable person. If she wasn't remarkable to start off with, the time spent in this particular setting would alter her intrinsically. We humans evolve to fit our surroundings.

I placed the copper baking dish in the oven. As I was refilling my wineglass . . . I heard something in the backyard. It was concerning. The downstairs tenant, if one existed, was not home. Who was in the backyard? The Straubs would definitely appreciate my checking on the situation.

I exited out the bifold doors and walked down the spiral staircase. "Hello!" I called out. A leafless cherry tree, dramatically lit, stood in the center of the yard surrounded by brown grass. Outside the garden apartment's back door was a small patio with two chairs and a side table. The downstairs resident was likely restricted to the patio. Amelia and Fritz wouldn't want to socialize or share space with a tenant. Would they?

I smelled something unusual. The Straubs would want me to check on a gas leak. They would be grateful for my conscientiousness. I knocked on the back door. "Hello!" Inside, the lights were still out, as they were when I arrived. I knocked again. No one answered.

I tried one of the extra keys, then the second extra key. Seconds later I was inside, standing in the open kitchen. I switched on the lights.

The apartment looked exactly as I'd hoped—as if it had been designed to conform to my tastes, with every architectural detail conceived and executed flawlessly. It was breathtaking.

Amelia (I assumed it was Amelia) had chosen more vivid colors for the garden apartment, such as smoky green in the living room and grayish purple in the hallway. I walked from one end of the apartment to the other. "Hello," I said loudly. If someone happened to be in, I would explain that I had smelled gas and was checking to make certain all was well.

The apartment had one large bedroom near the front entrance. A crisp white duvet cover appeared comparable to the linens in the master bedroom.

Two framed photos rested on the bedside table: A group of twentysomething women who looked to be on vacation in the Bahamas. A young homely woman and an older couple, maybe the woman's parents. Perhaps the homely woman lived here and rented the apartment. I wondered what she paid. I wondered what kind of work she did. I wondered if she was fucking Fritz. I opened her closet and saw several suits. Maybe a lawyer? Maybe finance? I examined her scant collection of imitation jewelry. She was meticulous. It takes one to know one. In that respect, she was an ideal tenant.

In the living room, I sat down on a dingy sofa that probably belonged to the tenant. I studied the recessed lights, the skim-coat paint job, the fine cabinetry. If the apartment was a rental, it was a highly unusual one. Perhaps Amelia and Fritz believed the entire house was a marketing opportunity, and it needed to represent their work accurately.

Before I left, I took a glass down from the kitchen cabinet and filled it with water. I poured the cup of water on the wood floor in the middle of the bedroom. A leak, she might think. I took a photo of the puddle so that I could replicate it in the future, if need be. Then I dried the glass and returned it to the cabinet.

• • •

When I finished eating dinner, I cleaned the Straubs' kitchen so it would look exactly as it had when I'd arrived. I washed the dishes by hand, dried them, and put them away. I placed all the garbage in a bag that I would throw out on my way to the train.

Before leaving, I checked on their home office, because I'd found useful information there in the past. I sat down at Amelia's desk, resting my hands on the smooth, rich walnut. In and among a stack of architectural drawings, I saw two new Post-its. One read: *surrogacy agency* with a phone number below. One read: *adoption agency* with a phone number below. A chill traveled across my scalp and down my back.

Amelia and Fritz could very well be moving forward on their quest to have a baby, and I wasn't privy to any of the pertinent information. I needed to understand their thought process so that I could guide them, so that I could help them.

•   •   •

Days later Ian sent me an extravagant flower arrangement with a card that read: *I'm in awe of you.* His mother, Paula, sent me a box of Godiva chocolates with a card that read: *You're brilliant.*

I emailed Ian to tell him that I was planning to be in his neighborhood in the West Village for work. We met for dinner at a small Japanese restaurant, decorated with antique Japanese panels.

Apparently, his mother had already received two offers on the apartment, with another potential one on the way, all greatly exceeding the asking price.

For the first half hour, Ian appeared tongue-tied and mildly flustered. "I really . . . I mean . . . Yeah, I know it was your photos," he said. "My mother is your friend for life. I can't even . . . I sent a couple of them to Amelia. She was blown away too."

He was especially grateful, he said, because he wanted to move things along quickly with his mother's apartment. "It reminds her of my dad," he said. "Once she moves out, she's planning to go to Florida." He paused. "You grew up in Florida, didn't you?"

"Orlando. My parents worked at Disney World."

"Wow." Ian blinked several times in a row. "A fairy-tale childhood."

"They were 'custodial cast members'—that's what Disney calls its janitors." My parents had hated their jobs and each other. It was probably each one's own personal hell.

"Wow."

Most people don't realize that *any* job at Disney World, maintenance staff or otherwise, has more dark than light, more pain than pleasure. "I lived in Disney housing for ten years."

"You're incredible."

"No." I smiled modestly.

"Overcoming . . . obstacles . . . hurdles."

I ate another piece of California roll. I'd mistakenly allowed Ian to order for both of us; obviously risk averse, he'd ordered the least interesting items on the menu. "I called Amelia yesterday," I said. "She sounded distressed."

Ian smoothed out the wrinkles in the tablecloth.

"She wouldn't tell me what was wrong." The waiter refilled our water glasses. "Do you know?" I had my own thoughts, but I was looking for Ian's history and perspective.

He sighed. "It's probably about the baby she wants to have."

I felt the muscles in my jaw release. "Yes?"

"Fritz says it's really hard."

"On their marriage?" I asked.

"Maybe."

"Of course it would be."

"Maybe they blame themselves or something. . . ."

"Solutions exist."

The waiter cleared our plates away.

Ian brushed away imaginary crumbs from the tablecloth. "Fritz says the whole adoption thing is rough. It's been two years."

"There's surrogacy," I said.

"Yeah." He rolled his chopsticks with the palms of his hands. "I know a guy who did that."

"Could be a friend or a relative," I said.

"I guess." He sighed.

The waiter brought the check.

"Ian, I'm so glad that we had this evening together," I said. "It's just, there's an ease. I feel like we've known each other forever." I gently placed my hand on his forearm and rested it there for several minutes. I put my arms around him when I said goodbye. It was an intentionally ambiguous gesture.

CHAPTER FIVE

My prints of Natalie's birthday party were ready on New Year's Day, the same day the Straubs returned from their vacation. I don't usually frame photos for my clients, but I couldn't resist in this case. I wanted to see my work in their home right away, and I didn't want to leave it to Amelia and Fritz, who might or might not get it done.

I framed five pictures and placed the best one—Natalie with her balloon unicorn, chin tilted up, laughing, hands up—in a sterling silver frame. I wrapped all of them in a heavy bronze-colored paper that I thought Amelia would like.

On the second of January, I brought the prints to the Straubs' house. I was nervous about seeing Amelia, and as I approached the front door, my anxiety escalated. I wondered if she'd missed me as much as I'd missed her.

When she opened the door to greet me, her words and gestures pulled me into the circle of light that surrounded her. "Delta Dawn!" she said. The bells sounded in my head again, but this time they transformed into a full orchestra performing an opera, probably Verdi's *Aida,* since that was the only opera I knew.

I handed her the wrapped packages. Would the silver frame strike her as an extravagant gift that wasn't warranted by our friendship? I feared that her response would be less than I'd imagined it to be. I needed her to recognize my work, the same way I recognized hers.

She unwrapped the one of Natalie with her balloon unicorn. Tears filled her eyes. "Darling Delta. There are no words." She embraced me.

My cup runneth over. That wasn't a phrase I'd ever thought about or used before, but right then it seemed apropos.

She placed three of the framed photos on their console table in the front library. And two in the great room. I couldn't have asked for more prominent placement.

•   •   •

In the New Year, Friday night babysitting at the Straubs became a pattern, and one or two additional nights often came up at the last minute, so I was averaging two nights a week at their house, one night a week with Ian, and found myself busy a great deal.

I got in the habit of picking up the Straubs' dry cleaning, and other odd errands, because such gestures gave me a reason to make extra visits to their house and because Amelia appreciated it so much. "Delta, you're a true miracle," she would say, interlacing her fingers below her chin in a prayerlike gesture.

One evening, as I approached the Straubs' brownstone to drop off the dry cleaning, I saw the lights on through their garden-level windows. I casually mentioned my observation to Fritz when he greeted me at the door. "Would you like me to shut those lights off?"

"That's quiet little Gwen who rents from us." He smiled. "She barely makes a peep. The best kind of tenant doesn't socialize."

I didn't spend a lot of time with Fritz in those early weeks, but I could tell he was attracted to me. I could sense his eyes locked on me when my back was turned. I, too, longed for a connection with him, perhaps because he was a central figure in Amelia's world.

On Fridays I would frequently arrive early, before Fritz and Natalie were home, because Amelia enjoyed having her own special time with me. The front door was occasionally unlocked in the daytime, so I'd let myself in. Sometimes Amelia didn't even hear me when I walked into her office. I would stand in the doorway and observe her working—her brow furrowed with concentration. Her beauty was impossible to separate from her dazzling mind.

I entered one afternoon and saw, on her monitor, the elevations of a town house. "Amelia, that's gorgeous." I was completely sincere.

"Oh, Delta, do you think so?" She looked like a child—so hopeful, so eager for praise.

"Yes, it's brilliant." Her supremely functional designs were always layered with ideas. She wasn't capable of drawing something commonplace.

Amelia was buoyed by my encouragement. I could tell by the change in her posture and the shift in the angle of her chin. "I get so lost in my work, and sometimes I don't know what's good and what isn't." She rested her fingers on my shoulder. "I can't tell you what your support means to me."

Fritz had probably stopped telling Amelia what she needed to hear. I could see her wilting when she didn't have sufficient praise. She needed someone to prop up her sense of herself.

After discussing her drawings, we would sit at the kitchen counter and she'd make us each a cup of herbal tea. These were some of my happiest moments. Without fail, I would try to steer the conversation in the direction of the baby that she yearned for. I was looking for the right time to address the subject directly and hadn't found it yet.

Sometimes she asked me about myself. "So I get reports from Ian but nothing from you," she said one day, a glimmer of curiosity in her eyes.

I sipped a warm mug of raspberry tea. "I feel so fortunate that you introduced us. How did you know?" I was seeing Ian regularly, but going slow on physical intimacy for as long as possible while still maintaining his interest.

Amelia beamed, clearly relishing the role of matchmaker. "It was intuition!"

"He's an amazing person," I said. "I feel like we've known each other for years."

"*You're* an amazing person." She squeezed my hand. "By the way, he showed me the photos of his mother's place. I hear Paula's planning the wedding already." She laughed. "And I don't blame her." The notes of her laughter rippled through the air.

•　　•　　•

R u free Thursday for lunch? It was a text from Amelia the following Monday. I felt light-headed. I didn't expect this. I'd been hoping that our relationship would extend beyond photography and babysitting, but I thought it would take several months. I didn't expect that we'd already be socializing, without the pretext of my babysitting Natalie.

Amelia suggested I meet her at a job site on the Upper East Side so she could show me the town house they'd just finished renovating. She wanted to spend time with me—to share her work with me. She'd already shared her drawings with me, but the invitation was an indication of our growing intimacy. It was a significant step forward in our relationship.

Wednesday night, I spent more than an hour choosing an outfit for my lunch with Amelia. I wanted her to be proud of me if she had occasion to introduce me to someone. I wanted to look like I belonged to the same socioeconomic class that she did. She might choose to take me to a fine restaurant, so I needed something slightly elevated but effortless. After trying on most of the clothes in my closet, I ended up choosing a gray cashmere sweater and black slacks. It wasn't a unique outfit, but Amelia would certainly notice that the pants and sweater were both very expensive.

When I arrived at the job site at noon the following day, three workers were finishing final touches on the house, installing the kitchen cabinetry, hardware, appliances, and light fixtures. I spotted Amelia. She was wearing a stylish brown coat and a silk scarf around her neck. "My beautiful Delta," she cried. "I'm so happy you're here!" It was freezing cold, but Amelia's words heated every inch of my body within seconds.

I noticed how the workers looked at her, the supreme respect they accorded her. They worshipped her. Her eyes darted to every corner of the kitchen, assessing what needed to be done. "Line up the pull and the hinge." "Center the sconce." "Raise the lantern two inches." When she gave a direction, her confidence and expertise were palpable.

She finished speaking to the workers, then led me through the parlor floor, describing the paths of circulation and the use of space. Not only was the renovation finished, the home was almost completely decorated. It appeared that many of the original walls were intact, as opposed to the first floor of the Straubs' home, which was largely open.

We entered the library in the back of the house. "The clients wanted to keep all the dark wood and the paneling," she said. "They think they're respecting history. I tried to tell them it was added in the sixties. And even if it was original, it's ugly.

"They saw our website," she said. "And I told them, listen, you say you like our work. Well, it's not going to look like that if you leave all the heavy wood everywhere." Amelia was surprisingly practical when speaking about her work. Yes, she was a true artist, and it was this aspect of her, above all else, that drew me to her. But she acknowledged the commercial side of her job without apology. Amelia and I had so much in common.

I found the home handsome—though not in the same league as the Straub house. Amelia led me up the stairs, pointing out details with which she was pleased, such as the design of the black iron newel posts, the steel balusters, and the gracefully curved mahogany handrails. The house didn't completely represent her aesthetics, but I could tell she was proud of it.

She showed me the master suite on the second floor and the children's bedrooms on the third floor. "We're submitting photos of our work for an award we were nominated for," she said. "The photographer we normally use totally flaked." We were about to head back down the stairs when she stopped and turned to face me, her eyes bright. "You know, I just had an idea," she said. "Would you take photos of the house for us?"

It took a minute for me to register what she'd said. When I did, I felt a hollow pit in my stomach. She'd asked me to lunch for this particular reason. I'd believed she was interested in spending time with me.

"We need someone brilliant who can fight against all the dark," she said. "Of course I'd pay you anything you ask."

I told myself that the request was flattering. She liked the photos of Ian's mother's place. Real friends do favors for each other. Just because Amelia had asked me for a favor, that didn't necessarily mean anything about our friendship.

But I felt foolish, and at that moment, when I tried to see myself through her eyes, I saw Natalie's babysitter and a party photographer. Not an artist. Not a peer.

•   •   •

When it came time for the shoot the following week, I overcame my despondency and was able to enjoy myself, largely because I had Amelia's undivided attention and her admiration. She followed me around like a puppy dog, just as Ian and Paula had done in Paula's apartment. Occasionally I allowed Amelia to look through the viewfinder. "How do you do it?" she said. "You're not misrepresenting the space, but you're interpreting it in the best possible way. You're a genius."

I hesitated when she asked what she owed me. If I were to take her money, then I would be solidifying an employer–employee relationship. But if I did not take her money, then I still wouldn't know if our friendship was purely one of convenience for her.

She'd been paying me to babysit Natalie and she wouldn't have it any other way. However, I considered the photographs to be in a separate category. For one thing, I typically charged a lot for my photographic skills. And something told me that Amelia was looking for a deal. She would be put off if I said my price was fifteen hundred for the day. But I couldn't devalue my work. It was all or nothing. I chose nothing.

·   ·   ·

In early February, Amelia and Fritz had a business trip. They were going to Rome for four days to meet with their biggest client. They asked me to stay with Natalie, and of course I agreed.

For those four days, each morning I made breakfast for Natalie and we walked to school together. Then I'd spend the majority of the day at my apartment, editing, if I didn't have a shoot. The hours in my apartment were growing difficult, because my body and brain were becoming accustomed to the scale and light in the Straubs' home, including the design of their windows and glass doors, which allowed the eye to borrow all the space outside their home as well. In the Straubs' house, I had the freedom to stretch and run, metaphorically speaking, with no constraints, whereas, in my own apartment, I felt myself shrink and compress.

Amelia had told me Natalie was old enough to be in their house alone for a couple of hours in the afternoon, but I didn't agree, so I made certain to return by four thirty, when Natalie arrived home, and often earlier.

I knew that Gwen, the tenant downstairs, was at work during

the day and it was possible to enter the garden apartment without fear of being observed. I felt that someone ought to be keeping tabs on her. I'd noticed several odd patterns of behavior. For instance, at the foot of her bed was a blanket that she always rolled into a tight cylinder—an indication that she was tightly wound and might be a loose cannon.

Sometimes I would arrive as early as 2 P.M. so that I could take a nap in the bed downstairs. I slept so soundly in that bed. It was perfect for me. I'd been repeating the puddle-of-water trick at least once a week, along with rearranging Gwen's clothing from time to time, just to keep her off-balance.

The garden apartment and the Straubs' future baby became linked in my thoughts. In my mind, the surrogate or birth mother who carried their baby belonged in the apartment. (It seemed to me that must have been the Straubs' intention all along.) Gwen was not that person.

Each evening, Natalie and I would do her homework, eat dinner together, and take Itzhak for a walk around the block. When she didn't have much homework, we stayed up late and played Scrabble. Before she went to sleep, we usually talked about school. Natalie told me various anecdotes about her friends.

"Hailey goes, 'Piper, remember the doughnuts we had at Madeleine's house?' And then she goes, 'Oh, Natalie, I forgot you weren't there.' But she didn't forget that I wasn't there. She wanted me to know that I wasn't invited to something."

I didn't offer advice, but I think Natalie felt better because I listened to her. It often took an hour or more for me to quiet her down. I couldn't have imagined how significant that time would be for me. And how I would long for it to continue.

•   •   •

On the third Friday of February, I was scheduled to babysit yet again, and this time Natalie was having a sleepover with Piper. I remembered her as the girl at Natalie's party who couldn't braid hair. I felt mildly hesitant, given what I'd learned of Natalie's friends. When I arrived, I set my laptop and a small shopping bag on the kitchen counter. Inside was a child's waterproof camera I'd purchased. It was a present for Jasper. I was hoping that someone would notice it.

I knocked on Natalie's door and poked my head in. "Hi, you two." Natalie and Piper were seated on the floor, immersed in painting their fingernails, and barely acknowledged me except for a slight wave. "I'll be downstairs," I said.

In the kitchen, I picked up a copy of the *Times* that was lying on the counter. Amelia and Fritz still subscribed to the paper edition. I sat down to read an article on a gang of counterfeiters from Lima, Peru. I learned that master counterfeiters are artists with a terrific desire for recognition. They're so hungry for praise that they often give themselves away inadvertently.

When I heard footsteps on the stairs, I refolded the newspaper as I'd found it, and left it on the counter. Fritz appeared in a becoming tuxedo, his face damp with perspiration. "Delta Dawn!"

He filled a glass with ice and filtered water and handed it to me, then filled a second glass for himself. "God, I hate this fucking monkey suit." He sat on the stool opposite me and glanced at the cover of the *Times,* then at the child's camera in my shopping bag.

"A little something I picked up for Jasper." I was pleased that my purchase had paid off.

"Right. I guess the apple doesn't fall far." He turned his water glass in a circle on the counter, as if he were inspecting it for a flaw. Then he sighed loudly. "Our clients . . ." He dropped his head back to look at the ceiling. "They're buying property in a fucking valley. Trees everywhere and dark as hell. They could buy anything. We told them and told them. They won't listen. It's the worst choice they could have made." He paused. "Man, I should stop talking, right?"

"I love hearing about your work, because it's all about light and shadow. Mine is too. When I walk into a space, any space, the first thing I see is the light and the shadow. Is that what you see?"

Fritz raised his eyebrows. "Yes!" He assessed me and I felt that his understanding of my abilities was coming into focus.

Backlit by the late-afternoon sun shining through the glass doors, he almost glowed. From behind his tortoiseshell glasses, his green eyes glistened brightly. I stifled a desire to pull out my Canon EOS. He laughed. "Unfortunately, I think that the star-chitects"—he chuckled at his pun—"and we're not star architects . . . even they still have to answer to someone. Someone else is paying for everything and making the decisions. Of course, we can walk off a job. But we haven't ever done that . . . not yet.

"These days, I come home to have a quick dinner with Natalie," he continued, "and then I work for another five hours. Amelia's worse than I am. When Natalie was younger, I was away a lot. Now it's the reverse. Amelia's more driven than anyone I've ever met." Fritz looked self-conscious, almost as if he'd forgotten I was sitting there. He studied a bubble in the handblown water glass. "You've been awesome to Natalie. It's just, we're juggling too much crap. Each year, a new crop of hotshots competes for the business. Anyway. I need to stop talking. And ask about you."

"I love observing children, discovering their personalities," I said. "The parents who hire me, some of them lack confidence. My pictures tell them that all of their choices have been the right ones, because their choices have led them to a life with joyful children who are thriving due to their love and care. I'm selling a self-image."

"Interesting." His eyes widened.

"You and Amelia too. I imagine a large part of what people buy from you is self-image. Living in a Straub house gives your clients confirmation that they belong to a cultured, sensitive, creative breed of elite."

I gathered that Fritz was pleased by what I said but didn't want to acknowledge it.

"They want to be *you*, don't they?" I said.

"Hell no." Fritz shook his head, as if amused by my outlandish idea, but I knew I had approached the core of what he considered to be the truth.

"It's an intimate act. To create someone's home," I said. "Your imagination, your intellect, your creativity, all of those things are funneled into your work. You're the artist. But the creation belongs to your clients. You give birth, and then you have to give your child up. The home becomes their child."

Fritz looked into my eyes and I knew we understood each other on a deeper level.

I stifled an urge to caress his face. I wondered what he would do if I took his hand and put it underneath my bra.

It was hard to explain my desire for Fritz. Even hard to explain it to myself. I didn't want Fritz or Amelia to have a personal life separate from me. The further I burrowed myself into them, both of them, the less likely I'd ever have to return to my own existence. The less likely they could disentangle themselves from me.

I heard footsteps on the stairs. Fritz stood, preparing to leave. Amelia, dressed in an alluring black dress with a long string of beads, entered the kitchen. She turned to face away from me, revealing the ivory skin on her back and a partially unzipped dress. "Delta darling." She gestured toward the zipper and I obliged.

She turned back around and smiled. "La Divina."

•   •   •

At 7 P.M., the doorbell rang and the pizza I'd ordered arrived. I called to the girls and they flew down the stairs and past me into the kitchen toward the small media room. Both girls were wearing capri pants and tank tops. Piper's top revealed her midriff. Natalie grabbed the remote.

"We're watching *Mean Girls* while we eat pizza," Natalie said.

"Yasss!" Piper said as she slid into a full split on the floor. She could do splits easily, and it was clear she wanted those around her to recognize her talent.

"Natalie, your parents OK with that?"

She rolled her eyes. "Of course."

I had the sense that Natalie wanted Piper to think she'd seen the movie before when she really hadn't—that she was trying to impress Piper with her prior knowledge of *Mean Girls*.

Natalie turned on Showtime and found the movie. Then the girls brought slices of pepperoni pizza on paper plates into the media room and settled into the sectional sofa with Itzhak at their feet.

I sat at the kitchen counter and worked for a while on my laptop, my eyes drifting to Lindsay Lohan on the television screen every few minutes.

Piper recited lines from the movie. "'What is that smell?' 'Oh, Regina gave me some perfume.' 'You smell like a baby prostitute!' Yasss!" She turned to Natalie. "OK, you're Janis and I'm Cady." Natalie acted as though she knew the dialogue too, but it was clear she didn't.

I pulled out my Canon EOS from my backpack; while the girls were engrossed in the movie, it was a good opportunity to take a few photographs of the house. I planned to keep the photos in my archives, in case I wanted to refer to them one day.

Natalie and Piper paused the movie halfway through to microwave popcorn and then resumed. When the credits were rolling at nine, I suggested it was time to brush teeth and change into pajamas. That was when Piper proposed *Mean Girls 2*. Natalie jumped on the idea.

"You can watch it over breakfast," I said. "It's too late to start a movie now."

"Whatevs," Piper said, tossing her hair.

"Mom and Dad let me stay up as late as I want when I have a sleepover." Natalie proceeded to look for *Mean Girls 2* on Showtime.

I didn't think this was exactly true, but I also didn't want to make her seem immature in front of Piper, who carried herself with a cool sophistication that was extreme for an eleven-year-old.

"I don't know." I made eye contact with Natalie, trying to read the situation.

"Please, Delta," she said quietly with wide, innocent eyes.

I already knew the dynamic with Piper was less than ideal. "OK, Natalie. Fine."

While the girls were watching the movie, I studied them. Piper had long, shiny black hair and golden skin. Her delineated features, her bone structure and its accompanying shadows and highlights, were unusual for a child. I look at children's faces for a living, so I know what I'm talking about. It takes a long time for a face to become what it is supposed to be. Some children have baby fat well into their teens. Then life experience forms a character and chisels out the lines of a face. Small children are often cute, but they're rarely beautiful, because real beauty has specificity.

Natalie hadn't yet become the person she was going to be, whereas Piper had. Even at eleven, Piper's face had lines and a form. How does that happen to a child? How does it not happen to a child? I don't know that I ever became the person I was meant to be.

After half an hour, Piper paused the movie. She stood up and shook her hips from side to side. "Damn, Gina, I need some candy!" She looked at me expectantly.

"There's none in the house." I knew that to be true because I checked the kitchen cabinets from time to time. If the Straubs were running low on any staples, I would stop by the market on my way to their house and pick up the items they needed. Amelia was always so grateful for such gestures.

"Skittles." Piper moved her hips in circles like she had a Hula-Hoop. "Woo-hoo!"

"Skittles!" Natalie chimed in, though she must have known that her parents didn't have Skittles in the house.

"I haven't seen any candy here." I found myself growing irritated by Piper and her demands.

"Ice cream!" Piper high-fived Natalie.

"Girls," I said. "Finish the movie. It's almost ten."

"Ice cream is a necessity," Piper said. They continued to dance, their arms in the air, their hips bumping each other.

I caved in and gave them coconut gelato, which I'd noticed in the freezer earlier.

After the movie, I followed them upstairs, but Natalie waved me away. "We're fine."

"Really?" I asked.

She closed the door behind her.

Later I checked back and the light was off in Natalie's room. I assumed that they were sleeping.

I straightened up the media room, fluffing the pillows on the sofa where the girls had flattened them down. A charm necklace had fallen in between two pillows. I assumed it was Natalie's. It appeared that she had made the clay charms herself. One charm resembled Itzhak. One was a little heart with a zigzagged line down the middle, meant to indicate that the heart was broken.

In the kitchen, as I was pouring boiling water over a tea bag, I heard a loud scream from upstairs. I raced up the stairs two at a time and opened the door to Natalie's room to find Natalie asleep in her bed. The pull-out trundle bed was empty. Piper was standing by the window, screaming. "There was a man! He had a knife! Help me!"

Natalie rustled in her bed, half-asleep. "What happened?"

"Shhh," I whispered to Piper. "You had a bad dream."

"What?" Natalie murmured again.

"Shhh." I patted Natalie's arm. "Go back to sleep. It's OK."

I tried to walk Piper to the door, but she jumped away from me and started screaming again. "No! No!" Even in the dark room, I could see the terror in her face. It wasn't a show. "I want my mom! You have to take me home!" Piper crouched on the floor, her body in a tight ball.

"Come with me and we'll call your mom." I pulled her to her feet and convinced her to follow me down the stairs.

Piper and I sat at the kitchen island. She was wearing a short red nightgown that could have been described as sexy. I've read that young children with a heightened sexual awareness have often been abused. In fifth grade I used to sit on top of the monkey bars in a dress and underwear, blocking the path, so that the boys would likely touch my crotch when they came swinging by.

"Do you want some milk?" I asked.

She nodded.

"Do you still want to call your mom?"

She cast her eyes down.

"OK, let's have some milk," I said, "and then we can decide what you want to do."

"And some cereal. Do they have any excellent cereal?"

I looked in the cabinet and found Special K and Lucky Charms, which surprised me. Piper chose Lucky Charms. I poured her a bowl of cereal and milk and placed the bowl and a spoon on the counter in front of her. I sat next to her while she ate.

Her frame of mind had shifted and she appeared to be recovering from her nightmare. "You know, you can buy a box that has only the Lucky Charms marshmallows," she said, "and none of the cereal."

"Wow."

"I remember you from Natalie's birthday party," she said. "You were taking pictures."

"Yeah."

She was painstakingly collecting only the marshmallows onto her spoon. "You're a photographer and a babysitter too? How come?"

I chose to view the question as innocent. "I like Natalie. I like her parents."

"You like babysitting?"

"Yes."

Piper took another bite of only marshmallows. I was struck by the definition of her lips, like a painted doll. "That's weird," she said.

"Why is it weird?" I asked.

"I saw you taking pictures of the house. Why were you taking pictures of the house?"

I didn't realize that Piper had noticed what I was doing while they were watching the movie. I experienced a familiar sharp tug in my abdomen. I knew my intentions were pure, but others might not understand.

"It's a beautiful house, right?"

"What are you going to do with the pictures?"

The faint smirk on her face elicited a burning sensation in my chest, similar to heartburn. "Someday when I buy a house," I said, "I'll refer to the pictures for ideas on how to decorate."

"Are you buying a house?"

"Not now."

"Are you married?"

"No."

"Why not?"

"Not everyone gets married."

"You don't want to get married?" Piper swished the milk around her bowl with her spoon.

"I didn't say that."

"Are you dating anyone?"

I paused. Ian would have described us as dating, but I didn't consider sharing that information with Piper.

"I'm divorced." Robert and Jasper were useful as a dam to block her questions.

"Then you were married before."

"I have a son."

"A son?"

"He lives with his dad."

"Oh." She licked the back of her spoon, like she was licking an ice cream cone. "Seems weird to me. That you're babysitting. Do you need the money?"

"That's not your business." I stood up and returned the box of Lucky Charms to the kitchen cabinet and the milk to the fridge. "You should go back to bed."

"D'you go out a lot?" she asked.

"Mm-hmm."

"Where do you go?"

"Wherever."

"So you have a lot of friends?"

What are friends? I go to three birthday parties a week. That's more socializing than anyone needs. When I lived in Florida, my best friend got married. She asked me to be her maid of honor and then she changed her mind. We'd had an unusually close bond. I cared for her when she fell and broke several bones. Her fiancé was probably threatened by the strength of our relationship. He couldn't handle the depth of her affection for me.

I heard the front door open and Amelia's and Fritz's footsteps. They appeared in the kitchen and saw me and Piper at the island. Dressed in winter coats and boots, eyes shining bright, faces flushed from the cold, they looked dashing.

"Hi, guys." Amelia furrowed her brow in confusion. She and Fritz threw their coats on the hall bench and removed their boots.

"Piper had a nightmare," I said.

"I'm OK." Piper brought her cereal bowl to the ceramic farmhouse sink. "The radiator in Natalie's room woke me up. Hashtag Noise. You guys should get it fixed. I don't know how Natalie sleeps in that room."

"Sure." Fritz pursed his lips, perhaps to indicate that he appreciated the gravity of the problem, or perhaps he was trying not to laugh.

Once Piper was safely upstairs, Amelia cut her eyes at me. "That kid is a piece of work."

I nodded, then gathered my belongings. "Listen, I'm sort of embarrassed to tell you this. I . . ."

"What?" Fritz asked.

"I took some pictures of your kitchen. It's exquisite. One day, when I buy a house, I want to have a kitchen that looks like yours." I gestured toward the cabinetry. "The workmanship on the cabinets. I took some photos so I don't forget. Is that OK?"

Amelia laughed. "My God, I don't care if you take pictures of the kitchen!"

Her laughter sounded like music to me, her voice lifting up to a high register, and then descending. In that instant I recognized my love for Amelia. I wasn't sure how to describe it. My feeling was bigger than any label I could come up with.

•   •   •

I woke to the sound of my cell phone ringing. It was my former colleague, Lana. She hadn't called me for three months. For a while she'd been calling every day. She found out I'd slept with the man she was dating. I'd had no idea they were in a relationship. I only saw them together twice. One night, about six months earlier, I'd bumped into Christopher at an overpriced bar on Vanderbilt, and we started talking about photography. He wanted to walk me home and he ended up spending the night. I hadn't talked to him since.

When Lana discovered what had happened, she said some vile things to me. She called me a whore and a parasite. It wasn't worth my time to fight with someone like her. She projected her own dishonesty and disloyalty onto other people. Years earlier she'd betrayed my trust, so our friendship was already on an inevitable decline. In the last couple of years, I'd barely seen her. It was even a stretch to describe her as a friend.

Lana's call went to voicemail. She rang again and it went to voicemail again.

I sat down at the kitchen counter with a cup of black coffee and a piece of toast and surveyed the living room and kitchen. I owned three expensive pieces of furniture: a solid rosewood coffee table and two leather chairs. The kitchen cabinets were well made, with high-quality chrome hardware, though I would have preferred polished nickel. My large walnut cutting board, prominently displayed on the kitchen counter, contrasted beautifully with the white Caesarstone countertops. But recently such details that had pleased me in the past failed to lift my spirits. I couldn't help comparing myself and my apartment to the Straubs and their house. The contrast left me feeling profoundly inadequate. I found it impossible to shut down the voices in my head that shouted out my inferiority.

Lately my brightest moments were derived from my personal photoshopping endeavors, particularly the ones involving the Straubs. I would usually allow myself to devote several hours to those projects later in the day, as soon as I'd finished my work. It was something to look forward to.

After breakfast I took a soothing hot shower and enjoyed the force of the water pounding onto my shoulders and arms. My shower was only thirty inches by thirty inches, though the glass walls on two sides gave the illusion of a larger shower. A small hexagon-shaped glass tile covered the shower floor, and a rose-colored subway tile covered the walls and gave off a warm glow. I should have painted the walls of the apartment the rose color instead of lavender. The lavender walls looked gray and flat in the northern light. Why hadn't I known that would be the case? If there was one thing I knew about, it was light. What kind of light made people and places shine.

CHAPTER SIX

On a Saturday afternoon in early March, I received a text from Amelia.

What r u up to during the day tomorrow?

Her question was one I'd hoped and prepared for.

going for a run over Brooklyn Bridge

I knew that Amelia enjoyed the route over the Brooklyn Bridge and through Brooklyn Bridge Park, because I'd overheard Natalie discussing it with Piper. I surmised that Amelia liked Brooklyn Bridge Park because she wanted to feel like she was part of the community. She liked the image of herself as someone who took advantage of the free things that the city had to offer, as if what she loved most about her life was accessible to anyone who lived in Brooklyn.

It wasn't an especially convenient route for me. Moreover, I disliked running. But I had a feeling that if I casually mentioned a plan to run over the bridge, Amelia would be tempted.

She wrote back: *I'd love to go with you.*

I spent a few minutes composing my response. I hoped to appear pleased, in a measured way, but not excited. In the end, I wrote: *Great.*

•   •   •

We met at 10 A.M. on Sunday morning and started by running north on the promenade. It was late winter, but still cold, so the walkway was relatively empty. The BQE below us was backed up with traffic and oppressively loud. For the first twenty minutes of our run, Amelia talked nonstop. "They'll move on to another architect in a heartbeat," she said. "And Fritz has a lazy confidence. He thinks the clients are loyal. He's always surprised if we lose them."

We approached the end of the promenade and continued down the long hill past the playground. In spite of the fact that Amelia was ten years older than me, she was a lot faster and in better shape. I tried to disguise my heavy breathing.

"He's leaving it to me, largely because he knows that I landed these clients and they're mostly interested in my ideas. Well, that doesn't have to be true." Amelia wasn't winded in the slightest. If I were just listening to her voice and didn't see her, I wouldn't have known she was running. "Fritz is devoting more and more of his time to pro bono jobs. A library for an underserved neighborhood. Fine. A homeless shelter. Fine. And he says he finds that more rewarding. But we have a hell of a lot of overhead. Fritz throws up his hands and he says it's time to downsize. Downsize, my ass. Twenty years ago he was driven. But he's lost his competitive edge." Amelia finished the speech and exhaled like it had taken a lot out of her. She sounded defensive and probably felt guilty about her criticism of Fritz. Even so, she really owned her story, perhaps more than anyone I'd ever met. It was intoxicating.

Once we approached the bridge, I looked below and could see the lights on Jane's Carousel, the century-old merry-go-round, sparkling inside a glass box, and could make out the carved wooden horses, no two exactly alike, and the chariots.

I'd photographed two birthday parties there. It was the most beautiful merry-go-round I'd ever seen. Up close, each horse has a distinct personality and decorative style. The older children prefer the "jumpers" and the littlest children like the "standers." The babies ride in the chariots.

I recognized this carousel as an original work of art. It differed from Cinderella's Golden Carousel and everything at Disney, all of which had an eye toward sales in its DNA.

So much talent and skill had gone into the restoration of Jane's Carousel and the design of the glass pavilion, situated on the East River between the two bridges. It was divine in its concept and execution. And how ironic that the children, the primary consumers, would never fully appreciate it. And neither would the adults. They would trivialize it as an amusement ride.

Amelia must have seen me looking in that direction. "Beautiful, isn't it?" She paused. "Do you ever take Jasper to the carousel when he's in town?"

My throat tightened. "Yes, he loves it."

"Same with Natalie. I used to take her there."

"How is Natalie?" I hadn't seen her for a week. She had gone to a friend's house Friday night, so Amelia hadn't needed me to babysit.

She paused. "Well . . . a couple of days ago, she heard us talking about having a baby. You know, I'm very open. I don't believe in hiding anything."

"Right."

"I worry about her. She's not tough. She doesn't have grit."

I thought it possible that Natalie was tougher than Amelia knew, but I didn't choose to share my opinion.

We ran across the bridge, then back again, then into the park with the river on our right. At this point, I was sweating profusely, and since I'd made the mistake of wearing cotton, my shirt was wet, cold, and clinging to my skin.

"So I need an update on you and Ian," Amelia said brightly.

"We've grown really close in such a short period of time," I said. "He has amazing stories from his childhood." Ian hadn't told me any amazing stories from his childhood. But it couldn't hurt for

Amelia to believe that Ian and I were serious. "I might be in love." I whispered the last words, as if I were embarrassed to admit it.

Amelia gasped with delight. She was clearly invested in my relationship with Ian. "If you two get engaged, I'm throwing you a brilliant party!"

I tried to laugh, but didn't have enough breath, so I had to make do with a smile.

"He's working on this apartment in Rome and our client adores him. Thanks to Ian, we have five new projects, all from the same client."

"Wow."

We ran along the water, past Pier 2, which offered endless choices of recreational activities: roller-skating, handball, bocce, basketball, kayaking. I've never been able to appreciate concepts like "recreation" and "fun." I don't viscerally understand what those words mean.

The wind was picking up, and my throat and lungs were burning in the cold air. Along with intermittent pain behind my knees, my shins were aching. Unfortunately, in talking to Amelia, I'd implied that I was a regular runner, so I needed to keep pace with her or risk appearing disingenuous.

We approached the Pier 4 Beach and the enormous residential complex up ahead.

"Do you have plans for the afternoon?" Amelia asked.

"Errands, laundry."

Amelia put her hand on my shoulder while we were running.

"Come back to the house with me. I bought a really good chicken soup at the market this morning." She had an eager expression on her face.

The invitation to join Amelia at her house gave me a powerful surge of energy and strength. In a matter of seconds, the pain in my shins and knees disappeared. My legs felt strong, and I could move forward with freedom. Even my breathing turned effortless.

•   •   •

Back at the Straub house, Amelia showered and changed. She offered me a change of clothes, but I told her I was fine, even though all my things were damp and I would have loved a hot shower. I sensed that she didn't *really* want to lend me anything—that she would have considered it an imposition.

Amelia made coffee and served Natalie and me chicken soup. The three of us sat at the kitchen counter, and Itzhak lay near Natalie's feet. Fritz was in Boston for the weekend, celebrating his brother's fiftieth birthday.

Natalie told us about her upcoming concert. Amelia listened for a few minutes, then checked her phone, sent a text, then checked her phone again.

"Delta," she said, "I totally forgot that I have to drop by one of our sites in Lower Manhattan. Would you mind hanging here with Natalie while I'm gone? Only if it's convenient, of course."

Once I'd processed her words, I felt a dull aching sensation in my chest, similar to how I'd felt when she asked me to photograph the town house. Amelia had invited me to her house for this reason specifically. Maybe she'd gone running with me for this reason too. Perhaps she could have left Natalie alone for a couple of hours. Or she could have had Natalie join her. But it was so much simpler to invite me over as the family friend who had nothing better to do.

While Amelia was out and Natalie was practicing the cello, I let myself into the garden apartment, having observed that no one was home. I moved a stack of books from the bedroom to the living room, opened the closet doors, and left a small puddle in the bedroom. Before leaving, I studied the photographs on Gwen's bedside table again. The picture of her in the Bahamas had probably been taken two years earlier, judging from the clothing the women were wearing and the quality of the photo. It was clear that Amelia and Fritz didn't think much of Gwen's personality. Yet, somehow, this woman had ten friends who wanted to spend their vacation with her in the Bahamas. What did she do to make them like her?

I returned to the main house before Natalie noticed I was gone. When Amelia came home in the late afternoon, I gathered my belongings. "Oh, don't leave yet," she said, her voice rising and falling in a lovely cadence. "I was hoping we'd have some time together."

I felt flushed and warm with pleasure. She had the capacity to alter the chemistry of the air around her instantaneously, as if a drug was pumped into the room when she entered and I was breathing it in involuntarily. I found it almost impossible to go against her will.

She poured us each a cup of coffee, and we sat together at the dining table. She spoke softly, but intently. "The thing is . . . I thought that Fritz and I were on the same page about having a baby."

The sound of Natalie playing a sonata on her cello drifted down the stairs.

I pressed the nails of my right hand into my left palm. "I understand how stressful it is," I said. "I'd like to help you in any way I can."

"You know, when a birth mother chooses us," she said, "we can't hesitate."

I took a sip of coffee, choosing my words carefully. "I understand."

"Adoption makes the most sense for us, but it's taking so long. If it doesn't happen soon, we'll have to go out of state for a surrogate." Amelia pushed her hair behind her ears.

I sipped my coffee again, mainly to distract from any telling signs of anxiety in my face or voice. "You're considering surrogacy, then?"

"I'm considering everything."

"What about a friend or a relative?"

"There isn't anyone, not someone I could ask." She pushed her hair behind her ears again.

I hesitated, looking for the right words.

"I'd do anything to help you, Amelia. You know that, right?"

"I know." She smiled at me.

"You're such an amazing mother to Natalie. If you want another child, you should be able to have another child. It shouldn't be so hard."

"Thank you, Delta."

The sun was low in the sky, shining through the glass doors into the great room. I took another sip of my coffee. "It doesn't seem fair. Pregnancy and childbirth were easy for me," I said. "So easy."

"You were lucky," she said, then paused at the sound of quick footsteps coming down the stairs.

Natalie appeared with a piece of paper in her hand. "Mom, I need you to sign this form for my field trip." Natalie lingered in the room after her mother had signed the paper. Amelia turned to sift through some mail on the kitchen counter. My window of opportunity had closed.

•   •   •

I was scheduled to shoot a birthday party the following Saturday at noon on the Upper West Side. The clients had a five-year-old daughter, Hazel. From one phone conversation with Hazel's mother, Brooke, I visualized her as a brunette with sun-damaged skin, an athletic build, and overdeveloped calf muscles. It was a game I often played with myself. After a phone conversation, I would create images in my head of the client and the family members. The majority of the time, my images would prove to be accurate.

The night before, I'd purposefully left my cardigan sweater at the Straubs' house so that I would have a reason to go by there after

Hazel's party and spend a few minutes in their house. Five minutes in the Straubs' home made a difference to me. The ache behind my sternum diminished quickly in their presence.

In freezing rain and sleet, I took a car from my apartment to the Upper West Side. Clients always covered my travel expenses, as I usually carried heavy equipment—a tripod and a ball head, external flash units, light stands, reflectors and diffusers, and my camera case with lenses, filters, and an exposure meter.

Hazel's family greeted me at the door, including all four grand-parents, Carmen and Sergio Fernandez, Sarah and Howard Cohen. I peeled off a couple of wet layers and entered the apartment, a classic six in a prewar doorman building. I identified Hazel's mother—the sun exposure and the overdeveloped calf muscles. But I got the hair color wrong. She was a redhead.

The grandmothers gathered around me. "I need a picture with Hazel," Sarah began, "for my next holiday card." Holiday cards. The bread and butter for a family photographer. What used to be a thoughtful gesture, a considerate note and good tidings for the holiday season, had become a self-promotional opportunity—with less reach than social media, but more of a tactile punch. My clients sent out holiday cards because they wanted their friends and family to know that they had beautiful children and a lot of money. It was a message that came across easily in my photos, if that was desired. Success, in its various forms, was what I sold, so conveying it and bringing it into relief was effortless for me.

"We have five other grandchildren," Howard said to Sarah. "You can't send out a picture of only one."

"She's the one who takes after me." I didn't see any physical resemblance between Sarah and her granddaughter.

"Happy fifth birthday, Hazel." I knelt so I could look her in the eye. She had a round face and a head of red curls, like Little Orphan Annie.

"I'm still four," she said apologetically. "My birthday is next week."

"I see."

Sarah led her granddaughter to the living room and sat down with Hazel in her lap. Sarah yanked Howard's arm. "What's her name, the girl who's taking pictures?" she said loudly.

"Delta." Howard put his finger to his mouth to shush his wife.

"Delta! Come here!" Sarah called to me.

Howard stood behind Sarah and Hazel for the group shot. I took several photos of them, and then Carmen and Sergio entered into the frame and leaned over Sarah's shoulder.

"*Feliz cumpleaños*, Hazel!" Carmen called out to the camera. She kissed Hazel on the forehead.

Sarah's expression morphed from joyful to irate. She turned to Howard. "I'd like one photograph with my little granddaughter. Without everyone breathing down my neck."

One after another, family members entered the apartment: aunts, uncles, cousins, grandparents, dressed for the occasion. I finally caught another glimpse of Hazel's parents. They looked amazed by their good fortune—amazed that a child such as Hazel had entered their lives. They seemed to believe in their child's brilliance and talent, the same way people believe in God.

"I don't know if I mentioned," Brooke said to me, "that Hazel is *also* a gifted ballerina. She'll be performing for us later." She came closer to me so that she could whisper in my ear. "I have an idea for Brian's birthday. I want to surprise him with a gallery wall—photos of Hazel dancing."

"Of course," I said. "Perfect."

Brooke was entirely undiscriminating in her opinions of her child—so different from Amelia. Amelia had high standards for herself, and those high standards extended to her daughter. She wasn't inclined to heap praise on Natalie if it wasn't warranted.

I concluded that all of Hazel's relatives at the party considered themselves an important part of the girl's life and had probably never missed a birthday. The child didn't realize what she had. Her significant place in people's lives. Her privilege was of a different kind than Natalie's. For all of Natalie's material advantages, she would never have the same kind of self-esteem that Hazel had. She simply wasn't that central. Natalie drifted on the periphery of the Straubs' lives, in an outer lane around their whirlpool.

Mack the Magician showed up on time. We'd seen each other at five birthdays in the last two months. I remember the first time we met. We were working on a party in the East Village and we left the clients' town house together. When we reached the sidewalk, he pointed at the brown leather biker jacket I was wearing. "Funny, I didn't see you arrive with that." I smiled and kept walking, but I've hated him ever since.

At two thirty, when Hazel's party was winding down, I slipped into the front vestibule to phone the Straubs' house.

"Delta?" Fritz picked up the phone.

"Hi, I left my sweater at your place last night. I—"

"Amelia missed her meeting in Dallas." Fritz was speaking quickly in a hoarse voice. "She left the house at five in the morning and was supposed to fly straight there, but she didn't show up. The clients called me. They can't reach her. I can't reach her. I left a message for Ian, but I haven't heard back."

"I'll be there soon." I attempted to keep my voice in a low, steady vocal range. Changes in pitch indicate fear or anxiety.

I packed up the camera equipment, which I'd already placed near the front door; it took longer than it normally would have because my arms and hands were trembling terribly and I found it difficult to zip and unzip my camera case.

I waited for my car on West End Avenue. The rain had stopped, but I could feel the harsh, bitter air cutting through my down jacket. All the blood in my body was rushing to my head. I was confronted with the possibility of losing Amelia. My love for her was as intense as any romantic love I had ever experienced. I needed her. I wanted to disappear inside her.

•   •   •

Fritz answered the door, his sandy-blond hair disheveled, his face unshaven, a glazed look in his eyes. "Natalie's in her room doing homework. I haven't told her anything yet."

I dropped my equipment in the vestibule, hung my coat, and followed him into the library.

"Why don't we sit down?" I motioned to the sofa. He rubbed his palms together, like his hands were cold. I was genuinely concerned for him. It occurred to me that I needed to behave in a calm and confident manner. It wasn't the role I wanted to play, but I really had no choice, because anything other than that would send Fritz into a state of greater panic and crisis.

"Let's just talk through everything," I said. "Do you know if Amelia took a car service to the airport this morning?"

"I wasn't awake." He held his hands to his mouth and blew hot air on them.

"Do you know if she boarded her flight?"

"Jesus Christ. Jesus fucking Christ," he said, covering his eyes with his hands.

"If she checked into her hotel?"

He opened his eyes, but didn't appear to process what I was saying.

"Do you know the airlines, what flight number?"

I remembered a conversation I'd had with Amelia. She'd described Fritz as fragile and said that he expected her to be the strong one. Now I saw how he broke down in a crisis.

He leaned his elbows onto his knees with his head resting in his hands. "I should have gone. Fuck. Fuck."

"In a little while, she'll call us, and we'll know that everything's fine," I said. "Maybe she sprained her ankle. Maybe she lost her cell phone." Blood was pumping in my head, like there was too much blood and not enough space. I hid my fear, not wanting to add to Fritz's worry.

He looked up at me. "Do you think I should file a missing person's report?'

"Not yet," I said, though I didn't actually know the answer. I took one of Fritz's large callused hands and held it in mine. The feeling of his hand in mine calmed my nerves slightly. "I understand how you feel."

He looked as though he might have a stroke or a heart attack. I gently placed my hand on his cheek. His face reddened slightly, but he didn't move my hand away. I needed to handle the situation for Amelia's sake. I needed to comfort Fritz and get him back to thinking straight. "This is so painful right now, but it won't last long. We'll find her." A river of tears poured from his bright green eyes, down his face, and soaked his T-shirt all the way through, as if he'd jumped into a pool. I'd never seen so many tears. He needed my help. I leaned in toward him and kissed his lips very lightly, in an attempt to alter his frame of mind. He didn't push me away. When I pulled back to look into his eyes and gauge his response, I was relieved to see some animation in his features. I tried to read his expression. It could have been shock, but I tended to think it was excitement. I felt that kissing him was the only way to shake him out of his state. Again I leaned toward him.

"Dad!" Natalie's voice called from upstairs.

Fritz stood up with a start, his face bright red. I could tell how intensely he wanted me.

"Madeleine's mom is taking me to chamber music," Natalie called down. "She's picking me up in five minutes."

"OK, honey."

Fritz motioned for me to stay where I was. He turned and ran down the hall and up the stairs. I said Amelia's name in my head, then tried to find an image of her in my mind, as if my subconscious might give me information on her whereabouts. But even visualizing her face was difficult and painful.

On their library console table were several of the framed photos from Natalie's birthday party: the one of Natalie with her balloon unicorn in a sterling silver frame. One of Amelia holding Natalie, kissing her daughter's forehead. They resembled each other in that both had large eyes spaced far apart. Natalie's hair was lighter. I remembered the original version of the photo. I'd edited Natalie's image because it had lacked sufficient lightness and joie de vivre.

My gaze returned to Amelia in the photo. I closed my eyes to see if I could place a background with her face and discern any clues to her location. I felt so connected to her—almost like we were one and the same person—I ought to know where she was. But nothing came to me.

I opened my eyes again and compared Amelia to her daughter in the photo: Amelia was clearly playing to an audience. I doubted that she could identify the line between her performance and her life.

In one revealing photo of Fritz and Amelia, they were saying goodbye to their guests, toward the end of the party. Amelia was resting her head on Fritz's shoulder. He was gripping her wrist. She wanted him to protect her. He wanted her to protect him. They both wanted to be saved. Amelia described herself as the organized one who always had to take charge. Fritz felt that she expected too much of him—that she was always slightly disappointed in him, and he was probably right.

I'd seen an unpaid tuition bill for Natalie's school in their office. Such questions of money could bring stress into a relationship. Enough stress to break a marriage. I knew, not because I had any firsthand experience. I knew because I'd seen it in subtle ways whenever I'd photographed a party. Some parents wouldn't notice whether I charged five hundred or five thousand for a birthday party.

But there were others, maybe bankers, traders, lawyers, or otherwise, who might have had a couple of lucrative years. Then there was an assumption it would continue like that. And maybe their expectations were set in a certain place. Luxuries crept in. And perhaps, they assumed, because they saw their peers, they assumed it could be done. They were wealthy. And they would stay that way.

The families would hire me one year and then they'd hire me

back the following year whether or not they could afford me. And the birthday party they'd have for the child—it would be as lavish as it was the prior year. Maybe it was a matter of pride or positive thinking. If we believe we have the money, we will. So it was in those cases where I could see the tension starting to eat away at the family. And I could see it was right under the surface, just like Amelia and Fritz. And the mom was snapping at the dad because she was angry. Because they'd hired a photographer and a magician, and they had a fancy cake, but the kid was screaming his head off. Tension. And on some level, the mom probably knew that they spent the money and it wasn't worth it because of what it was doing and would do to their relationship. And she was probably angry at herself. But she felt angry at her husband because, well, in Amelia's case, she was the wage earner for all intents and purposes. But he was supposed to be. She wasn't supposed to be worried about money. That was the unspoken arrangement. She's not supposed to wake up one morning and feel her way of life slipping away from her, out from underneath her. And he feels angry at her. Why is the burden on him? And why is she the one who's running up the tab? And why, why, why.

Because someone lied to them. Someone told them that every year would be a little better than the last one. These were people who were working hard. They heard the silent promise floating through the air. And they probably believed it. Until one credit card bill after another started to pile up. And the private school tuitions were too much. And maybe we need to pull our kids out. Or move out because New York's too expensive. And experience the shame because our friends would know why. And our children would know that this was never the plan. And for some of them, the children loved the school. And the children would be so sad. It all comes crashing down. It all comes crashing in on you. That can happen when you have too much. Like some people do.

But Fritz and Amelia were different. They were truly deserving and generous. *Truly.* They were raising a principled daughter and they were instilling decent values in her. Fritz and Amelia were talented, sensitive, cultured, intellectual types with fine sensibilities, well read, with sophisticated taste. I felt myself to be so very fortunate—that Fritz and Amelia and Natalie had entered into my life. All that they were. And it was because I knew that I was my best version of myself when I was with them. *Yes.* When I was in their house. In their company. I became the person I'd always wanted to be. Possibilities opened up for me. I knew I could help them. First and foremost, I could help Fritz to find Amelia.

And later, when Amelia returned . . . I could help them have the baby they longed to have. It was clearer than ever to me now. In life, sometimes we have an opportunity to choose our family. I couldn't imagine there were any other people in the world with whom I'd have had such a strong connection. It was a certain kind of ecstasy to know where I belonged.

•   •   •

Fritz descended the stairs holding Natalie's hand. I didn't want her to see me, so I stepped back into the library and around the corner. A car horn beeped outside. Natalie kissed her father. Cello case in hand, she headed out the door, knowing nothing of her mother's absence. The door closed behind her.

The house was now empty except for Fritz and me. I thought about the Straubs' king-size bed, the mountain of pillows, their organic cotton sheets, and felt my body sliding under the sheets next to Fritz, his body on mine. I would help him get through this. He needed me right now. I needed him too. Holding Fritz close to me might ease the pain I was feeling. The excruciating pain of Amelia's absence. I moved back into his line of sight.

He took a step back. "The important thing here is I need to find Amelia."

"Yes."

He was sinking, melting into quicksand. "Nothing else," he said.

"Yes." And I knew that he was right. I wanted Fritz's hands on me. But more than that, I wanted Amelia back in the house.

Fritz and I looked out the window next to the door. I saw Natalie climb into the back seat of the Toyota Highlander that had pulled into the Straubs' private driveway. The car door slammed shut. Her friend's mother waved out the car window. I heard the car accelerating onto the street. Fritz finally looked back at me.

"Do you have access to Amelia's calendar?" I asked.

•   •   •

In the daytime, the Straubs' home office looked as if it were completely open to the side deck; one entire wall was made up of sliding doors with glass so clean, you wouldn't even know it was there. Outside, I saw the snow beginning to melt. The rain had washed much of it away. I could almost make out the lines of the landscaping. A few potted plants, which had been covered with snow up until now, were starting to reveal themselves.

Fritz turned on Amelia's computer. I sat next to him so I could look over his shoulder. His strong body odor filled the room.

Over the course of an hour, we looked through each and every meeting and call that had taken place that year, starting in January, as well as those that were scheduled to take place in late March and April.

"There was one time," he said, "maybe five years ago, when I thought Amelia was having an affair. I was gone a lot. And I think she was lonely. I didn't blame her. . . ." I heard a layer of darkness in his voice. "But it takes a toll."

In my mind's eye, I saw Amelia in bed with a woman, not a man. When I tried to make out the woman's face, I realized it was mine.

"Recently she seems anxious," I said.

Fritz continued to scroll through the calendar. "The whole baby thing."

"I know." My stomach clenched. He'd brought the subject up himself.

"Yeah, we've been looking at adopting," he said. "Looking at surrogates."

Amelia's absence had led to an opening for the surrogate conversation. Here was an opportunity and I couldn't turn away from it. "Did she find a surrogate?"

"We were . . . arguing. Amelia thinks a surrogate would confuse Natalie. And she doesn't want her baby in a stranger's body."

"Of course."

"It's a decision with fucking zero information, all these donors, surrogates, birth mothers, for Christ's sake. And you don't know a goddamn thing about anyone."

Patience. I needed patience and a level head. "You should hire someone you know to be the surrogate."

Fritz combed his fingers through his hair, starting from his forehead and going straight back.

"It might give you a measure of comfort." I patted Itzhak, who had followed us into the office. I could tell the dog was also troubled by Amelia's absence.

"Nothing's giving me comfort right now, Delta." He repeated that gesture of running his fingers through his hair. "I don't know where the fuck my wife is."

Fritz was obviously agitated. Even so, I needed to see the subject through to its logical conclusion. Granted, it was not the best timing, but it wasn't likely that surrogacy would come up again in an organic way. "Listen," I said, "there might be a woman who wants the experience of being pregnant. Or someone who loved being pregnant and wants that experience a second time. Or someone who needs the money. There are health benefits. Your risk of cancer and heart disease go down."

"OK." Fritz was staring at the monitor and didn't respond.

"All of those reasons would pale compared to the reasons that a friend would do it. A good friend who cared about you would want to see you happy. I know that I would."

He shifted his jaw to one side. "Yeah?" He was finally listening to me.

"I would do it for a good friend."

He squinted. "For us?"

My whole body was vibrating with uncontainable energy. I tried to maintain poise and stillness. I didn't want Fritz to know how high the stakes were for me. The lengths to which I would go. "Fritz, you and Amelia"—I took his hand in mine in a purposefully platonic gesture—"I love both of you. And I love Natalie too. I don't think it's appropriate. . . . Amelia is the one who should be having the conversation."

"She's not here. Did you notice?" His voice sounded choked and sarcastic all at once. "And it's just as much my decision."

"Is it?" I placed my other hand on top of his. "I think . . . I don't want to offend you."

Fritz looked down at the floor, clearly angered. "Fine. Talk to Amelia about it. If she's not dead."

I heard a noise in the doorway, looked up, and was stunned to see Amelia standing there.

CHAPTER SEVEN

Amelia wore an expression of divine bliss and looked strikingly pretty in spite of her wrinkled dress and faded makeup. The western light streamed through the wall of glass doors and across her face. She seemed to glow from the inside out.

Fritz stood up quickly.

With her chin tilted up and her chest expanded, Amelia was relishing the drama of her entrance. "I found our birth mother," she announced. "I found our baby."

Her words knocked the wind out of me.

Fritz's eyes narrowed into thin slits in his face. His jaw was clenched. He pounded the desk with his fist. "Amelia, you can't disappear for eight hours."

"I found our baby," she said. "There was no time this morning—I had to go straight to her house in New Jersey. She left me a message. Then I lost my cell phone; I left it in the car."

My breath felt restricted, as if I were hiking at a high altitude. Now that Amelia had found a birth mother, I would have difficulty reversing her course.

I stood up. "Tell us, Amelia." I did my best to smile.

Amelia took in my presence, but didn't appear bothered by it. I might as well have been their dog. For an instant I recognized the modicum of space I occupied in her mind, but my love for her was not diminished. If anything, I wanted her affection even more.

"Fritz, this girl, Lucia"—Amelia looked directly at Fritz, her voice at a higher pitch than normal—"she's a girl, she's nineteen, but not an idiot. She's Catholic and Latinx. She knows she's not in a position to raise the baby. She gets it. No money, no resources, no husband. And so someone else should." It was as if Amelia and Fritz were the only two people in the room now. She wasn't aware that she was sharing the information with me or not sharing it. "Different cultures have different priorities, and it's not for us to judge. They leave their children in their country and come here to work and send money each week. Or the grandparents raise them. It's quite practical, really. And it's smart. She's smart. And she's very pretty. White teeth. Clear skin. Glossy hair. And she's slender. I mean, she's pregnant, but her hips are slim." She motioned in the air with her hands to outline the contours of the girl's slim hips. "It's not good for a pregnant woman to be fat, because then the baby will be too. I said yes to the baby."

I felt as though all the oxygen were leaving the room. This was so wrong. It was all wrong. I needed to convince Amelia that she was making a mistake.

Fritz's lips were white and his face had developed a grayish hue. His anger was simmering. He leaned against the sliding glass door and fixed his gaze on the exterior landscape.

"There was another couple." Amelia was speaking rapidly and still in a high register. "I actually saw them leaving Lucia's house. I saw their photo. They live in Manhattan and they want the baby too. Lucia told me they're attorneys, but the woman plans to stop working and stay at home, or so she said to Lucia." She perched on the edge of her desk. "Still, I'm pretty sure Lucia's going to choose us. I told her all about you, Fritz. What a terrific father you are. I told her about Natalie—how excited she was for a little sister. It's a girl, by the way. Lucia is having a girl."

"I thought you were dead!" Fritz exploded, spitting at her. He slammed his fist into the nearby wall. He picked up a book from his desk and threw it across the room. "You have no fucking concern for anyone but yourself."

I inhaled and exhaled slowly, in an effort to quiet my nervous system.

"I lost my phone!" Amelia said. "It slipped out of my purse, I suppose." She examined her leather bag, the interior pockets, as if she was trying to figure out how the phone could possibly have fallen out. "And when I arrived, it was a *sensitive moment*. Lucia's mother was there, and I needed to show immense respect. They take this very seriously. They're religious people. It would have been a big mistake to make it all about my lost phone," she said. "I needed to communicate the right narrative."

I interjected. "There's not another chance to make a first impression."

"Exactly," Amelia said.

Fritz pushed his glasses up onto the bridge of his nose.

"Fritz," Amelia said, "you need to meet Lucia and the family. We need to go together tomorrow."

"I don't think so." He wiped saliva from the sides of his mouth.

"What?" Amelia said.

"Maybe you should invite her to come here," I said, digging the nails from my right hand into the palm of my left hand. "She would meet Natalie. And she would see the warmth and love in your family."

"Good idea." Amelia brightened. Strands of her hair were taken over by static and sticking straight up in the air.

"When is her baby due?" Fritz asked.

"It's important for us to say 'the baby,' not 'her baby.' We have to send the right energy into the universe." Amelia motioned up and out with both hands. "Language is powerful."

"When is the baby due?" he repeated.

"May tenth."

A timer was set on a ticking bomb. I had two months in which to shift the outcome. Long, slow, deep breaths.

"I don't think she should come here," Fritz said. "No one's committed to anything."

"Well, sweetheart . . ." Amelia paused.

I could see her mental calculations. How much should she pretend to take Fritz's opinion into consideration? "I haven't had any kind of clarity about any of this—for over a year. And I feel good about Lucia. You're going to feel that way too. And if you don't, then we'll just let her know that we changed our mind."

Fritz's gaze wandered toward me. Was he thinking of our earlier conversation? He picked up his cell phone, apparently to read a text.

"Fritz, please." Amelia was making a concentrated effort to soften her voice and her face.

"I won't pretend that I've agreed to this," he said. "I don't know shit about her, or the father."

"As long as you have an open mind." Amelia crossed the room to put her arms around Fritz, who barely reciprocated. "I'll invite her to come here tomorrow. But I'll make it clear that you and she need to meet so everyone is fully on board."

She walked into the kitchen, ostensibly to make the phone call. Fritz followed, as did I. Now that Amelia was safely home, I didn't have a good reason to stay. I had chills and a headache behind my eyes, as if my body were depleted of oxygen.

Amelia sat down at the small desk in the kitchen, next to the only landline in the house. She seemed mildly oblivious to the anger in Fritz's eyes.

I heard the sound of the front door opening and slamming shut.

"Natalie doesn't know that you were missing," he whispered to Amelia.

"I wasn't."

Natalie's footsteps pattered down the hall. She appeared in the kitchen with her cello. "Hi, Mom."

Amelia stood and wrapped her arms tightly around Natalie and held her. "I love you so much."

"You're back from Texas?"

"Honey, we've found our baby. The baby girl who will be your little sister."

Natalie's face whitened. Her lips pressed together tightly. She looked down and fumbled with the latch on her cello case, which had come partially open. "Where is she?"

"The woman I met today is pregnant with a baby girl. And I just have a feeling this could be so wonderful for us."

Natalie tried again to close the latch on her cello case. "Why doesn't she want her baby?"

"It's not that she doesn't want her," Amelia said. "It's that she can't provide for her. And she's not married."

"You don't need to be married to have a baby," Natalie said.

"It's hard."

When Natalie finally succeeded in closing the case, she leaned it against the wall and sat on the floor to pet Itzhak. "I feel sorry for the baby," she said.

"I'm going to be her mother."

Fritz raised his voice. "That is not decided."

Amelia and Fritz made eye contact. Silent communication passed between them. Each of them had a different way they wanted their daughter to view the situation. They mistakenly thought that Natalie didn't register the entire exchange.

"Natalie," I said. "How about one game of Scrabble before I take off?"

Natalie perked up at the suggestion. "OK."

Her parents looked relieved. I'd figured out a way to serve a purpose and a reason to stay in the house. Natalie and I settled in at the dining table.

Amelia called Lucia several times without reaching her. I could hear her leaving messages. Several minutes into our game of Scrabble, I heard Amelia talking to someone. I missed the first few words of her conversation.

"You're working tomorrow?" Amelia said, the disappointment in her voice impossible to disguise. "She's working tomorrow," she said to Fritz. "Tonight? Yes. Yes. Eight is perfect." Amelia hung up the phone. "She's coming over after dinner!"

I was relieved by this turn of events—and pleased at my own skill in directing us toward the desired outcome.

Natalie turned to see what the commotion was. "Who's coming?"

"Lucia is coming to meet us, honey." Amelia approached and leaned over to encircle Natalie in her arms.

I stood up. "I should go now. This is a time for your immediate family." It was a calculated risk, because I wanted to stay.

"We just started our game," Natalie said.

"We'll play another time." I spoke firmly so none of them would question my determination.

Fritz interjected. "No, it would be great for you to stay. Please." Fritz gave me a meaningful look. Was he thinking about our earlier conversation?

"It'd be nice for Natalie to have a pal," Amelia said cheerfully.

I did my best to maintain a neutral expression. I practiced inhaling and exhaling through my nose, taking slow, deep breaths. Amelia was underestimating the importance of the birth mother role—focused only on the girl's gait, carriage, and temperament. It was my moral obligation to alter Amelia's course.

Lucia was scheduled to arrive in one hour. Natalie and I continued our game. Meanwhile, Fritz took a pizza out of the freezer and put it in the microwave.

"We don't want Lucia to see that." Amelia pointed to the pizza box like it was a dead mouse. "Don't forget to throw it away."

Fritz barely acknowledged her.

Natalie and I ate pizza and drank seltzer while continuing on with Scrabble, and Amelia prepared a beautiful platter of raw vegetables and homemade cucumber dill dip, along with a platter of fresh fruit.

"Where's that homemade pumpkin bread?" Amelia called out from the kitchen.

"What?" Fritz asked.

"Got it."

Their house was so over-the-top clean that Amelia and Fritz had nothing to tidy. In fact, they had the opposite problem. Their house did not reveal the presence of a child, almost as if there was some shame attached to the fact that a child lived there and it might have been preferable if she didn't. Her belongings were all confined to her bedroom. There was very little evidence of Natalie in the downstairs living areas. Interestingly, Amelia must have recognized this, because she disappeared and, a few minutes later, appeared with a number of Natalie's toys, books, dolls, and art supplies.

Natalie spotted her mother with an armful of her belongings. "What are you doing?"

Amelia didn't register embarrassment. "I want Lucia to know that you have great toys and that your little sister would too."

"Oh." Natalie looked relatively satisfied with the answer.

Amelia placed a stack of Natalie's dog-eared books on the glass coffee table next to her large, glossy art books. Then, in an apparently haphazard manner, she placed some slutty-looking Barbie dolls gone wrong, a Spirograph set, and jewelry-making paraphernalia in various strategic locations throughout the downstairs living area. One would have assumed that Natalie had been playing and neglected to put the items away. I was impressed with the execution.

Amelia built a fire in the library, and then she and Fritz went upstairs to change while Natalie and I concluded our game of Scrabble.

I thought that Natalie had mixed feelings when she witnessed her mother's level of desperation for a baby. And I couldn't blame her. I felt a kinship with Natalie. It was clear she craved her parents' attention and rarely got enough of their time or energy. Another child would presumably mean even less time for Natalie.

"It's a special day," I said. Even though I had good letters, I traded them in, because I wanted Natalie to win the game.

"It's not definite, though. The baby sister." She frowned and rearranged her letters on her Scrabble rack.

"Of course it's not." Long, slow, deep breaths.

Itzhak rested his head on Natalie's lap. She studied her letters.

"Your parents want you to be involved in the decision too," I said. Natalie was an extremely perceptive child and able to identify deceit. But I was telling her the version of circumstances that ought to be true. So it was true, in a sense.

Natalie cocked her head. "I don't know."

"I believe they do. And they want you to feel ownership over the whole process." I brushed some stray hairs away from her face. "You want Lucia to know everything about your family. Because the worst of all possible outcomes would be that your mom gets her hopes up and then Lucia backs out at the last minute."

She rearranged her letters again.

I inhaled, breathing low into my core. "Like she finds out

something she didn't know and then she decides, oh, she really wants to choose a different family. I know a few families who went through that. At the last minute, the birth mother—that's what Lucia is—she can change her mind whenever she wants to. Even after the baby is born."

She looked up from her letters. "Really?"

"Yes."

Natalie finally placed her letters: *C-O-N-T-R-O-L* next to the word *L-E-D* that was already on the board, to spell *CONTROLLED*. She smiled ever so slightly.

"*Control* is seven letters," I said. "*Controlled* is fifty extra points, beyond the points on the tiles."

She was clearly pleased with herself.

She twisted one small section of her hair tightly around her finger. "Why would Lucia change her mind?"

"All kinds of reasons. These decisions—sometimes they're not purely rational. Religion sometimes. Culture, sensibility. Sometimes people want a similar value system."

"We're Jewish."

"Right." I held my breath.

"We're not religious." She twisted the same section of hair again.

"Right." I paused and counted to five in my head. "I'm sure she'll be fine with that. The important thing about tonight is that everything's on the table. No secrets, no surprises."

CHAPTER EIGHT

The doorbell rang at 8 P.M. on the dot.

Amelia rushed to the door, and Fritz followed. In anticipation of Lucia's arrival, Amelia had changed into a navy turtleneck dress that fell below her knees. The layers of her dark glossy shoulder-length hair framed her cheekbones perfectly. I could recognize the skill of a high-priced hairstylist. Amelia was wearing a pearl necklace and matching earrings. Perhaps she thought a prim and proper look would appeal to Lucia.

Fritz, on the other hand, even after having showered, still looked disheveled. His button-down shirt was wrinkled and his hair appeared to be uncombed. He had a patchy five o'clock shadow. He had the capacity to look stylish, but the events of the day had broken him down.

Natalie and I walked into the front hallway so that we both had a view of the door. I picked up my digital Canon EOS and put the strap around my neck.

Amelia opened the front door to reveal Lucia, a girl with a jet-black ponytail and olive skin. She looked to be sixteen, as opposed to nineteen, partly because she was so short, not much taller than Natalie.

The explosion of rage I felt when confronted with Lucia's presence was unreasonable, perhaps. But I didn't understand: Why wouldn't Amelia and Fritz recognize my love for them and look to me for assistance instead of looking to a total stranger?

Lucia was wearing a red woolen coat that she'd clearly borrowed from someone much taller than she was, because it almost hit the ground in spite of her high-heeled boots. And she wore a thin red scarf.

"Lucia!" Amelia embraced the girl as if they were related. "Thank you for coming, sweetheart."

Lucia timidly stepped inside the house, her nose and cheeks pink from the cold. She removed her boots and left them at the door while Amelia hung her coat. Without a coat on, it was obvious how pregnant Lucia was. Amelia led her to the library and offered everyone a glass of water. Fritz left the room and returned with a bottle of IPA for himself.

I sat next to Lucia on one of the sofas, resentment rising up into my throat. Fritz and Amelia sat on the opposite sofa, and Natalie perched on the arm next to her father. My breath was shallow and restricted, like I might hyperventilate. I needed to calm my nerves. I needed to think clearly.

"You have a beautiful home," Lucia said. She adjusted her body so that she could lean her lower back against the throw pillows on the sofa.

"Thank you," Amelia and Fritz said in unison.

Natalie made no attempt to hide the fact that she was staring at Lucia. Natalie's eyes moved to Lucia's face, probably assessing her purple eye shadow, then dropped down to her hands and her fingernails and her floral nail art.

"I recognize how important it is for you to know and understand the family who will adopt the child," Amelia said. "You need to feel a hundred percent confident in your decision. We all need to feel that way."

I focused on slow and sustained breathing, low into my core.

Fritz interjected. "So what are you looking for here?"

I detected a hint of hostility in his voice, and it seemed Lucia did too.

"Um . . ." Lucia hesitated.

A hard glint flashed in Amelia's eyes. "What Fritz means," she said, "and what we all know, is that you want to find—"

Fritz interrupted. "Let Lucia answer."

"I can't support the baby," she said. "I can barely support myself." She looked down at her fingernails self-consciously. Perhaps she'd noticed Natalie studying them. She examined her thumbnail closely, as if dissatisfied with that one in particular. Lucia had all of the power in this situation, but didn't appear to recognize her leverage.

"Where's the father?" Fritz asked. I was glad that subject was on the table, because it went straight to the question of character.

Amelia leaned over the marble coffee table and handed Lucia a platter of strawberries and grapes.

Lucia took the platter and held it in her lap, though it was a serving tray and not intended for her to keep. "I don't speak to him." Her face flushed slightly.

Fritz adjusted his glasses on his nose. "Were you in a relationship with him?"

"It depends on what you say a relationship is." Lucia attempted a laugh.

"Did you live together?" Fritz sipped his IPA, then set the bottle on the coffee table in front of him.

"For a little while." Lucia gripped the sides of the fruit platter.

"If he came back?"

Lucia looked down and realized that she was still holding the platter. She put a grape in her mouth and then placed the fruit tray on the coffee table. "He won't."

"But if he did, would you change your mind?"

She bit her lip and shook her head.

I could tell that Lucia wasn't accustomed to lying. It didn't come easily to her. Good liars propel their brains and their bodies toward their story with momentum, and they stick the landing. A moment's hesitation will kill you.

Fritz squinted. He didn't believe Lucia. Granted, he was asking about an unlikely scenario, but still it was obvious to him and to me that she would definitely change her mind if her boyfriend returned.

"It's wonderful that you're so close to your mother." Amelia pushed her hair behind her ears. "Just terrific." Amelia's desperation hung in the air. "You know what I didn't mention is that you and Natalie have something in common. You both really like to draw!"

"Wow," Lucia said. As soon as she addressed Natalie, she became far more relaxed. "That's cool. What do you draw?" Lucia rested one hand on her lower abdomen. I wondered if the baby was kicking.

"Unicorns mostly." Natalie spoke in a barely audible whisper.

"I love unicorns," Lucia said with apparent sincerity.

Natalie smiled with half of her mouth.

"You two have a lot in common!" Amelia cried. She was trying to fill the room with enough merriment to distract from her daughter's unfriendly tone.

Natalie made eye contact with Lucia. "What are your religious beliefs?"

A tingling sensation traveled down my limbs. This line of discussion was the best chance I had.

Amelia's body jerked in Natalie's general direction. Her hand reached toward Natalie's face as if she might be able to stop the words coming out of her daughter's mouth.

Lucia placed both hands on her abdomen. "I'm Catholic."

"We're Jewish." Natalie projected her voice through the room like a stage actor.

"OK," Lucia said.

"Do you go to church?" Natalie asked.

"Sometimes." Lucia scratched her arm and then her shoulder, like she had more than one bug bite.

"We don't go to synagogue. Dad's a lapsed Jew." Natalie spoke as if she were describing the weather on a particularly lovely day. "Mom's agnostic."

When I saw the color drain from Amelia's face, I had a pang of guilt, but the guilt didn't last long. For the most part, I felt relief and pride in the role I'd played helping Natalie to find her voice. Wasn't she just speaking her truth?

"OK." Lucia crossed her legs, a stab at modesty, perhaps, but a considerable effort for a pregnant woman.

Fritz appeared pleased by the exchange. Was he thinking of me? Of our earlier conversation?

"The house is warm." Amelia fanned herself. She made a show of going to the thermostat and turning it down. The house wasn't actually warm at all. She returned to offer Lucia more fruit and vegetables, which Lucia declined. She offered her pumpkin bread, which Lucia also declined.

Natalie knelt on the floor next to the pumpkin bread and

picked up the sharp knife. "My Aunt Marjorie made us the pumpkin bread," Natalie said as she gestured with the knife in her hand. "Aunt Marjorie's a stay-at-home mom, so she has time for stuff like that. Mom works really hard. She uses her brain in a lot of different ways. But not for pumpkin bread." She put half a slice of bread in her mouth.

I could sense Amelia's dismay, but I doubt that Lucia was able to.

"Lucia, do you like to cook?" Amelia asked.

"Mm-hmm."

"I love to cook. It doesn't come naturally, but I do try. What's most important to me is the idea of a home. That's why I wanted to study architecture, because I was drawn to the idea that the design of a home can bring together a family. Fritz and I work on residences." She turned to Fritz and clasped his hand in hers. He allowed her to take his hand. "We work with families to help create a unifying space. I think that cooking is another way to bring together a family. It's all part of the same thing, which is how do you use your home, how do you live in your home, how do you bring your family together in your home?"

It was a good save. I was impressed with Amelia's dexterity.

Lucia uncrossed and crossed her legs again. *Give it up, girlfriend,* I wanted to tell her.

"Do you have a lot of family nearby?" Lucia addressed Amelia and Fritz.

"We see my sister, Marjorie, almost every weekend," Amelia

said. "My parents retired and they moved to Florida, but they visit several times a year. And same with Fritz's parents; they're regular visitors!"

I studied Fritz's face, then Natalie's, trying to judge how much of the statement was true, but neither betrayed anything. I had never heard Marjorie's name mentioned or been aware of any family member visiting the Straubs so far. Amelia was a good liar.

"Who stays with Natalie when you're both working?" Lucia asked.

"Delta is our wonderful family friend." Amelia stood and held her hands out in my direction as if presenting me at court. "And she stays with Natalie a lot."

"Oh, I didn't realize you were their babysitter?" Lucia seemed to like me more once she had this piece of information.

"Well, no," Amelia jumped in. "Delta's an amazing photographer. She has a son too. Jasper. She just babysits because she *loves* Natalie. That's not like . . . what she does."

"I used to babysit a lot," Lucia said. "I still do."

Amelia beamed. "Babysitting is a great thing to do."

"How old were the children you babysat for?" Natalie asked.

"Babies mostly. Infants."

"Maybe you should babysit for *your* baby," Natalie said, "after someone adopts her."

A silence fell over the room. Amelia ate several grapes at once.

"I love spending time with Natalie," I said.

I saw several ways to slow the progress of the adoption, if not prevent it altogether. However, now the whole idea might self-destruct on its own, in which case, no need to risk a perception of meddling.

"May I use your restroom?" Lucia asked.

I jumped up. "I'll show you where it is." I walked ahead of Lucia down the hall. As we had both removed our shoes at the door, our socks slid on the reclaimed elm wood floor. Once out of the Straubs' earshot, I turned back to her. "I really hope it works out." I placed my hand on her shoulder and smiled warmly. Across the front of her knit sweater, pale blue and silver reversible sequins spelled out the word WONDER, except the O in WONDER was replaced by a heart. "I think Natalie's terribly lonely. It would be great for her to have a sister. That way, the two girls would have each other. And then it wouldn't even matter if their parents weren't . . ." I paused and counted to three. "A sisterly bond is so important."

Lucia studied me as though I were a strange animal she had never seen before.

"I'd love to take your photograph." I patted the camera around my neck. "The light across your face right now is breathtaking."

She shrugged and smiled.

I snapped thirty shots of her, which took all of ten seconds on my digital camera. One or two of them would be superb.

"If they turn out well, I'd like to use a photo of you on the maternity section of my website. And in return, I'd give you as many prints as you'd like."

Lucia nodded, which I took to mean yes. I quickly typed her email address into my phone.

"Pregnancy does something to certain women and, all of a sudden, it's like everything beautiful in the world is in their eyes and in their body," I said. "Everything that's positive and inspiring and lifts us up to God and to the angels. I see all of that in you. It's the beginning of a life with complete and absolute potential there. And the woman who carries the baby, she's the creator of that life. She has a little bit of God inside her." I was doing my best to layer in Madonna and Child subtext, along with the suggestion that motherhood might be Lucia's calling.

I think I succeeded with my message, because she placed her hand on her midriff, and her expression turned wistful.

"Does he know?" I asked.

"Hmm?" She knew exactly what I was asking.

"The father of the child. Does he know he has a baby?" I asked gently.

Lucia looked out at the backyard, as if something there had distracted her.

I tried to infuse my voice with tenderness. "You should send him one of the photos. It's the right thing to do."

•   •   •

As I was reentering the library, I saw Amelia and Natalie standing in the far corner, near the fireplace and bookshelves. Amelia was speaking to Natalie in a hushed voice: "You should be able to figure that out on your own."

"Don't you want her to know who we are?" Natalie chewed on her nails.

"Your father and I will take the lead. It is not your place." Amelia rounded her shoulders and back, exactly as my cat, Eliza, sometimes did. Her feline bearing came into sharp relief when she'd been crossed. I imagined using Photoshop to create an amalgam of Amelia's image and my cat's. A cat woman.

Fritz interjected from across the room. "I disagree—"

"Fritz," Amelia cut him off.

I wondered if Fritz and Natalie heard the steeliness in Amelia's voice.

Lucia appeared seconds later. Amelia led her back to the sofa, then picked up a photo album from the coffee table and sat next to Lucia in my seat. "These are photos of Natalie as a baby." Together, they flipped through the pages.

"I don't think I've seen that album." I walked behind the sofa so that I had a view over Lucia's shoulder. Long, slow, deep breaths.

The majority of the pictures were poorly shot photos of Amelia and Natalie on the beach. I surmised that Fritz had taken them, because he wasn't in any of them. Natalie looked to be a year old, like she had only just learned to walk. She was wearing a bikini that was covered with watermelon slices and a matching watermelon sun hat. In one photo, her feet were buried in the sand with only the tips of her toes peeking out. She was laughing. In the next photo, Natalie held a handful of sand and appeared to be dropping her sand into a bucket of water. Next, she was back at the waves, adding water to her bucket. In another photo, she was splashing in the waves. Wet sand covered her legs and arms completely and was also caked into her hair. Amelia, who was visible in the background, was sitting on a beach chair reading a magazine. She looked well groomed, as though she had just had her hair blown out. No sand on her face or body.

For some reason, Amelia (I assumed it was Amelia) had also chosen to include a photo of Natalie crying. I never include photos of children crying. It's a rookie mistake. The kid looks bad and the parents look worse. In this case, the child was crying and Amelia appeared to be at a loss, lacking any maternal instinct. From the photo, I was able to see Amelia's limitations. As soon as her child started to cry, as soon as she had something unpleasant to contend with, she was inclined to hand the child off.

"Natalie, you were a beautiful baby," Amelia said to her daughter, who'd taken her place back on the arm of the sofa.

"She's a beautiful girl," I said. Amelia missed so many opportunities to boost Natalie's self-confidence.

"That was the year we went to Florida for my father's seventieth birthday celebration," Amelia said. "We spent every day at the ocean. When we got back to Brooklyn, Natalie kept asking for the water. She was always a water baby."

"I like the water too," Lucia said.

"Me too," I said.

"Lucia, want me to show you around the house?" Fritz asked.

I was surprised by Fritz's question. Surprised that he was engaging with Lucia to such a degree. Maybe he saw this as his only opportunity to question her without Amelia hovering over his shoulder. Maybe he wanted her. I had a much better body than Lucia, but I wasn't nineteen. An image of Fritz and Lucia in the master bedroom flashed through my mind.

Lucia followed him up the stairs.

Amelia appeared irritated. She was unwise not to follow them. She turned to Natalie, picking up on their earlier conversation: "It's really important to me," she whispered. "I need your help."

Natalie didn't answer, which probably infuriated her mother.

Standing behind Amelia, I placed my hand on her shoulder. "Lucia is very pretty."

She turned around to look at me and smiled gratefully. "Yes. I know."

"And bright."

"Yes." Amelia stood and circled the sofa to approach me. "But she does seem concerned about something."

"Uneasy," I said. "Under the circumstances."

"Do you think—"

"It could be—" I stopped mid-sentence.

"Yes?" Amelia asked.

I put my arms around Amelia's shoulders and could feel her body trembling. "I'm so happy that you found her."

"It could be what?"

"She's obviously a caring person."

"Yes?"

"And I would guess that she'll care for the baby."

A dark cloud came over Amelia's brow. She leaned toward me so she could whisper and still be heard. "You think she'll change her mind?"

"I think she'll care for the baby," I said quietly, "meaning she'll want what's best for the baby."

"I don't think that's what you were going to say." Amelia pushed her hair behind her ears again, a nervous gesture to which I was growing accustomed.

"No. I really don't think she'll change her mind," I said.

Her hands were so tense, it looked like electric currents were shooting through them.

"If she makes a commitment," I said, "I think she'll stick to that commitment. She strikes me as that kind of person."

"Right."

Natalie was silent. I felt almost certain she wanted the same thing I did.

Amelia paced the room, from one end to the other and then back again.

"Is the father Latinx too?" I asked.

"What?" Amelia stopped her pacing and stood still.

"Just wondering if the baby's father is Latinx?" I had a feeling that the question of the child's race and ethnicity was floating around in the back of Amelia's mind, and I thought it was to my advantage to flush it out. Nevertheless, I knew I was treading on dangerous ground.

"The father's race is not important." Amelia's mouth pinched into a hard, straight line.

"I didn't know . . . if you and Fritz care whether the baby looks like you," I said, "or like Natalie's sibling."

"The father is white," she said. "However, it's irrelevant. Lucia's family is from the Dominican Republic, but she's perfectly lovely, and she has relatively light skin." She smiled.

I hadn't realized that the father was white. It was possible my strategy was backfiring. I knew that Amelia would have preferred that the mother be white too, but she didn't want to acknowledge that the race of the child made a difference to her, so she might dig her heels in even more, just to prove something.

"Would you like me to take some photographs of Lucia and you together?" I asked.

"What?"

"Shoot some photographs?" I pointed to the camera, which was still around my neck.

"Why?" She held her hands over her eyes, as if shielding them from bright sunlight.

"Just documentation." I thought a photo of Lucia and Amelia together could highlight their differences—differences I could make even starker with a little editing.

"No!" she said.

I felt pressure in my lungs.

"I can't imagine anything less appropriate than that," she said. "Are you crazy?"

I felt the blood behind my eyes. I felt my scalp burning. "It's possible that you'll end up with several choices. And you may want a reminder of who she is and what she looks like." I focused on slow and sustained breathing.

"I appreciate your desire to be helpful, Delta. But, no."

"OK. Just tell me how I can help you."

"This is how you can help me." She looked at me, and then at Natalie. "Both of you." She scanned the room and I wasn't positive what she was looking for. "Just keep your mouth shut." Amelia turned her back and picked up several used dishes and glasses from the coffee table.

"Just keep your mouth shut," Natalie quietly mocked her mother's voice. Amelia didn't seem to hear. She walked down the hall to deposit the dishes in the kitchen sink.

I pretended not to hear. I was still recovering from Amelia's dismissive and hurtful comments. Moreover, if I had heard, I would have had to say something or do something. I didn't want to cause any friction in their relationship. I wanted to support their family. Honestly, I did. My goal was to strengthen the bond between Amelia and Natalie, but still provide Natalie with a sounding board and another badly needed perspective. I wanted Natalie to have a warm, loving home. To the degree that Amelia was absent and unable to attend to Natalie, I would step in and offer my assistance. I wanted Amelia to have the baby that she dreamed of having, and I strongly believed that I could help her. Together, we could achieve her dream.

I knew that Lucia's baby was not the right one for the Straubs. I loved them. I wanted what was best for them.

CHAPTER NINE

"What a beautiful home," Lucia said. "Natalie, I love your unicorn collection." She and Fritz returned to the library after touring the house.

Natalie forced a tight smile. "Thanks." She was looking more like her mother all the time: her face was getting thinner and she had a growing air of sophistication. Not sophisticated in her clothing or her language or her ideas, but sophisticated in that her innocence was leaving or had already left. Maybe the right word was *worldliness*. Over the last couple of months, her carefree spirit had been replaced by a quiet understanding of the emotional landscape she lived in. I felt as though she were seeing her home for the first time. And witnessing a divide between her parents. One that she'd probably witnessed in the past, but in this situation, that divide could not be ignored.

Perhaps she was also seeing her mother's actions more clearly. Amelia's actions had little to do with promoting the interests of her family. I understood Amelia's need for a baby. It was a desire to pull herself from the abyss. To be lifted out of her suffering. To leave her own body and become someone else.

"Have a seat," Amelia said to Lucia, gesturing to the sofa, and sat down across from her. Natalie was sitting tense and cross-legged on the arm of the sofa. I sat down between her and her mother.

"Lucia," Amelia said, "your medical bills must be a burden." She clasped her hands in her lap in an earnest-looking pose. "And you mentioned that you had to cut your hours back at work because you haven't been feeling well. Pregnancy takes such a toll on a woman's body. Such a toll. I remember it well. I think . . . it's important to have support. Assuming that this works out, and that we all feel comfortable, I'd like to provide the kind of support that would allow you to rest, to study, to exercise, and to have proper nutrition."

Amelia was successfully managing a maternal tone, as if the only difference between her and Lucia was age.

"Assuming that it works out," Amelia said, "I'd like to cover all your expenses—medical, food, transportation—retroactively and for the duration of your pregnancy. It's the least Fritz and I can do."

She looked at Fritz like she was hoping for a nod of affirmation, but she received none. She quickly turned back to Lucia, who appeared to be confused by Amelia's offer. "Furthermore, I recognize that your pregnancy interrupted your studies, so I'd like to cover the remainder of your college tuition. Wherever you choose to go."

Lucia held the end of her red scarf in her fingers and twisted the tassels. She didn't smile or say thank you. Maybe she recognized the semi-bribe for what it was and was insulted. Maybe she saw in Amelia an easy target and planned to squeeze her for all she was worth.

Leaning his back against the doorway to the library, Fritz removed his glasses, revealing a red indentation on either side of his nose, and cleaned the lenses meticulously with the bottom of his undershirt. I gathered he and Amelia had not discussed the subject prior to Lucia's arrival. I gathered he was angry.

I sensed Natalie feeling her importance in the family slipping out from underneath her. Amelia's offer to Lucia would have a financial impact on their lives. I thought about that unpaid tuition bill.

Amelia moved to the opposite sofa, next to Lucia, and she took the girl's hand in her own. "Thank you for coming to our house tonight. It means the world to me. And I know that Fritz and Natalie feel the same way." Fritz checked his watch. Natalie glued her eyes to the floor and chewed her nails.

The meeting was coming to a close. I needed for Amelia and Fritz to view Lucia's state of mind accurately, and I only had a few

minutes left in which to shine a light on the cracks in their understanding of her.

"What is the baby's name?" I asked.

"Nina," Lucia said.

Perhaps my question was ill timed, but I knew I wouldn't have
another chance.

"Who gets to name the baby?" Natalie was suddenly reen-
gaged.

"The baby's parents name the baby." Amelia spoke with an
edge in her voice.

"Who counts as the baby's parents?" Natalie asked.

A silence fell over the room. I could feel Amelia's anger ema-
nating like a hot stove.

"That's an odd question, Natalie." Amelia made an effort to
sound lighthearted. "Because Lucia is the child's birth mother. But
someone will adopt the baby and that person or those people will
be the baby's adoptive parents."

"So who names the baby?" Natalie asked again, her voice and
face now animated.

There was a brief silence before Fritz interjected. "Honey, the
adoptive parents usually name the baby. The baby takes their last
name, and they choose a first name for the baby."

Natalie had released her limbs from their constricted position
and seemed to be regaining control of her voice and her body.
She addressed Lucia directly. "So why did you choose a name already?"

Lucia paused. "The baby's inside me." She placed her hand on her middle. "Right now I'm the child's mother. And I need to talk to my baby. So I call her Nina."

"Well, won't that be confusing for her?" Natalie asked everyone. "Now she hears Lucia calling her Nina, but then later she has a different name. I don't think that's fair to the baby. If her name is Nina now, it should stay Nina. It's a nice name anyway."

"Wow," Amelia said. "I didn't realize what time it was. It's almost ten. Lucia, you need to get some rest."

"Yeah." Fritz checked his watch again.

"Let's get you a car home." Amelia picked up her iPad from the coffee table to call a car.

Amelia and Lucia both stood. Amelia planted a kiss on Lucia's forehead. It was almost a religious gesture, very unlike Amelia. "I want you to take care of yourself. Promise me you will," she said.

Lucia nodded self-consciously.

"Bye, Lucia." Fritz gave Lucia an awkward thumbs-up and then disappeared into the kitchen.

Amelia helped to bundle Lucia into her red coat. Then she slipped on her sneakers, which were next to the front door, and walked Lucia outside to the car. I stood in the doorway with my hand on Natalie's shoulder and watched the interaction between the two women on the sidewalk. Amelia, who had neglected to wear a coat herself, must have been freezing cold with her bare legs and sneakers. She put her hand to Lucia's cheek. Lucia, with her high ponytail and round face, looked like a little girl compared to

Amelia. Once Lucia climbed into the car, Amelia blew her a kiss through the window, then clasped her hands to her heart. As the car pulled away, Amelia waved both hands in the air as if she were saying goodbye to her daughter. And I suppose, in her mind, she was.

·　　·　　·

I opened the hall closet and found my coat. It was next to Amelia's shiny purple Moncler. I'd tried on the exact same one at a store recently. One day I planned to ask Amelia if I could borrow her coat, but today was probably not the best day for that.

I didn't want to leave, but I also didn't want to face a moment when the Straubs wished I wasn't there.

Amelia walked back up the front path, shivering from the cold. I kissed Natalie on the cheek.

"Delta." Amelia stood in the doorway. "Why did you ask the baby's name?"

The hostility in her voice gave me a sinking sensation.

She closed the door behind her. "The baby doesn't have a name." Amelia's words came at a fast clip. "In the Jewish religion, you never name a baby before it's born. Neither do you buy clothes or a crib for a baby, or you might draw the attention of the 'evil eye.'"

"I'm sorry . . . I was curious," I said, "because I overheard her talking to the baby when I walked her to the bathroom. The baby is probably better off with a birth mother who is invested in the child's well-being. No?"

"No. Yes. No." Amelia kicked her sneakers off by the coat closet. I followed her down the hallway toward the kitchen, where Fritz was sitting on one of the counter stools, drinking another beer and eating a large bag of chips. She leaned her torso all the way forward onto the Calacatta marble of the island, her arms crossed to create a pillow for her head. After a minute of silence, she stood up and faced me again. "Lucia has decided that she is not the baby's mother. That's her decision. Whether she chooses us or another family, she has no right to name the baby. She has no rights at all regarding this baby." Amelia stood uncomfortable in her body, almost as if it belonged to someone else.

Next to the open refrigerator, Natalie held a container of milk in her hands. Inside the refrigerator, at least ten bottles of champagne, lying sideways, covered one of the shelves. Perhaps they'd had a party recently or were going to have a party. One I hadn't been invited to.

"Of course," I said, "her rights will be terminated as a birth parent. After the baby is born."

Amelia's hands involuntarily flicked in the direction of the floor, like she was shaking water off them.

"Amelia," I continued, "it's just I sense ambivalence about her decision. I'm scared you might be hurt."

"No one's made any decision yet." Fritz tossed the empty bag of chips into the trash under the sink and slammed the cabinet. "Not Lucia. Not us. And this conversation is bullshit."

Apparently, Fritz and Amelia had little regard for Natalie's presence in the room and how she might be processing their conversation. They prided themselves on being transparent with their child.

Natalie reached up high to pull a tall blue tumbler from one of the open shelves. She poured the last few ounces of milk into her glass. She looked exhausted.

"I have to invest in this baby," Amelia said, her voice devoid of inflection. "I don't have a choice. I have to invest in this baby."

"No, Amelia," Fritz said. "You will not force this down my throat."

"Amelia," I said, "you have options."

I tried to envision an Amelia who was not overflowing with confidence.

Tears filled her eyes. It seemed to me that she was encouraging the tears. She didn't have an answer for Fritz and, strategically, probably thought that crying was her best response. Not to suggest that she wasn't impulsive and dramatic. She was. But, to achieve her end, I believed that Amelia could control her behavior. She and I were alike in that way.

I had never felt a strong urge to have a baby. The urge for me was to be a surrogate for Amelia and Fritz. The intimacy of that act. The importance. Very soon after the baby's arrival, Amelia would return to working long hours. I could bond with the baby. I could potentially have a stronger bond with the child than Amelia would. And perhaps even more critical, my presence would be forever integrated into the Straubs' lives.

It wasn't the right time to introduce the subject to Amelia. I didn't want to appear to be invested in any particular outcome. Amelia covered her face and wept, her body caving in. Something about her crumpled form made me know that I wouldn't be able to repair the rift today. I needed to come at it from another angle.

"You all should get some rest." I put my arms around Natalie and kissed her. Leaving the house took tremendous willpower. I told my legs to walk and they didn't. An undefinable magnetic force held me in place.

Fritz moved toward the door, expecting me to follow. I forced my feet to lift and step in that direction.

"Call me if you need anything," I said to Fritz. I wanted to touch him. I wanted him to know how much I cared about him and his well-being.

"Thanks, Delta." He leaned forward, as if he might embrace me, but then thought better of it and stepped back.

That night, I had a recurring dream. I was running toward a baby, and then I became the baby that I was running toward. Someone's arms were wrapped around my body. I felt encompassed by warmth and love. I belonged to someone.

CHAPTER TEN

—————————

I woke up early with Lucia's face etched in my mind. I pulled up the photos of her and clicked through all of them until I landed on the one. She was the Madonna. She was an Angel. A Child.

The photo needed more sex if it were to achieve its intended result. Making a pregnant woman look sexy is a subtle art. If I made any alterations, they would have to be indiscernible so that Lucia wouldn't catch them. After some careful scrutiny, I developed a game plan: I darkened the shadows around her breasts. I took a sliver off her waist to make it slightly smaller than it actually was. I moved her hand so that it was closer to her crotch. I layered beads of moisture on her face. And I parted her lips a little bit.

When Lucia's boyfriend saw the photo, he would see a woman who was sexually aroused, notwithstanding her angelic innocence. He would imagine fucking her again. At the same time, he would see the mother of his child. And he would see his unborn child inside her. It would be difficult to resist all of that. Maybe impossible.

When my work was finished, I emailed Lucia the photo. *Lucia, I had to send you this. Don't forget what we discussed.*

For the remainder of the day, I checked my email constantly. It was close to midnight when she wrote back. *Wow. Thanks, Delta.*

I felt certain she would send her boyfriend the photo. I had extreme confidence in my work. I knew how he would react to the picture of Lucia. He would want to claim her and her baby as his property. Right away, before someone else did.

•   •   •

The Straubs and I had established a routine; they assumed I would babysit Natalie every Friday. But given the nature of our last exchange, I could no longer take the routine for granted. I texted Amelia on Friday morning. She didn't respond.

I tried to distract myself with errands and activities that day.

Friday evening I returned home and gave Eliza her dinner, and afterward we sat together on the sofa for several minutes, at which time I stroked the soft fur on her back and told her about my day. If she had been able to speak, she would have asked me not to leave her for so many hours. She would have asked me to bring her along next time. She would have told me that loneliness made her want to end her life—that the walls of the apartment we shared were inching imperceptibly toward each other, so that she feared she would one day be crushed.

I took a glass of wine to my office and spent two hours on-line researching adoption in New York State. I learned that a birth mother can decide whether an adoption is "open," and if she stipulates, she can see the child as often as she chooses to. That kind of ongoing connection to Lucia would be an albatross around Amelia's neck, especially if Lucia were struggling financially. The Straubs might find themselves coerced into supporting Lucia's whole family.

I also researched surrogacy laws. From a conversation with Amelia, I'd already gathered that paid surrogacy wasn't legal in New York. I'd have a significant advantage as an "altruistic surrogate," if the Straubs were to go that route. A whole layer of logistical complication could be eliminated, though they wouldn't have an enforceable contract. In New York, a woman who gives birth is presumed to be the legal mother at birth and she has preferred parental status. If I were the surrogate, they would have to trust me.

Later that night, I opened up one of the folders on my hard drive. It contained photos of the Straubs' kitchen, the ones I took when I was babysitting Natalie and Piper. I couldn't help dwelling on the high ceilings, the exquisite finishes, the various touches of brass, copper, nickel all working in unison with glass to create a shimmery vision. I remember when I first saw that kitchen. It appeared to be made out of crystal because it sparkled so much.

I pulled up the photos of myself that I'd used for my website. Five years earlier, Lana had shot them as a favor to me. They were by far the best photos of myself that I'd ever had taken. The close-ups emphasized my bright blue eyes, creamy skin, and silky hair. The long shots highlighted my hourglass figure. I'd enjoyed designing my website, primarily because it had been an opportunity to showcase the photos. Once finished with my website, I'd sought out other occasions to use them. I considered it a waste to leave such extraordinary pictures sitting unused on my computer, so I placed my image in advertisements I found online and created photos of myself skiing or hiking or scuba diving. The activity was amusing, but since I didn't know the other people in the frame, and I'd never been to the locations, it was hard for me to believe in the pictures. Whereas, I discovered that inserting myself into my clients' photos wasn't such a stretch for my imagination, and, as a result, I found it much more gratifying.

When I layered my image into the Straubs' kitchen, it was a way to spend time with the Straubs, all of whom I missed terribly, and a way to fully inhabit their home and their life. I found stock photos of pots and pans online and layered them into the scene too, along with cutting boards, knives, vegetables, and fruit. I already had photos of Natalie and Piper watching *Mean Girls*. And now I had photos of myself cooking. I cut back and forth between the images to create a short slideshow. One would have inferred that I was their mother, or possibly Natalie's big sister. Then I cut to photos of Natalie and Piper sound asleep in Natalie's room. That came afterward in the sequence. Then, at the end of the evening, I cut to photos of me and

Fritz. We were making love in the Straubs' bedroom. I had already taken independent photos of Fritz, me, and the Straubs' bedroom. I just had to layer our bodies on their bed. Fritz's naked body posed a bit of a challenge, but I combined a few different images, some I had taken myself and some from Amelia's Instagram account—pictures of him in his swimsuit. As luck would have it, the light in all of these was coming from the same direction, hitting him at the same angle. I had more than one AI "undressing" app on my computer. All I had to do was input Fritz's image in a swimsuit, and after a couple of minutes, I'd get Fritz completely nude, front, back and side views. The computer's best guess of what he'd look like naked was close, but inferior to my best guess, so I tweaked the computer-generated image, changing the skin tone and muscle tone slightly.

I was pleased with my creation.

I inserted a photo of Amelia and me together in the cooking section. She was reading a recipe to me and I was mixing the ingredients in a bowl. It looked to be my home and I was cooking with my dear friend Amelia. I found it comforting to play the slideshow for myself and watched it several times. I especially liked the section with me and Fritz in the Straubs' bed, our bodies pressed together. When I looked at the photos, I felt connected to a world and a life. I thought about replacing Fritz's body with Amelia's—an image of me and Amelia, our bodies pressed against each other. That would also be an uplifting vision, but I instinctively felt it would be a little harder to achieve.

I was about to go to sleep when I realized that I hadn't included

Jasper. I experienced a stab of guilt: I hadn't thought about my son, and now it wasn't clear how to incorporate him. Where had Jasper been the whole time? I finally decided that he had been sleeping the entire evening. That was plausible. He was only five years old, after all. So I created a bed for him in Natalie's room, and layered his delicate little body onto that bed. It was Natalie and Jasper, as opposed to Natalie and Piper, who were asleep in Natalie's room. It was as if Piper had gone home after the movie, and Jasper and Natalie were asleep in their beds.

•   •   •

I texted Amelia again Saturday morning and didn't hear back. I felt increasingly unmoored and didn't know what to do with myself. I needed contact with the Straubs. I hadn't seen them or spoken to them for a week.

Ian was now my only source of information. I made plans to meet him for dinner at a gastropub in the West Village. After dinner, we bundled up and walked down Greenwich Avenue through the crowd of pedestrians. After several blocks, we came to a red light and he checked his watch. "Do you want to have a drink with me?" His breath escaped from his mouth in a misty cloud.

This was what I'd been hoping for. I took his gloved hand in mine, looked him in the eye, and nodded. Behind him was a group of rowdy teenagers. One of the heavier girls was holding a lamppost and pretending to do a striptease, with one knee hooked around the pole.

"At my apartment, I meant to say."

"I know," I said.

The teenagers laughed at the pretend striptease. They chanted: "Donna! Donna!"

"I haven't been on too many dates recently," Ian said shyly. "I forget the protocol."

I pressed my fingers into his palm.

We crossed the street and passed a group of loud tourists, maps in hand, young women with bare shoulders and cleavages exposed in spite of the mid-March frost. Even before I moved to New York, when I'd visited for a weekend, I despised the tourists, though I myself was one. I could see how different we were from real New Yorkers. Less sophisticated, less educated, less everything. Even then, I wanted people to believe that I lived here. I understood how important it was to fit in. Emily Miller had been helpful in that respect. She'd grown up with money and understood the landscape. When I was working on her weddings, I watched her. I listened to her. She'd pretend to let her hair down, but she was performing the entire time—not unlike Amelia Straub. A consummate professional, Emily never said or did anything by accident.

• • •

Ian's one-bedroom apartment, on the second floor of a prewar walk-up, appeared to have been renovated recently, and the masculine furniture was in good taste relative to his fashion sense. The black frames of the enormous uncovered windows contrasted with the crisp white walls, as did the polished dark wood on the back of his white bookshelves. The surfaces were bare, except for a few carefully selected items, probably purchased on his travels, like a Balinese wooden sculpture.

Ian disappeared into his kitchen and returned with two glasses of red wine, which he placed on the coffee table in front of the sofa. I took several sips, deposited my wine on the table, and turned to him. I saw no point in wasting time. I leaned in toward him and we kissed. He smelled like aftershave and garlic. My hand on his crotch. Then my legs around his waist. We crossed to his bed, and then I allowed him to take the lead.

I let him undress me and then we screwed. I enjoyed having sex with Ian and liked the fact that he was smitten with me. But if I were to measure the gravitational pull that I felt toward the Straubs versus Ian, there was no comparison.

After, I suggested another glass of wine. Sex and wine were both helpful in getting the information I needed. Ian pulled his boxers on. He left the room and returned with the half-empty bottle of red wine and our two glasses. He poured us each a glass. I pulled the sheet up over my chest, and positioned two pillows behind me so that I could sit up in bed and drink.

Ian ran his fingers through my hair. "God, you're beautiful, Delta."

I looked down, as though embarrassed by the compliment.

"Each time I see you, you're more beautiful." He laughed. "I don't know exactly how that works."

I looked into Ian's eyes and saw a generosity of spirit and kindness. But I also saw mediocrity. I didn't see someone who planned to succeed at the highest level. I saw someone who was content to lead an average life.

"Maybe because I'm trying to impress you," I said.

Under the sheet, Ian placed a warm hand on my thigh. I kissed his neck.

When finished with my wine, I climbed on top of him and rested my head next to his on his pillow. "Is it OK with you if I spend the night?"

Ian looked more relaxed than he had several hours earlier, with far less tension in his face. "I wouldn't let you go home now. It's two in the morning."

"I want to be close to you," I whispered in his ear.

He wrapped his arms tightly around my body.

I pushed my pelvis up against his, just to keep his mind whirling and defenses down. "I can't stop thinking about Amelia and Fritz. I'm worried about them."

He kissed my cheek. "I think they're doing pretty well."

"Yes?"

"I spoke to Fritz yesterday," he said.

"And?"

"It looks like that baby . . . the baby they want to adopt . . ." He traced his finger over the outline of my mouth.

"Yes?"

"It's going to happen. He said it's going to happen."

I focused on my breath, low in my body. Shallow, high breathing leads to anxiety and vice versa. "Wow. Is he happy?"

"Maybe," he said.

"But he's going along with it?"

"He thinks it's too late to turn back because Amelia's frantic. He thinks that she'd lose her mind if he stopped her."

I rolled off Ian and lay next to him, my head on his shoulder, until he fell asleep. I looked at his digital clock periodically throughout the night, almost every hour, and counted the minutes until I could go home. Ian slept soundly.

The next day, I had a genuine excuse to leave—an early-morning job shooting newborn twins. He insisted on making me a cappuccino with his shiny red Nespresso machine. Before I left, we confirmed our date for the following week. I couldn't risk losing momentum.

CHAPTER ELEVEN

It was the week of March 21. I had a sinking sensation every morning when I woke up and looked at my phone. I was hoping for a message from Amelia, but received none. It was almost two weeks since I'd seen the Straubs. I feared that I'd lost my place in their life. I'd had a growing conviction that Amelia was attached to me. And then there was the shattering episode with Lucia, and the fear that she was going to replace me.

I gathered that I'd handled certain things poorly. Maybe Amelia felt that I hadn't been helpful in facilitating the adoption. Amelia and I were very close, as long as the ground rules were understood: We were both working on making her life better. Her life was the one we were focusing on. I didn't mind that aspect of our relationship. In fact, the ground rules usually served me well, since scrutiny of my own life wasn't an option.

On Friday morning I sent Amelia another text asking if she'd like me to babysit Natalie. I received no response. That evening, I turned on my computer and clicked through some photos of the Straubs. I went back to the day that I first met them at Natalie's birthday party. I remembered feeling Amelia's attention like the sun. Her gaze could warm, brighten, and heal me. I craved it. I felt a physical need for her presence, and without it, my body was responding with symptoms of withdrawal. I'd had headaches off and on all week, along with shaky hands, a significant handicap in my profession. I'd canceled two jobs, and the quality of my work was clearly suffering.

I turned toward photoshopping as a means of relief from the vast emptiness in front of me. I opened the folder labeled Straub, Alternates. By now it held more images than all my other private folders combined. I started with a captivating photo of Amelia in profile, wearing dark glasses and a leather jacket. She was holding her arm up in the air, waving to someone. I layered that image onto an exterior shot of Court Street in Cobble Hill, as well as an image of myself coming from the opposite direction. We were meeting up for a shopping excursion.

I focused on the image of Amelia waving to me, allowing my eyes to rest on the picture while breathing deeply. In a few minutes, I felt better.

I created another photo of us drinking cocktails at Buttermilk Channel. Amelia was touching my hand. Her welcoming expression in each image mirrored the way she looked the first time I'd met her. I would never forget that day. No one had ever recognized me so fully.

Lastly I created a photo of the two of us running across the Brooklyn Bridge. I felt it was a shame that the event hadn't been recorded at all. But it was easy to layer each of us onto the bridge. From a distance, the shot had more to do with the backdrop than seeing our faces, but our body language suggested an animated conversation.

I returned to the photo of us on Court Street. I replaced my own image with a version of myself looking seven months pregnant. Amelia was beside herself with joy.

In these photos, I could see Amelia's affection right in front of my eyes. Not only could I see it, I could feel my body respond, a gradual relaxing of my muscles, a sensation of expansion. The hollow part of my stomach was filled in. The sharp pain in my gut gave way to a feeling of warmth and ease.

·   ·   ·

When I arrived at Ian's apartment on Saturday evening, the beef Bourguignon was on the stove and the salad was in the fridge. The candles were lit. "Bohemian Rhapsody" by Queen was playing. Ian's faded jeans and long-sleeve T-shirt were a departure from his usual wardrobe. His hair had grown out a little longer. Overall, the more relaxed appearance suited him.

"Your mom sent me another present," I said. "A silk scarf." It was the third present Paula had sent me since we'd met. This time, the card read: *To my future daughter-in-law (shhh!)* with a smiley face drawn on the side. I didn't mention the card to Ian.

"You're kidding," he said. "She's the cheapest person I know."

"She has good taste." I smiled.

Laughter and chatter made its way from the street to Ian's second-floor window, which was barely open.

Halfway through dinner, he refilled my glass of cabernet. I was pleased to see he was pouring a fifty-dollar bottle.

"Tell me more about Jasper," he said.

My throat tightened. I wondered why he was asking.

"He's so smart," I said. "And adorable."

Ian served me more beef Bourguignon. "You said he'd be away for a few months?"

"He'll definitely return by September. He'll start kindergarten here." I wiped my mouth with a dark green linen napkin. Such details are unusual for a straight bachelor.

"I don't want to pry, but . . ."

"I don't have secrets." I smiled again.

"What happened to your marriage?"

"Robert had an affair." I sipped the cabernet. "He fell in love with another woman."

"I'm sorry."

"It's OK now. We're friends. Sort of."

"Does Robert have a place in LA?" The voices outside were

louder. Ian walked to the window and lowered it, then returned to the table.

"In Santa Monica, close to his office."

"Who stays with Jasper when he's working?"

I could still hear a man laughing outside. "He's in daycare."

"What about the woman?"

The wine had dulled my brain. "Which woman?"

"The other woman."

"Oh." I looked down at my hands in my lap while I collected my thoughts. I wasn't usually sloppy with my details.

"Where is she?" he asked.

"She lives in New York."

He looked confused. "He's single now?"

"Yes."

"What's Robert's last name?"

Fuck you. "Why do you ask?" I said politely.

"You mentioned that he works in film. I have some friends in entertainment."

I paused. "I'd rather not talk about Robert anymore. It's a painful subject."

Ian looked at the ground, his index finger to his mouth, like he was trying to remember something. "Where does your sister live?" he asked.

He was sharper than I'd realized. "We're not in touch."

"Is she married?"

"I know she was with a guy."

He thought I was lying to him.

"I don't think you trust me." He frowned.

"I don't trust anyone." I laughed. That was true, but I didn't exactly mean to say it. It wasn't a good look. People think there's something wrong with a woman who doesn't trust.

"I don't care about your sister or your ex," he mumbled. "But I've got to start with something. Whatever was there. It doesn't just go away, you know."

I saw something in Ian's eyes, affection maybe, and I wished for a moment that I was a different person. "Too bad. It would be nice if it did. Go away, that is." I finished the rest of my wine. "What about you? You haven't told me about your past."

"I dated someone for eight years. She said she didn't believe in marriage. But I thought she'd change her mind." He shrugged. "Well, she didn't change her mind. She broke up with me." Ian spoke quickly, in an upbeat manner. I thought he was making an effort to sound casual.

"I'm sorry."

"I can't be mad," he said. "She never pretended to be someone she wasn't."

Was he challenging me? I studied his face. No, he wasn't. He trusted me.

•   •   •

After we had sex, I lay on top of Ian's body. My face was right next to Ian's on his pillow, the tip of my nose touching his cheek. His hair was wet from perspiration, as was the pillow underneath us. "Cheap Thrills" by Sia played on the bedroom speaker.

"Natalie loves this song." I paused for several seconds. "Have you seen her lately?" I hadn't seen Natalie for two weeks. I hadn't told Ian about the strain in my relationship with the Straubs, and I hoped they hadn't mentioned it to him.

"No," he said, "but I saw Fritz at work yesterday. Did you hear about their birth mother?"

"No."

"She got back together with her boyfriend. He reappeared."

A hard knot inside my abdomen released, and a pleasurable tingling feeling traveled from my organs to my extremities. My body felt buoyant, like I might float up to the ceiling. My photography had brought them together. *I knew that.* I knew it for a fact. No one could do what I could do.

"Amelia is scared that Lucia's going to change her mind," he said.

I needed to see Amelia and Fritz. I needed them to understand that I could help them.

"I feel awful for her," I said.

"Fritz says she's a wreck," he said. "It's almost like she thinks that's the only baby she can possibly have."

"She's wrong."

"They've been trying for a while."

My body still on top of his, I allowed my fingers to trail over the side of his hips. I shifted so that my legs were staggered with his—one of my legs over one of his. "There are alternatives."

"I guess."

"Like surrogacy."

He shifted his body underneath me. "Seems complicated."

"Not always. It's exhilarating to create a life. And for some women, it's the best thing they've ever done." I kissed his neck. "I would enjoy doing it."

"What?" he said.

I breathed into his neck. "I would enjoy doing it."

"No!" He laughed and pulled on a strand of my hair.

"Why not?" I found it hard to swallow, as if my throat were swollen.

"No way, José." He pulled away from me so he could look at my face. Maybe he was trying to assess whether I was joking.

I didn't have enough saliva in my mouth. "I loved being pregnant."

He seemed to recognize that I was serious; the smile on his face vanished. "What if I want you for myself?"

Ian had grown too attached to me. I hadn't judged the situation accurately. He didn't want to lose my body to the Straubs and the Straubs' baby. I was angry with myself for my shortsightedness. Still, he was my primary connection to the Straubs, and I needed him.

•   •   •

I had a chance to reestablish myself in the Straubs' lives and a possibility of claiming a permanent place. In the last two weeks, I'd grown to understand how crucial it was for me to cement my relationship with them. I had a vision of myself as the central source of power in their home and family, without which nothing could function—essential to their well-being and indispensable.

In the morning, I sent Amelia a text. *Hope you're feeling OK.* She didn't respond.

The following day, I sent another one: *Thinking of you.* She didn't respond.

The day after, I wrote: *I would love to visit you and see Natalie. Picking up the dry cleaning. If OK, I'll swing by and drop it off.*

This time, she wrote back: *Sure.*

In less than a minute, my coat and boots were on and I was out the door—on my way to see Amelia again.

·   ·   ·

I rang the doorbell, dry cleaning in hand. Amelia answered the door. My joy in seeing her was swiftly undercut by the silhouette of a pregnant Lucia behind her and down the hallway. Why was Lucia in the house? I took it as a bad sign. The chorus of "London Bridge Is Falling Down" (which I'd heard at a recent birthday party) was stuck in my head. I once read that the lyrics had to do with burying children alive in the foundation of the bridge as a sacrifice.

Lucia looked much more pregnant than she had two weeks earlier, but she also appeared more sophisticated and poised. She was wearing a subtle brown eye shadow as opposed to bright purple. The new and improved Lucia likely posed a greater threat to me.

I feared she might bring up our email exchange.

"Delta, you shouldn't have." Amelia took the dry cleaning from my hand and hung it in the hall closet. The colors of her mustard-green blouse and kelly-green pants were disconcertingly off and clashing. Her foundation was not applied evenly and visibly caked on her forehead. She was losing the polish that created distance between her and the rest of the world. I was conflicted, because I'd always wanted to bridge that distance. But I was also mildly disappointed that she looked ordinary. More concerning, however, was her exposure in front of Lucia. I didn't want her to let down her guard in front of this woman who wasn't her friend.

Lucia approached closer to the front door. Itzhak trailed behind her, wagging his tail.

"Lucia, do you remember our friend, Delta?"

"Yes." She looked through me, avoiding eye contact. Fortunately, it appeared that Lucia did not want to acknowledge our previous interaction either.

"The date is fast approaching." I hadn't expected that I'd ever see Lucia in person again. The sight of her was hard to take.

Amelia motioned us down the hall and to the dining table. I sat down across from Lucia.

"What a lovely sunset." I chose to concentrate on the brilliant pink sky through the glass doors until I got my bearings.

Amelia poured wine for me and sparkling water for Lucia. Over the last few months, I'd developed a distaste for inferior wine. Cheap wine made me view myself in a certain light, as belonging to a certain socioeconomic class. So I was astonished, frankly, when

I saw Amelia with an eight-dollar bottle of wine in her hand. Perhaps someone had given her the bottle and she hadn't paid attention to the label.

Amelia sat down next to me and across from Lucia. "Lucia and I . . . we're discussing some of the options she has," Amelia said in a careful and controlled tone of voice. "We've had a few conversations over the past week, just talking it all through."

I patted Itzhak, who had sidled up next to me. The dog provided me with a welcome point of focus.

"But I've decided already. . . . I'm not still deciding," Lucia said. "Ron wants to be with me and the baby. I came here because I thought I should apologize, because I'm sorry I said yes before." Lucia clearly felt guilty. She was rambling, but she wasn't confused.

I had that same sensation of lightness and buoyancy again. Two pictures of Ron alternated in my brain: 1.) a shifty slacker who operated just barely inside the law; 2.) an ambitious and outwardly respectable guy who didn't want to get strapped with a wife and baby, both of whom would limit his future prospects.

No matter his profile, my photograph of Lucia had succeeded in exerting power over him.

"I'm very sorry." Lucia looked down at the ground.

Amelia's catlike movements and sounds came to the fore when she was on edge. She was the opposite of approachable. If I were able to see inside her mouth, I was sure I would have seen her biting her tongue so hard that she was drawing blood.

I noticed a silver ring on Lucia's right middle finger that I hadn't seen before. Perhaps it was a promise ring. She was too young to know how meaningless a promise ring was.

"He loves me. Ron knows what he wants." Lucia appeared to feel less vulnerable than the last time I saw her. Obviously, she believed that she had an ally in Ron. And maybe she did.

"Sweetheart." Amelia smiled broadly, showing her teeth. The smile was an attempt at friendliness but veered toward a grimace. She took a large sip of her wine. "I believe he's in love with you. Who wouldn't be? But it's a lot of pressure to put on your relationship. Financial and emotional pressure." She studied Lucia's face, as if looking for agreement. I noticed Lucia's jaw tighten. Amelia smoothed her blouse down, then meticulously rolled up her sleeves. "What do you think, Delta?" she said amiably. There was a right answer and a wrong answer to the question.

"I think that you and Ron should be together," I said to Lucia.

Amelia's body stiffened.

"But you're very young to have a baby," I said.

"Ron wants to be a father," Lucia said.

"In a few years, of course," Amelia said calmly, "when you've finished school and have a job. There's time for everything." She spoke as if she had some real authority over the girl, as if Lucia were obliged to follow her directions. Amelia was so accustomed to her demands being acceded. She considered herself wiser than everyone in the room and thought others ought to be grateful for her superior opinion. I wondered if her demeanor was a strategy, developed in order to get her own way. In this case, the strategy looked to be backfiring.

"Ron loves our baby." Lucia put her hand on her belly. "*This* baby." I saw the almost imperceptible smile on Lucia's face as she touched the baby and I knew that Amelia's chances had diminished. Lucia had allowed herself to fall in love with her child. Even if Ron didn't stick around, the adoption prospects didn't look strong for Amelia.

I doubted that Amelia saw what I did. Maybe she chose not to. She was focused on Lucia's words. "Sweetheart, he disappeared for six months." She continued to speak in a calm, slow, and deliberate voice, but I could tell that it was an effort to do so.

"He was struggling," Lucia said.

"Drugs?" Amelia licked her lips twice.

Lucia shrugged.

"Addiction issues?"

Lucia moved her head very slightly. I wasn't positive if she was nodding or just looking down.

Here Amelia's careful tone and manner started to disintegrate. "*That* shit never goes away." It was as if she'd run out of the lubricating oil she'd been applying to her voice and, all of a sudden, we could hear its true, shrill quality.

Lucia visibly flinched, like she'd been cut.

"You need to know the truth," Amelia continued. "Before the baby turns one, Ron will take off, best-case scenario. Worst, he'll stay and slap you around when he's had a few too many."

I needed to eliminate Lucia, but Amelia was doing a better job alienating her than I'd ever be able to on my own. With Amelia's last speech, Lucia turned off. It was clear to me she'd made up her mind and there was no going back.

"You don't know him." Lucia's distress surrounded her like a dense fog. She was unreachable.

"I know enough," Amelia said.

"I need to leave." Lucia pushed her chair back and stood up, using the table to support her weight.

Amelia froze for an instant. It was as if she were drunk and someone had thrown a glass of ice water in her face. She rushed around to the opposite side of the table. "Sweetheart, I didn't mean that. I didn't mean that." She tried to push Lucia back down into the chair.

"I understand you." Lucia elbowed her aside. She was stronger than I'd realized.

I saw the markings of unspeakable pain and loss etched on Amelia's face. It was like gravity's weight on her had increased tenfold in the last three minutes. "I'm feeling so anxious," she said to Lucia. "Please forgive me."

"You don't know him. You really don't." Lucia had no need to convince Amelia of Ron's character. But I could tell that she wanted to. The disparaging statements about Ron were painful to her.

"Please give yourself a few days," Amelia said. "To weigh all the information you have."

Lucia nodded reluctantly, but we all knew which way this was going.

While Amelia called a car for Lucia and walked her outside, I found my coat and boots. I felt that it would be in my best interest to leave quickly.

As I was on my way out the door, Amelia stopped me. "Stay for a minute, Delta." She reached for my hand with cold fingers and a searching look in her eyes.

I followed her to the back of the house and sat down across from her at the dining table. She leaned toward me so she could speak quietly and still be heard, though we were alone in the house. "I offered Ron money to give up the baby."

This was beyond what I'd expected, but I was nevertheless impressed and strangely proud. I admired her audacity.

"When did you talk to him?" I asked.

She spoke in a small, tight voice. "I went to Lucia's house last week. Ron was there."

Itzhak moaned lightly and repositioned himself on the hardwood floor.

"Did she hear you?"

"She was out of the room."

"Well, let's see. . . ." I didn't want Amelia to end up in jail, nor did I want a PR scandal. At the same time, I didn't believe it would be constructive to criticize her for actions already taken.

Her eyes filled with tears. "Ron is . . . everything you wouldn't want for your daughter . . . opportunistic, dull, arrogant, lazy . . . it would be a mother's deepest heartache to see a daughter with a man like him. And Lucia's mother, her pain, her pain, I can't imagine, to see it all unfolding before her eyes. The potential *death of her daughter's future.*"

"But the baby, then . . . Your baby would be biologically related to Ron. Would that concern you?"

"You think I don't know that?" Her words and saliva came toward me all at once.

I was surprised by the fury in her voice. It was an indication of her instability. Her madness.

"Yes," she said. "There is risk in adoption."

"I didn't mean . . ."

"That loser is not sticking around to raise the child." She pushed her hair behind her ears. "And Lucia's an idiot. Because she thinks he is. He wants to get laid and he wants to tell his loser friends he has a kid, because that's proof he got laid. Proof of his manhood."

"But if that's her decision . . ." I tried to point out the obvious, hoping she'd recognize that the path of Lucia was closed.

"You think I don't see that I have nothing? No power and nothing. I get it, Delta. I get it."

From my point of view, Amelia had limitless power. I thought about possible responses that wouldn't anger her. "I think you could fix the situation, if you want to."

"It's too late." She looked down and ran her thumb through the grooves in the antique farmhouse table.

"What did you say to him?" I tried to modulate my voice so it wouldn't sound at all critical.

"That I would be happy to loan him fifty thousand." Her eyes remained glued to the table.

"Loan?" I was relieved to hear the word *loan*. How could you go to jail for loaning money to someone?

"Yes, but I think he knew. That the 'loan' . . . it was conditional and euphemistic. He's not the brightest bulb, but he probably understands that much."

"Does Fritz know?"

Amelia rubbed a water-ring stain on the table with her finger, as if she might be able to remove it. "Well, I already talked about her tuition and other kinds of expenses."

"You could say—"

Amelia began to cry. "Whatever I say . . . it's not going to make a difference. She wants to keep the baby. She hates me."

I walked around the table to where she was sitting and put my arms around her shoulders. "It's OK, Amelia. It's going to be OK. She doesn't hate you. Let's just wait to see what happens."

Amelia continued to cry.

"It may be all right."

CHAPTER TWELVE

It was clear that Lucia wanted to keep her baby. But it was hard to judge how greedy Ron was. On the off chance that Lucia and Ron came back, Lucia needed to know that Amelia had tried to bribe Ron. I felt mild guilt about my plan, but any child of Ron's was likely to have long-term problems, with potential addiction issues, and make the Straubs miserable eventually.

I woke up on Thursday morning, drank two cups of coffee, and called Lucia. She sounded surprised to hear my voice.

"Amelia feels bad," I said. "She said things she didn't mean."

"It's OK." Lucia spoke with finality, as if hoping to get off the phone quickly.

"She feels bad about *both* conversations." I attempted a somber tone when I said the word *both* that would imply something untoward.

"Both?"

"The one at your house too."

"Yes?" She sounded confused.

"You know . . ." I paused for four seconds. "That she had the conversation with Ron when you weren't in the room. I mean, she knew he'd talk to you about it later. It wasn't like she was trying to hide anything. It's just . . . she doesn't want you to think she was offering to pay Ron for the baby."

There were a few seconds of silence.

"Excuse me?" Lucia's voice came through the phone receiver clipped and high.

"Well . . . the fifty thousand . . ." I paused again. "It was a *loan*."

"What are you talking about?" For the first time, I heard an edge in Lucia's voice.

"She wasn't offering to pay Ron for the baby," I said.

I heard her breath come through the receiver. "Don't call me again," she said in a low, steady voice. She hung up the phone.

Lucia was gone from our lives for good. And opportunities were opening up for me.

•   •   •

On Friday I sent Amelia a text and asked if she'd like me to babysit.

Ten minutes later she wrote back. She said yes. She said yes.

I had barely survived the strain of the previous three weeks. I felt as though I'd been drowning and Amelia's text was a life preserver tossed in my direction.

When I arrived at the Straubs' house late that afternoon, Natalie answered the door. I'd missed Natalie terribly. The sight of her face fortified me.

She brightened when she saw me. Maybe she'd missed me too.

I kissed her forehead. "How are you, honey?"

I hung my down coat on one of several glass hooks in the hallway.

"Mom and Dad are . . . crazy." Natalie walked in the direction of the kitchen, and I followed. "Mainly Mom. The whole baby thing. I don't know what their problem is." She was wearing tight jeans and a glittery T-shirt with a picture of a purple unicorn on it. I could see her sharp shoulder blades and ribs through her shirt. I could see her hip bones, too, and wondered whether she was eating. Whether her parents' anxiety had infected her.

She sat down at the kitchen island, on one of the leather-and-stainless kitchen stools, and I sat next to her. Her eyes appeared huge in her face and her skin was even more translucent than usual. She chewed on her fingernails or her fingers. I couldn't tell which.

Itzhak lay in his usual spot on the kitchen floor nearby. He whimpered quietly.

"Mom said that you have a son in California. Why don't you ever talk about him?"

I wasn't troubled by Natalie's comment. I'd known that the Straubs were eventually going to ask more about my son. But I'd grown to understand who Jasper was in a fuller way and would actually relish talking about him. "I haven't wanted to bother you or your mom with my troubles."

Natalie examined her fingernails, which were bitten down to the quick. "I know you're divorced. Piper's parents got divorced. Sometimes I think my parents should too. They act like they hate each other." She wore a bracelet made out of colored beads that spelled her name. "Piper said her parents are better friends now that they're divorced."

"All marriages have problems, but they usually work out."

"Why didn't yours?"

The late-afternoon sun flooded in through the three sets of bifold doors behind Natalie, casting long shadows into the room.

"There are exceptions. You need to make a good choice." I squinted in order to see her.

"What's your son's name?" she asked.

"Jasper." I could see Jasper in my mind's eye, golden skin, dark locks of hair, large brown eyes, small and wiry body. I visualized him in California with his father, at the beach among the waves and whitecaps, his toes sinking into the wet sand beneath him.

Itzhak rearranged himself on the floor. Natalie petted him with her bare foot. "When is your son coming back?"

"Soon, I hope." The sun moved behind a large branch of the

Straubs' cherry tree, so I was temporarily relieved from the glare in my eyes.

She picked up a pencil resting on the kitchen counter and twirled it in her fingers. "I'd like to meet him."

"One day." Jasper was my creation, just as a child from my womb would be my creation, were I to have one. And because I knew him so intimately, every eyelash, each toenail, I could speak about him with complete candor. Without apology.

She set the pencil back down on the counter and twirled it in place.

The sound of Itzhak's labored breathing filled the room. Natalie turned her attention toward the dog again. "I'm scared that Itzhak's going to die."

"Oh, honey."

"He sleeps almost all the time. When I come home from school, he doesn't run to say hi anymore. I think it's his heart condition."

At this time of day, the suspended glass cabinet glowed, as did every wineglass inside it.

"His eyesight and his hearing aren't good either," she said. "He can still smell me though. Itzhak has an incredible sense of smell. Did you know that a bloodhound's nose is ten to one hundred million times more sensitive than a human's?" She sniffed the air as if testing the sensitivity of her own nose.

"That's amazing."

Now one side of Natalie's face was bathed in light. Her gray eyes had small flecks of yellow. I took several long, slow breaths. The ache behind my sternum was subsiding.

"Some bloodhounds can detect who has touched a pipe bomb after the pipe bomb already exploded." Natalie got down from the kitchen stool and sat cross-legged on the hardwood floor, next to Itzhak. "They can detect one milligram of human sweat among one hundred million cubic meters of air. Those detective dogs are so cool. I'd love to meet one of them."

Itzhak rolled over onto his back. She scratched him behind his ears. "You're my best friend. Right, buddy?"

"Itzhak loves you so much," I said.

"I read that some dogs go away to die." She rubbed his stomach. "Is that true?"

The sun was quickly sinking behind the Straubs' shrubbery at the back of their yard. "Itzhak, please don't," she said. "I'm scared that one day I'll come home and he won't be here anymore. No one will know where he went." The whole house dimmed. Itzhak stood and limped away from Natalie and toward the tall glass doors.

"Maybe dogs who go away to die are hoping to spare their masters the pain of witnessing their death." I'd been by myself with my uncle when he'd had a heart attack. I was twelve at the time. I called the paramedics, but, unfortunately, he died before they arrived.

Natalie hugged her skinny legs into her ribs. "I think it would be worse. The not knowing."

Amelia and Fritz were going to return soon, but I was relishing my time with Natalie and wanted a few more minutes of uninterrupted conversation.

"Remember Lucia?" Natalie sat back down on the kitchen stool.

"Hmm?"

"She's keeping her baby."

I felt dust in my throat and coughed.

"I think you knew that already." Natalie made eye contact with me. The yellow flecks in her eyes danced. I saw acuity in her gaze.

"I wasn't sure." I was very aware of the muscles in my face.

"Her boyfriend came back. He decided to be the dad." She studied me, as if anticipating a reaction.

I tried to maintain a semi-neutral expression of detached concern.

She swiveled her stool 360 degrees and then back the other way. "Mom's dying for a baby. It's pathetic." Again, she swiveled and reversed.

Itzhak circled in order to find a comfortable spot near Natalie.

"They don't need a baby," she said. "They have me."

"You're not a baby." I envisioned the chaos of any baby compromising Amelia's desire for order and infringing on her circumscribed life.

"I'm their real daughter," Natalie said. "Why bring some other gene pool into the house?"

I looked at her face to determine if she was making a joke, but saw no trace of humor.

"I want to say to them: You're too old for another baby." She swiveled, then caught herself mid-revolution each time, and pushed off in the opposite direction.

I held her stool in place to keep her from swiveling.

"Your parents adore you," I said.

"They don't adore spending time with me."

I heard a car pulling into the Straubs' driveway. Itzhak's ears perked up. He stood, as if he were considering running to the front door out of duty, but then an expression of defeat fell across his face and he lay back down.

I heard the front door open, followed by the sound of forceful wind, along with boots stomping on the doormat. The door clicked shut. Then footsteps in the hall. I recognized the footsteps as belonging to Fritz.

In a baseball cap and jeans, he appeared brooding and intensely handsome. He flicked a switch and every light in the back half of the house was illuminated. He rubbed his hands together. The cold air from the front door had traveled down the hall, toward the back of the house, and even the kitchen felt chilly. It was the last day of March, but the temperature was still below freezing.

"Hi, Delta," he said. "Hi, Toots." Fritz kissed Natalie on her forehead. I noticed that his beard had grown in.

"Rough day?" I asked.

"It's three grand to replace the car's fucking transmission." He opened the Sub-Zero refrigerator and then turned away from the open door, distracted, as if he forgot what he was looking for. He removed his baseball cap and threw it across the room, where it landed on the sofa.

"Sorry to hear that."

The refrigerator beeped to indicate it was still open.

He turned back to the fridge and pulled out a bottle of IPA. "Lucia decided to keep her baby. Did you know?"

I tried to read him. Was he thinking of our conversation from a few weeks earlier? I held my face still and expressionless. "A temporary change of heart, perhaps?"

He widened his eyes. "Amelia's a disaster."

"Dad," Natalie said. "Mom needs to get a grip."

"I know." He studied his bottle of beer, as if deciding how to open it.

"Maybe she needs to talk to our rabbi," Natalie said.

Fritz reached into a drawer and pulled out a ninety-nine-cent bottle opener, one of the only mundane items I'd noticed in the Straub household, not in the same league as my brass-and-marble bottle opener. The bottle cap fell to the floor. He left it there.

"Piper says Mom needs spiritual guidance."

"Your mom doesn't want spiritual guidance." Fritz looked out toward the backyard. His attention seemed to be caught by something he heard. I observed his rounded shoulders. The endless exchanges with Amelia had taken a toll on his body. Though an exceedingly attractive man, his hair was thinning, his hairline receding.

"She doesn't know what she wants." Natalie seemed irritated at her father's distraction.

Fritz continued to gaze absentmindedly at the cherry tree, the dead brown grass, the lavender sky.

"Mom's damaged," Natalie said, raising her voice to get his attention. She sounded strident.

He pressed his eyes closed tightly.

"Spiritual guidance could be helpful," I said. Still seated at the kitchen island, with Natalie next to me, I gently placed my hand on hers, and, as I did, I noticed that it was almost as large as mine. The skin on her knuckles felt rough from the harsh winter air. "Amelia's experienced a loss because she was counting on Lucia's baby. There are people who can help her with that."

Fritz laughed thinly. He cast his eyes in my direction.

"I grew up Catholic," I said. "I used to talk to the priest at our church when I was having difficulty." I'd barely known the priest, and only spoken to him once, when he took me aside to ask me about my parents' divorce. I was wearing a white blouse with bell sleeves that day. I remember wishing for a pair of scissors so that I could cut off my sleeves and cover his mouth with them, to mask the nauseating smell of his breath. "In fact, even recently, I called the priest from my church for counsel on my custody situation."

Fritz cleared his throat, as if he expected me to say more, but I didn't.

It wasn't in my best interest to be spiritual. Maybe one day, when I had what Amelia already had—money, family, love, success—on that day, I could afford to look for God. But right now it wasn't the best use of my time.

Amelia, however, was a different story. Natalie was right that she needed guidance of some kind. Opening her heart up to God, her pain might disappear entirely. It worked for some people. She might look around and say, *Wow. I'm fortunate. Thank you, God.*

But first she'd have to acknowledge her blessings. She'd have to notice, for example, that I was standing in front of her, eager to help.

"Fritz, if you don't mind my saying so, you and Amelia should try to communicate with Natalie during the whole process so that she understands your thinking."

A muscle in his cheek twitched. "Thanks, Delta. I think we got this."

Natalie rolled her eyes. "Really?" She pushed her ash-colored hair behind her ears, a habit not dissimilar to Amelia's. "How's that?"

My stomach turned. I didn't want him to associate me with Natalie's rebellion.

"Why don't you go practice the cello?" he said to her.

He opened one set of bifold doors and walked outside without closing them behind him. Itzhak followed him to the door, but just stood there with the wind blowing his hair and ears back and chose not to go out. Cold air made its way through the house again. Natalie shivered. Fritz walked down the spiral staircase and to the far end of their backyard, where he appeared to examine their cherry tree. He'd told me it was glorious in full bloom, but I liked it now, when the tree's angular silhouette carved out negative space in the sky. Fritz circled the tree methodically, looking closely at the bark and the roots, as if he were an arborist. I wondered if he knew anything at all about trees.

I walked to the stove, picking up Fritz's bottle cap on my way, and turned on one of the burners to boil some water.

"Fritz," I called outside through the open door. "Would you like a cup of tea?"

"He doesn't drink tea. He drinks beer." Natalie's tone of voice was sharp. I felt chastised.

"Would you like a cup of tea?" I asked her.

Natalie sighed loudly and stared at the ceiling. "No."

I took down two large rust-colored ceramic mugs from the cabinet—two of a set of twelve, probably handmade—and removed two expensive-looking tea sachets from a tin container.

I walked back to the kitchen island and sat down next to her. "I think you should talk to your mom."

Itzhak lay back down next to Natalie. His breathing sounded like a broken radiator.

"I want to help you all," I said.

Fritz reappeared and closed the doors behind him.

The teakettle shrieked loudly. It sounded like an ambulance siren. I poured boiling water into the ceramic mugs and let the tea steep.

Fritz joined us at the kitchen island. "It looks good." He held his beer bottle in one hand and placed his other hand on the handle of the mug.

"You hate tea," Natalie said.

"I do?" He adjusted his glasses on his nose.

The phone rang and Fritz picked up. "Nat, it's Piper."

Natalie took the portable phone down the hall.

Fritz and I were now alone in the kitchen. Our previous conversation hung in the air between us, as did our previous physical contact.

"My back . . . it's killing me." Fritz rubbed his shoulder. His hands looked masculine, like they belonged to a blue-collar worker. The way my father's hands looked. The way my uncle's hands looked.

"I used to be a masseuse."

He glanced at me. Perhaps he interpreted my statement as an overture. Perhaps it was.

"It's probably in spasm," I said. I stood behind him and placed my hand on his shoulder. His shirt was still cold from having been outside. "Is this where it hurts?" I pressed my thumb down on what I thought might be a pressure point. The Australian masseur I'd dated several years earlier had shown me a few. That relationship lasted longer than most, until his roommate made absurd accusations and changed the locks on their apartment.

My fingers lingered on the carotid pulse in Fritz's neck and I could feel it quicken.

"I have a headache too." He put his hand to his head.

"Usually tension in the shoulder contributes to a headache. The constriction of blood flow." My hands moved to his forehead and his temples, often the source of a headache. I used my fingers to place pressure on his temples and his jaw, all potential causes of tension. "Here is the problem," I said, "right here." Then I moved down his arms to his hands. He released his tight hold on the bottle and a few drops of beer spilled onto the floor.

"Delta, you're really good at this." He shifted on his stool. "Thank you."

I massaged one of his hands, then the other. I felt the calluses covering his palms. "The hands have pressure points connected to every part of the body. Pain in one part of your hand is an indication of a larger problem." After his hands, I massaged his lower back. Then I turned his body on the stool so that he was facing away from the counter and toward me and I would have more access to the front of his body. His face was flushed and damp with perspiration. I wanted him. My desire for Fritz didn't completely align with my grander vision, but I couldn't talk myself out of it. I wanted to be in the center—with no secrets between Amelia and Fritz that I didn't have access to.

I willed Fritz to put his hand between my legs. He needed something to take his mind off the failed adoption and Amelia. I closed my eyes and imagined his hand on my thigh, then further up on my crotch.

How long would Natalie be on the phone with Piper?

In my mind, I saw myself: I walked toward the Straubs' side office and looked back so that he would follow me and, in my mind, he did. Fritz closed the door behind him and locked it. In the background, I could still hear Natalie on the phone. We didn't have much time. I lay my upper body facedown on Fritz's desk and pulled my dress up. I understood him. He was angry at everyone. Maybe even angry at me for offering sex to him. And angry at himself for accepting the offer. Rage was driving him. I know what that's like.

When I opened my eyes, I was standing in front of Fritz in the kitchen. His eyes were still closed. His head had dropped forward slightly. My hands were still on his shoulders.

I heard Natalie say goodbye to Piper then her footsteps approaching. Fritz opened his eyes. We made eye contact. I felt the pounding of my heart in my body. Then he looked away. Natalie joined us in the kitchen and sat on the floor, petting Itzhak while Fritz drank his beer. He didn't touch the tea.

CHAPTER THIRTEEN

I heard the front door open, the wind shrieking, and then silence after the door slammed shut. Amelia appeared in the kitchen. She had dark circles underneath her red, swollen eyes and appeared thinner than the last time I'd seen her.

Without a word, she crossed to the sink, turned on the faucet, and vigorously splashed water onto her face, spilling it onto her dress and the floor as well. She dried her hands with a paper towel, but didn't bother to wipe up the puddle on the floor.

Amelia carefully dabbed her lips with the paper towel, then her forehead and then her cheeks. "I have a right to say goodbye to the baby."

"What do you mean?" Fritz took a large sip of his beer.

"I believed that I was her mother." Amelia's voice shifted into a higher register. "I bonded with the baby. My heart has been ripped from my chest." She rolled the wet paper towel into a small ball.

Fritz crossed toward Amelia and put his hands on her shoulders. "You have us, babe."

She pushed him away as if his hands burnt her skin through her dress. "I'm dying."

Seated on the floor next to Itzhak, Natalie twisted a rubber band around her hair to create a ponytail.

"Amelia," Fritz said. "You need a therapist or a counselor."

"It's deep grief." Amelia pulled on her ear, like a baby with an earache.

"You need spiritual guidance." Natalie stood and sat back down on one of the counter stools.

Amelia turned to look at Natalie as if noticing her for the first time. "Hmm?"

"Maybe our rabbi," Natalie said.

"We don't have a rabbi."

"At the synagogue."

"We don't have a synagogue."

"Any synagogue will do."

Amelia looked at her daughter as though she were speaking another language. The frayed hem of Amelia's dress and the scuff marks on her boots did not comport with the charismatic, glamorous woman I'd met several months earlier. The roots of her hair were gray and greasy. Her shine had completely worn off. She wasn't trying and failing. She had stopped trying altogether.

Amelia had yet to recognize my presence. I was used to feeling invisible, but even so, her lack of acknowledgment elicited a hollow feeling in my gut.

I considered excusing myself, out of a sense of propriety, but I owed it to myself to embrace the opportunities I'd created.

"I don't want a baby if this is what happens to you." Fritz spoke in a dry voice. "I don't know you."

"Then I suppose we go our separate ways." Amelia opened up one of the kitchen cabinets. She looked at the expiration date on a box of crackers and tossed it into the trash. I questioned whether the crackers were actually expired.

"Jesus Christ." Fritz downed the last of his beer and deposited the bottle under the sink with a loud crash. "Do you have any concern for your daughter's feelings?" I imagined that he said the line "concern for your daughter's feelings" often and by rote because it made him sound responsible and caring.

Fritz crossed to the fridge for another beer.

Amelia picked up a bottle of Fernando Pensato olive oil and studied the label, again looking for an expiration date. She poured the bottle of expensive olive oil into the sink. It splashed onto her blouse, but she seemed oblivious to it. She smelled the opening of the empty bottle and wrinkled her nose, confirming to herself that she'd been right in pouring it out.

"You have no compassion," she said to Fritz. "You have no empathy."

I stood and clasped my hands together. "Can I try to help you both? I want to help you have a child."

Amelia startled at the sound of my voice. She turned to me with a bewildered expression. She had the glassy eyes and blotchy cheeks of someone with a high fever. "What are you going to do?"

"Whatever you want me to do." In order to achieve my dream, I needed to believe that this was true—that I was willing to do anything in order to help their family.

"What are you *talking* about?" She put her head in her hands and looked to the heavens in a dramatic gesture.

"Carrying the baby?" Fritz's eyes locked on mine, and then he turned to Amelia. "I think she means carrying the baby."

I heard faint bells in the distance. "I mean anything."

"Carrying the child. Surrogacy." Amelia steadied herself with one hand, her fingers clutching the kitchen island so hard, they turned white.

"Yes, surrogacy." I didn't have enough saliva in my mouth to swallow easily. "Or anything else."

I looked for answers in Amelia but just saw confusion and rigidity.

"I don't even understand what *surrogacy* means," Natalie said, swiveling on her chair.

Amelia furrowed her brow. I could tell she wasn't in the mood for explanations.

"Well," Fritz began tentatively, "a surrogate is a woman who helps people have a baby."

"How?" Natalie asked.

"She carries the baby for someone who can't," he said.

"In her stomach?"

"Yes."

"That's weird," Natalie said. "Like she's a mom but she's not a mom."

"Shut up, Natalie!" Amelia said.

I couldn't bear to hear Amelia speak harshly to her daughter. I walked over to where Natalie was seated and stood behind her protectively. Her frame looked so vulnerable from behind. I could practically feel Amelia's words penetrating her.

"Delta, I need to understand." Amelia's hand wandered through her hair like a butterfly, without any real direction. "Are you offering to be a surrogate for our family?"

"I love your family so much." Everything I wanted was in front of me, but I sensed that one mistake could undermine all of it.

Amelia held me by my forearms, her fingers covered in olive oil. "If you're offering to be a surrogate for our family"—she looked into my eyes—"my answer is yes and my gratitude knows no bounds."

A current of air lifted me up off the ground.

I didn't respond to her. I feared that my voice would give away my excitement. If I were able to see myself in a mirror, I would have looked sixteen, the effects of gravity on my body having been reversed. I was weightless.

Tears fell from Amelia's eyes. She spoke through her sobs. "But you can't betray us, betray our trust. I can't survive with this kind of pain again."

"I don't know." Fritz frowned and looked down. "This . . . It feels like too much to ask." His voice shook. He didn't seem completely comfortable with the idea, but neither did he have the energy to challenge Amelia directly.

"We want you to be our surrogate," Amelia sobbed, then bit her lip and swallowed. "Of course, we'd figure out a way to compensate you."

"I wouldn't accept money."

"Some kind of compensation," she said. "It wouldn't be right otherwise." I could hear underlying panic in her voice. It was the fear that I might say no. Or that I might say yes and then change my mind. Amelia was desperate and her desperation made her vulnerable.

"Money isn't . . ."

"We would be eternally grateful," Amelia said.

"Of course," Fritz said, "we'd be grateful."

"Why would Delta want to?" Natalie chewed on her nails.

I placed my hand on Natalie's shoulder. "The joy of bringing a life into the world."

Her shoulder blades trembled. "I don't believe that."

"Natalie!" Amelia snapped.

"Don't pretend that it's any kind of favor to *me*." Natalie stood and backed away from us.

"Stop it," Amelia said to Natalie. "I apologize for Natalie's behavior." Amelia bowed her head. "You can't know what a huge gift you're giving us."

"I want to be in a different family," Natalie said.

Fritz held both hands up. "Enough."

"Last week, Mom slapped me," Natalie said loudly.

"Go to your room!" Amelia said.

Natalie ran to the stairs. We listened to the sound of her feet climbing two flights of stairs.

"Did you hit her?" Fritz said quietly.

"How dare you?" Amelia's fury filled the room like smoke.

"I just don't understand. . . ." he said.

"Go fuck yourself."

"Everyone's nerves are frayed," I said. "It's so hard on all of you. Is it OK with you if I talk to her?" I looked at each of them, one at a time, waiting for a response. I took their silence as acquiescence.

•   •   •

Natalie's door was ajar. I knocked softly.

"Come in." She was lying on her bed, on top of the purple unicorn comforter.

I closed the door behind me.

"I hate this house," Natalie said. "I want to live someplace else." She lifted her legs up in the air, then alternated kicking them one at a time. "My mom didn't actually slap me."

"Of course she didn't." I was relieved, but at the same time I experienced a slight letdown. I wanted Natalie to need me. I wanted to be essential.

"My mom just wants a baby." She rolled over onto her side so she could see me.

"I know."

"She wants a baby so much more than she wants me. It's ridiculous." She made her mouth into a small O and blew out a tunnel of air. "I'm not that interesting."

"Natalie . . ."

She sat up on her bed and hugged her knees into her chest. "She says she's the only one in the family who carries her weight."

"You're a child."

"She has to take care of everything." She removed her bracelet. "Dad doesn't work as hard as she does." She pulled both ends of the elastic out, then let them snap back in. "My mom says she's drowning." She snapped the bracelet again. "She wishes I were more helpful."

"Your mom is feeling bad lately, but it has absolutely nothing to do with you." I studied the framed photograph of Natalie and her father on her desk. He was pushing her on a swing at a playground.

"I'm not making her happy." She snapped the bracelet again and this time I was sure it would break. "She probably thought that I would at first."

"Honey, you can't expect to fix everything." Natalie couldn't, but I could. Astonishingly. I was in a position to make Amelia happy. The feeling of weightlessness from earlier returned.

Natalie held my gaze. "Sometimes I think some relative died and my mom and dad had to take me in. My mom acts like I ought to be someone else's responsibility."

She stood and walked to the window. Her third-floor bedroom, with its two large windows, faced a quiet street. In and among tree branches, it felt like a tree house.

She leaned her hands on the panes and pressed her face up to the glass. "I want to live with you," she said.

"Natalie . . ." My pulse quickened. My shirt was damp with perspiration. I needed my relationship with Natalie to work alongside the surrogacy, not in competition. I thought about the most appropriate way to respond to her. She might repeat what I said to her parents. "I would do anything for you."

"Let me stay with you," she said.

"I'd love for you to stay with me. For a night or a weekend or even longer."

"I mean live with you."

"You don't really want that. You . . . you just need time to process everything."

"I've had a whole life with them," she said. "I don't need time."

"Honey, it's a rough patch," I said. "Things will get better."

"Please don't be a surrogate," she said. "You were *my* friend. And now they've taken you for themselves."

I had increasing anxiety, recognizing that Natalie wasn't going to accept the surrogacy easily. I needed to find a way to appease her. For my own peace of mind. I didn't realize how much her unhappiness would weigh on me.

"Whether or not I'm a surrogate, it doesn't change our friendship."

She stared out the window. She was quiet for a few minutes.

My eyes landed on her green science folder. "How's your science project going?"

She crossed to the desk, opened the science folder, and looked over her completed pages of work.

Natalie had spent time explaining each unicorn in her room to me, but hadn't ever mentioned the large black unicorn lamp on her desk, and I hadn't noticed it, perhaps because it was an abstract sculpture. Unless you were up close, you wouldn't necessarily identify the lamp as a unicorn, but once you did, it was mildly unsettling.

She flipped through several pages and then stopped. "This is wrong." She sat down and took a pencil, eraser, and sharpener from her desk drawer. She erased several formulas.

"All of this is hard for you," I said.

"I want them to give it up." She started over, writing several formulas in a column.

"I understand how you feel."

Through the window, a bright red cardinal, perched on a nearby branch, was calling out to its mate.

"How come you don't visit your son?" She erased her work

again, and this time she erased so hard that she tore a small hole in the paper. "Goddamn it." She threw the eraser at the window in an apparent attempt to startle the cardinal. But the bird just fluttered its wings. "Everyone's talking about a baby that doesn't even exist."

"I miss my son." I did. I missed Jasper from the bottom of my heart. I ached to hold him in my arms. I'd worked hard to create memories, and over time my child had grown so clear to me. I could hold on to the notion that I would be reunited with Jasper. I thought about the work I could do in my studio, creating even more memories that would provide me with hours of happiness. The pain I was experiencing was the pain of a mother, an artist, a creator. Jasper was my creation, but eventually I would have to release him. With love comes loss.

"I long for Jasper," I said. "We FaceTime every day."

"Can I FaceTime with him?"

"He's shy."

Natalie looked down at her homework. "What does he like?"

"Surfing. He lives near the beach in Venice."

She drew spirals on the side of the page.

"He has an imaginary friend named Spiro," I said.

She smiled for the first time since I'd arrived at their house that day. "Jasper could visit you. You could visit him."

"I'm visiting him next week."

"Oh." Her spirals grew larger.

"I know it's probably hard for you to understand the surrogacy. I care about you and your mom and your dad. I love all of you."

"You haven't known us that long."

"I feel as if I've known you forever." That was true. From the moment I'd met Amelia, I felt like she knew me, and I knew her.

Natalie shifted from spirals to a vortex.

I paused, trying to find the right words: "I don't think your mom is going to give up on the idea of a baby."

She continued drawing a vortex that appeared to be spinning around a black hole. "I just want to get out of here," she said.

My pulse quickened again. I took her hand in mine. "I think that as soon as your mom has a baby, she'll act the way you want her to act."

"You're wrong."

The cardinal landed on a branch that was even closer to Natalie's window.

"What do you think would make you feel better?" I asked.

"I want my parents to die."

Her bedroom felt warm and close. I had a strong urge to open the window.

"I want my mom to be my mom," she said. "Just because she cries, doesn't mean that she's a good person. My mom wants people to pay attention to her. That's why she cries."

She turned her eyes to look out the window. I followed her gaze. The bird appeared to be staring at us.

"I never cry anymore," she said.

I understood why. Amelia had taken the role of the person who cries.

Natalie stood and walked to the window. "Why is it looking at us?" The bird didn't move. "My mom wasn't like this before she was obsessed by a baby. She didn't cry all the time. She just worked."

She collapsed her body onto the large beanbag in the middle of the room. "Sometimes people came to take a tour of the house. Mom was happy because they'd say it was beautiful."

She leaned back on the beanbag and pulled her knees tightly into her chest. "And then sometimes, on those days, me and Mom went to the bookstore and got ice cream sundaes."

"You'll do those things again."

I heard a loud noise and turned in time to see the bird crashing head-on into the window. Natalie screamed. The cardinal dropped toward the ground.

Natalie leapt to the far side of the room, away from the windows. "Help!"

"It's OK." I walked to the window and looked down.

A minute later Fritz appeared in the bedroom doorway. "What's wrong?"

"That bird tried to break into the house!" Natalie cried.

"A cardinal sometimes attacks its reflection in the glass," Fritz said. "It thinks it sees another bird."

Natalie was still breathing heavily. "Is he dead?" she asked me.

"I think so," I said.

She chewed on her nails in an agitated manner. She seemed to feel complicit in the bird's death because she'd witnessed it. "It's such a stupid bird." She approached the window. "Why couldn't he tell it was a reflection?" She gestured toward her own barely visible image in the glass. "It doesn't look real. It doesn't look like anything."

I put my arm around her shoulders.

"Let's go downstairs for a drink," Fritz said, "to take the edge off."

CHAPTER FOURTEEN

Downstairs I found Amelia frenetically cleaning the kitchen counters, though they appeared clean already. She was rubbing one spot repeatedly, as if it were stained. She looked up when I entered.

"I think we should celebrate," she said. "I think we should draw up a legal document." She was speaking fast, and her eyes were bouncing around the room.

Natalie turned on the television in the media room. Fritz sat at the dining table with a bourbon and soda to sort a stack of mail. Amelia and Fritz were acting as if they'd forgotten about their plans to go out.

"You two should leave whenever you need to," I said.

"Amelia," Fritz said, "we've gotta make an appearance." He pushed the stack of mail aside and disappeared upstairs with his bourbon and soda.

"The last two years," she said to me, "it's been a heartbreaking time for me. I can't keep track of all the disappointments." Her syllables came out on top of one another, blurring her speech.

"I understand."

"Delta, I can't have my hopes dashed again. I can't survive if that happens again. I need to know that you will see this through."

The sound of bells returned and grew slightly louder than before. "I'm honored that you've asked me to be your surrogate." It was an effort to stay in the room with Amelia, because I couldn't resist watching the scene unfold—watching my dreams come to fruition.

Amelia looked at me in earnest. "Would you like to see *my* doctor? My OB?" she asked hopefully.

"I have an amazing doctor," I said. "A brilliant woman." I tried to conjure up the image of the physician I saw recently at the walk-in urgent care facility I frequented.

"That's terrific." Amelia's expression turned serious. "I want you to know that if you'd like to participate in the child's life, I would be a hundred percent on board with that."

I felt warmth in my core. My life was changing. *My life was changing.*

Amelia stiffened. Something had occurred to her. "What will Ian say?"

I didn't believe Amelia cared how Ian felt, but I suppose she thought that she ought to care. She wanted me to see her as a self-less person who kept everyone else's needs top of mind. Or perhaps she was scared he'd interfere.

"He knows where my heart is," I said. "I hope to have a baby with Ian. One day. He understands that. I dream of Jasper coming back to Brooklyn and living with me and Ian and our baby. Those are the happy thoughts that put me to sleep at night." I had never even considered living with Ian, and I had no desire to have a baby with him. But I had a sense that the narrative might satisfy Amelia's desire to understand me and my priorities. In any case, it wouldn't serve her to delve too deep. She wanted to believe what she wanted to believe.

"And Jasper?" she asked. "How will he feel?"

I felt a burning sensation in my throat, similar to acid reflux. "Jasper knows I love him." In my mind, I could see Jasper building a sandcastle on the beach, his damp hair clinging to the base of his neck.

Amelia put her arms around me and rested her head on my shoulder. "I am so grateful, Delta." Moisture from her tears landed on my shoulder. She lifted her head. With no makeup, her color-less lips had disappeared. "Help me explain things to Natalie. She trusts you." She whispered loudly, inadvertently spitting in my ear. "I know it's hard for her, but she has to recognize that I have needs too."

She opened the refrigerator and took a bottle of white wine out of the side compartment. She poured herself a large glass. I enjoyed wine as much as she did, but I knew she wasn't going to offer me any, because I was Natalie's babysitter and now the surrogate for her baby. After Natalie went to bed, I planned to have a small glass, not enough that anyone would notice.

Amelia swirled her wine in the glass and raised it toward the light to observe the streaks, then downed all of it quickly and set her glass in the sink. Several minutes later she and Fritz walked out the door. She hadn't changed her clothes or even brushed through her matted hair.

After her parents left, Natalie and I played Scrabble and watched *The Hunger Games*. By the time she went to bed, she'd moved on from the subject of surrogacy, at least for the night.

•   •   •

I awoke to Amelia's hand on my shoulder.

"Delta, darling," she said.

I looked up and saw her face inches from mine, so close that it was distorted. I could identify the individual hairs of her eyebrows. I had a strong urge to kiss her. I sat up on the leather sofa in the media room, embarrassed to have fallen asleep. I didn't sleep very deeply or very much. In my youth, I'd learned to sleep with one eye open, especially when certain members of the family were visiting.

I could feel her breath on my face as she spoke. "Stay downstairs tonight, in the garden apartment. It's so late." Bells sounded in my head. I'd intuitively understood that the surrogacy and the apartment were cosmically linked, only I hadn't known which would happen first, or if the two things would happen simultaneously.

"Our tenant moved out last week," she explained.

A triumphant refrain from *Aida* replaced the bells. The apartment's vacancy was official. (I already knew Gwen had moved out, and, to some extent, I'd orchestrated the move. In addition to occasional puddles on the floor, I'd been rearranging her belongings in subtle but unsettling ways. A month earlier I'd noticed flyers from an open house on the kitchen counter. Then she'd started to pack, and a week later everything had disappeared.)

"Don't worry," she said, "we have brand-new sheets and towels. You won't get cooties." Amelia's mood had shifted dramatically over the last three hours. She was a different person. She'd miraculously pulled out of a spiraling dive.

Fritz appeared in the doorway, still wearing his coat. "Please, Delta." He sounded genuinely concerned.

"OK." I could smell the alcohol on Amelia's breath.

"Have breakfast with us in the morning?" Amelia said.

A few minutes later Fritz walked me down the steps, unlocked the garden apartment, and turned on the recessed lights in the front hall.

In a way, I was seeing the apartment for the first time, because now I could allow myself to indulge in my dream. I believed it was only a matter of time before the apartment belonged to me. "It's stunning."

"Get some sleep," Fritz said. His gaze traveled from my eyes, slowly downward. I sensed that he wanted to stay with me. The opportunity was before us. Amelia was so drunk that, invariably, she would have fallen asleep immediately. She wasn't going to notice what time Fritz returned. Any minute he was going to step toward me and unbutton my blouse. I would have liked to tell him it was OK. I wanted him too.

At no time did my desire for Fritz eclipse my love for Amelia. The two things coexisted and fed off each other. I hoped to be the center of their worlds.

"Good night." Once he made the decision to leave, his face drooped down and his shoulders rounded. He turned and walked out the front door. His departure was mildly disappointing, but I couldn't dwell on it, given all that I'd accomplished in the last twelve hours.

Now I had unlimited time to admire every aspect of the apartment anew, with the knowledge that I was going to spend the entire night there. The design, the materials, and the workmanship were on par with the main house. The reclaimed elm wood floor, high-end appliances, marble countertops, plumbing fixtures, hardware, tile backsplash, recessed lighting, the windows, and the cabinetry.

A number of years earlier I'd been involved with a highly skilled cabinetmaker, so I knew about the time and expense involved in bookshelves like these. The attention to detail. The cabinetmaker and his wife had occupied an apartment down the hall from me when I lived in Queens. I was close friends with his wife, but eventually she found out that he and I were having sex in my kitchen in exchange for my cabinets.

Amelia had lent me a pair of her pajamas. The faint smell of her lemon-and-bergamot perfume still lingered on them. I knew she would never wear them again after I did. She would either give them away or throw them out. She assumed that I'd love wearing her pajamas. She was right.

That night, I dreamed that I was trying to escape from a dragon. I found a temporary refuge—a small cardboard house, the size of a child's playhouse. I stepped inside the playhouse and closed the door. I could hear the dragon outside. When it started to rain, the playhouse collapsed into a pile of mush, and then the dragon saw me with the crumbled playhouse all around me and he realized how vulnerable I was. Only then did he go in for the kill.

•   •   •

After having showered and dressed in the same clothes from the day before, I had a chance to study the apartment in daylight. The living room had sliding glass doors that opened up to a small patio and the backyard. I wondered whether Gwen had been allowed to use the entire yard, or whether she'd been confined to the patio.

At 10 A.M., I joined everyone upstairs for a late breakfast.

"Hello, beauty!" Amelia called out in a vibrant, positive voice.

I didn't often experience the Straub house in the morning light. The southern light streamed in through the skylight from above—an intense, unfiltered, unrelenting California kind of light.

I had a fresh surge of appreciation for the Straubs' architectural talent.

The dining table was already set, including a place for me. I sat down and Fritz brought me a cappuccino. Amelia served me a plate of scrambled eggs and bacon. Her appearance had improved significantly overnight. She'd obviously washed her hair, and her gray roots were less noticeable because she'd pulled her hair back in a ponytail. The circles underneath her eyes had disappeared, likely with the help of her seventy-dollar concealer, which she'd applied for the first time in weeks.

"What if you rent our apartment from us for the rest of the year?" she asked.

Bells echoed in my head, and then *Aida* again. I feared that my voice would crack if I answered, so I said nothing, hoping that my silence would indicate thoughtfulness, as opposed to hyperventilation or euphoria.

I took a sip of my cappuccino and wiped the foam off my upper lip.

"You'd be close by." Amelia took a seat next to Natalie.

I thought Amelia expected me to voice an objection or a concern. "My cat," I said.

Amelia placed her hand on Natalie's shoulder. "It would be incredible for Natalie." Natalie looked at her mother's hand as if it were a bug.

"You can pay the same rent you're paying now," Amelia said. "Babysitting would be so much easier."

"Your cat would like it too," Natalie said. She was wearing pajamas decorated with question marks of varying colors and sizes. Her long lashes stood out against her pale skin.

I didn't reply, but, of course, of course, I knew what my answer was.

"Just consider it," Amelia said. "Especially given what we discussed yesterday. It all makes so much sense." She raised her eyebrows meaningfully.

I looked at Natalie to see if I detected a reaction, but fortunately, she'd backed away from the confrontation with her mother.

"It's a beautiful apartment," I said.

Fritz sat next to me and served himself bacon and eggs. He took a bite of his undercooked bacon. I sensed a fissure in the family. "Only downside is you'll get sucked into babysitting more often than you want to." He laughed in a self-deprecating manner.

I wasn't listening anymore. I was suspended above my body, watching my new life emerge.

●   ●   ●

The lease on my Crown Heights apartment was up May 15. I tried and failed to get out early. Since I had enough money in the bank to cover both apartments for an overlapping month, I never mentioned the situation to the Straubs. The extra rent was a small price to pay. I didn't want to wait.

Once I began packing, my cat, Eliza, tried to sabotage the move. She stood in front of the kitchen cabinet that held my pots and pans so I couldn't reach them. When I tried to pack the dishes, she blocked that cabinet too. Eventually I gave up and locked her in my bedroom.

The move proved an opportunity for me to streamline my belongings and part with old clothing, photos, and knickknacks that were weighing me down, literally and figuratively. In the process, I cleaned up the digital files on my hard drive that I no longer needed. I had folders full of images dating back ten years. I held on to the best ones, in case the clients returned for more prints, but deleted many of them.

I had twenty-two folders of my private photoshopped images, representing twenty-two families. Of course, the twenty-two folders were a small fraction of all my clients. But those were the families who had made an impression on me. In certain cases, there was a story to be told, with groups of images that conveyed something about a life I'd shared with someone. In other cases, it was just a matter of one or two gratifying pictures.

I opened the Straub, Alternates folder. Clicking through the photos, I stopped when I came to the pictures of me and Fritz in bed together. I had done impressive work in making the photos feel alive. In my estimation, they were artistic creations. I'd successfully fabricated an expression of ecstasy on Fritz's face. Some of the photos were tight on our body parts and some allowed a view of the whole scene. I stopped again when I came to the photoshopped pictures of Amelia and me and took a few minutes to savor the image of us sharing a piece of birthday cake. I felt uneasy leaving all the images on my hard drive, now that I would be living in the Straub home. So, painful though it was, I deleted each photo individually, followed by the entire folder.

· · ·

Ian and I were having coffee around the corner from my apartment, at his insistence. The coffee shop was mostly empty, except for one woman with headphones working on her laptop in the far corner.

He was angry when he learned about my being the Straubs' surrogate. But I wasn't inclined to discuss my choices with him.

"Have you ever heard of generosity?" I said.

"It's not generosity," he said. "You can't bear to be in your own skin."

I felt pressure in my sinuses and ears, like I was on an airplane. Ian was trying to provoke me. I couldn't allow him to see that he'd succeeded. He felt he had the right to talk to me like that because we were having sex. In his mind, we were in a relationship. I resented his presumption. I've always considered the contents of my brain private.

I wiped up a little coffee that had spilled on the table in front of me.

"If you want to get pregnant so badly, then have a baby with me," he said. "The idea of being someone's surrogate. I don't even get what you think it does for you."

I wasn't interested in Ian's idea of normal behavior. He thought that the surrogacy was fulfilling some short-term desire, at the expense of my long-term happiness. He didn't realize that my definition of *long-term happiness* had nothing to do with his.

"It's an end in itself," I said.

"What does your son think of it?" I saw some challenge in his gaze.

"No one is asking for your opinion."

"Do you really have a son?" His eyes bored into me.

"Of course."

A twentysomething man entered the coffee shop and walked to the counter to order. Cold air rushed in behind him.

"I don't think you do." Ian spoke in a low voice.

I laughed. "You have no idea who I am."

"Does anyone?"

I felt a compression of my rib cage.

Ian put his thumb and forefinger on the bridge of his nose and squeezed his eyes shut, like he had a headache. "Is it about Amelia and Fritz?"

I nodded. "I want to help them."

CHAPTER FIFTEEN

In mid-April, two Polish men with thick accents knocked on my door. My father was Polish, so I recognized the movers' accents as being similar to my two uncles'. The men wrapped my couch in plastic wrap, then blankets, like they were swaddling a baby, then walked it out the door. I'd never hired professional movers. I'd never owned decent enough furniture to make it worthwhile.

Eliza hissed at the men when they entered, and clawed one of them on his pants. I had a feeling she understood our future home to be precarious. She knew that we were undergoing a sea change. And she also sensed my anxiety. I locked her in the bedroom again.

I had invested a lot of my artistic self in the apartment over the last several years: painting the walls, hanging the drapes. And over the last few months, I'd hung photos of Jasper everywhere. The home in which my son and I had lived would soon be vacated. I was giving up all that I had for something uncertain.

Since moving to New York, I'd lived in several different apartments, most of them dumps. I shared my first apartment with Lana and one other roommate. Lana got me my first job in New York as a photographer's assistant, working for Emily Miller, who was considered the grande dame of event planning at the time. (I'd done similar work in Florida, on occasion, so I already had many of the necessary skills.)

One day Emily's lead photographer had a family emergency. I flew to Puerto Vallarta and shot a wedding that night. The pictures were remarkable, especially the ones of the children. Within a year, her clients were calling me to photograph their kids.

In the end, she and I had a falling-out. She mistakenly thought I was going to give her a cut of my business. She viewed me as being indebted to her and thought I ought to be grateful. I suppose she'd always considered herself superior to me, but I'd chosen not to see it.

I quit my job waiting tables. After two years I had a regular roster of clients and I'd doubled my rates, so I moved into my present apartment, which wasn't gorgeous, but it was respectable and more my home than any other place had ever been.

"Cute kid," one of the movers said when he removed a photo of Jasper that had been hanging on the wall in order to wrap it.

"Thanks."

"Where is he now?"

"With his dad."

He nodded knowingly and covered the picture in bubble wrap.

"I got a kid," he said. "Two years old. Man, what a lot of work. How old's your kid?"

"Five."

"Ohh."

"He's hearing impaired. He goes to a special school." Why did I say that?

"Too bad."

"Right now he's at school."

A minute earlier I'd said he was with his father. I was angry with myself for such an unnecessary stumble. And angry with myself for caring what the man thought of me.

When the men left, I opened the door of the bedroom and my cat raced out. Sitting on the floor of the kitchen, I leaned my back against the cabinets. Eliza ran in circles through the apartment. As she passed me, she hissed. I pushed her away. Then she lifted one paw and scratched me across my chest, above the neckline of my shirt. Red raised lines appeared on my skin, along with a drop of blood. For a minute I thought about throwing her out the window. She must have seen the hatred in my eyes. She hissed at me again.

"What is it?"

She stood completely still.

"What the fuck's your problem?"

She made a mental calculation and must have decided that she was better off appealing to my vanity rather than alienating me. She knew it was in her interest to remain docile and subservient to me—to give me love, whether or not it was genuine. How would I ever know if Eliza was just pretending to love me because she needed food and shelter? I suddenly had disdain for her. She was a whore, willing to sell her emotions to the highest bidder. She was willing to be the cat I needed her to be, if it meant that she would retain her position. If it meant her life wouldn't be threatened and she'd have a roof over her head.

I opened the door to her kennel. She walked in without missing a beat. I closed it. I could just leave her. I didn't need to bring her with me to my new home, and she knew it. She was completely at my mercy.

Before leaving, I walked through each room one last time, kissing each wall goodbye. In this apartment, I'd secured a measure of safety. I tried to hold on to that feeling, in case I never experienced it again.

•   •   •

The movers deposited my furniture, dishes, linens, clothing, cameras, and computers in the designated locations of my new apartment. My exquisite apartment. The Straubs could have charged six thousand a month, but they were renting it to me for two thousand.

I brought the rosewood coffee table, the leather chairs, and the dining table and chairs. (I sold the rest. I couldn't bear for the

Straubs to see that I owned any mediocre furniture.) I never could have dreamed of living in an apartment with this level of luxury—a luxury of exquisite design and exquisite execution of the design. It was a magazine life.

A whole world was opening up to me. I was now physically connected to the Straubs' lives in a variety of different ways. I was living in their building, in close proximity to them at all times. I was also the caregiver, tutor, and confidante for Natalie. More and more, I was inextricably linked to them. Natalie was going to come to me for help with her homework even more often because now I was readily accessible. Amelia was going to rely on me more and more as a babysitter. And soon I would be carrying their child.

Ever since our agreement, Amelia had assumed an intense intimacy with me, along with a kind of proprietary manner. She had chosen me and my womb, and I belonged to her. Amelia now felt justified in keeping tabs on me. I can't say that I minded. It had been so long since anyone cared what I did or where I went. Her attention, almost oppressive in its concentration, was a wild departure from what I was used to.

The Straubs gave me a key to the main house and told me to come and go as I liked. It was a feeling of welcome and inclusion unlike any that I'd had before. I was no longer hovering on the edge of something. I had reached the center. I had arrived.

On my second day in my new apartment, I spent several hours unpacking. I decided to borrow some garbage bags from the Straubs and was jittery with excitement at the thought of using my personal key to their house for the first time. I felt a surge of energy as I unlocked their front door.

Standing in the entry, I overheard Amelia's voice. "Delta can fend for herself."

I was surprised to hear Ian's voice: "She's derailing her life. You don't see that?"

I resented Ian's interference and was about to tell him so, when I turned and saw Itzhak several feet away from me. The dog's body was tense and low to the ground, and his tail was stiff. Itzhak lunged toward me, jaw open, and his teeth closed on my ankle. I screamed.

Amelia and Ian appeared in the stair hall, both of them stunned. "Noooo!" Amelia yelled at the dog, and yanked his collar. "Get away from her!"

Itzhak crouched, growling.

"Delta, are you OK?" Ian looked shaken. He put his hand on my arm.

My heart was pounding in my chest. I was trembling. I sat on the hall bench, and Ian sat next to me. I pulled my sock down to reveal bite marks. The dog's teeth had broken the skin, but barely.

"This is crazy." Amelia's voice was strident. She was extremely agitated. "He never bites anyone." Pulling him by the collar, Amelia led Itzhak away to the home office. I heard her close the door.

I was ashamed that the dog had bitten me. I feared the incident would undermine Amelia's belief that I was part of the family.

She reappeared a few moments later with antiseptic and a bandage.

"It's not a big deal." I was trying to speak in a calm voice. "I had a tetanus shot last year." I didn't want to reveal how much the dog had frightened me.

"I'm so sorry, Delta." She looked stricken.

I must have caught Itzhak by surprise. That's what I told myself repeatedly. His eyesight was poor and he was confused about who I was. Even so, it took several days for me to shake off the episode and return to my former feeling of optimism.

•　　•　　•

A week later Amelia and Fritz accompanied me to the Manhattan fertility clinic they'd chosen. The reception area, with its marble floors, high-vaulted ceilings, and enormous windows resembled a ballroom. I wondered how much the fertility doctors charged, in order to pay for all the marble. We each filled out our respective questionnaire and waited before Dr. Krasnov called us into his office. I saw him assess Amelia when she entered the office. She was wearing a peach-colored dress, a peach scarf, and matching lipstick. On someone else, the outfit might have appeared cloying, but her acute sense of style overrode any such possibility. Her silky hair fell toward her face.

The doctor probably smelled Amelia's money and her desperation. That was his job—to monetize her desperation. He fed off people's deficits. He wasn't invested in her happiness. But I was. Truly, I was.

I admired Krasnov's skill and emotional intelligence in navigating the charged situation. He knew not to offend anyone, even with his subtle nods or tone of voice, or turn of the head, or gesture of the hand. He understood the power dynamics. Amelia and Fritz had one kind of power. I had another kind. I had the power to bear a child. I had something Amelia yearned for. She and Fritz had money and a superior socioeconomic status.

He most likely dealt with many people who had some explicit or implicit financial gain at stake. I felt certain he had never seen a surrogate with my level of apparent breeding. I say apparent because I've had to play catch-up. It was only after graduating from college that I had opportunities to improve my lot in life. And frankly, most surrogates are similar to my own parents in their socioeconomic status. He had seen women who were struggling, but savvy enough to make it appear that they were not struggling too much. Those women wanted to avoid the impression that they had ever taken drugs or entered into high-risk situations with abusive boyfriends or spouses. That they had ever drank alcohol to excess or smoked cigarettes at all. They wanted to give the impression that they lived moderate, wholesome, and health-conscious lives. Because any really trashy genes, they might soak into the baby in undefined and inarticulable ways.

The doctor had already reviewed our questionnaires, looking for discrepancies in terms of our expectations. The only question

I'd hesitated to answer was the question about my access to the child after it was born. My desire was to be a presence in the child's life forever. But at the same time, I didn't want to give the Straubs cause to question my agenda. Not at this stage.

On a scale of 1 to 5, on the question of how much time I'd like to spend with the child once he or she was born, I circled 3.

Amelia suggested that I circle 4. "It takes a village." She laughed.

I changed my answer, then studied her face afterward, trying to determine if I detected any discomfort.

I had agreed to consult with the Straubs on all medical decisions along the way and to allow them to take the lead on where the baby would be delivered. They would have input on my diet and lifestyle during the pregnancy. If the child had birth defects, it would be terminated. If I had more than two embryos, one would be terminated. We weren't working with a surrogacy agency because Amelia said she feared an agency would slow the process down. But I thought she really feared that someone's mind would change—maybe Fritz's, maybe mine. I hypothesized that she wanted to rush the surrogacy through. She needn't have worried that my mind was going to change. I wanted the baby as much as she did.

Across from the doctor, I was seated between Amelia and Fritz, as if *I* were their child. Periodically, Amelia patted my shoulder or my hand.

"Why does surrogacy interest you, Delta?" the doctor asked.

"Why do you want to be a surrogate?" He leaned back in his chair and crossed his ankles.

I'd been hoping that he'd direct most of his questions to Amelia and Fritz. "I love Amelia. I love Fritz."

"But why do you want to be their surrogate?" He crossed his arms over his chest. His sleeve hiked up slightly, revealing his Patek Philippe watch.

"We were discussing that yesterday." I looked to Amelia for assistance.

"We're like family," Amelia said. "Delta, Fritz, Natalie, and I . . . we feel like we're family."

She beamed at me throughout the entire interview, as if she were so proud of me. And I recognized that, because I was going to bear her child, she saw me as her child too. And it was one of the most wonderful experiences I'd ever had. Feeling like I mattered to that degree. Amelia couldn't lavish her attention on the baby yet. But she could lavish her attention on me. The moment I met Amelia, I had longed to be her child. This was the closest I would ever come.

"But you're *not* family." The doctor tilted his head down and peered at us over the top of his glasses in an accusatory fashion.

"How do you define *family*?" Amelia's tone had some defiance.

The doctor turned his body away from us and toward his monitor. I sensed he was irritated by Amelia's question and her attitude, though he did well disguising it.

Fritz looked up at the plaques on the doctor's walls—

announcing the awards he'd won and the degrees conferred upon him.

The doctor appeared to be searching for something on his computer. "You've known each other less than a year?"

"I will feel fulfilled if I'm able to help Amelia and Fritz." I made an effort to speak at a normal volume and at a normal pace.

"How does it benefit you?" The doctor peered over his glasses again.

"Bringing a child into the world." I pressed the heel of one of my shoes deep into my other foot, hoping the pain would distract me from my self-consciousness.

"You have a son?" The doctor pursed his lips.

"Yes." My heart rate quickened. I felt perspiration under my clothing.

"How old is he?" He smiled benignly.

"Five."

The doctor sighed and placed his fingertips together, making the shape of a roof in front of his chin. "Your personal situation, it's not the typical profile I see."

I looked down and noticed the hem of my pants was loose.

"So I have to be cautious." He sighed. "And I expect Amelia and Fritz to be especially cautious. Why don't you want to have another child of your *own*?"

"I might one day."

"Yes?" He collapsed the roof of his fingers down, then brought them back up.

"I loved how my body felt when I was pregnant." I placed my hand on my abdomen.

"Where did you deliver?"

"Hmmm?" I feared that sweat stains were showing under my arms.

"Where did you deliver your son?"

Breathing in my core, low in my center. I'd practiced my answers. "California."

"The hospital and doctor?"

"A natural birth center. It was . . . a midwife."

The doctor smiled and squinted. "Vaginal?"

"Mm-hmm." Could he prove that I had or had not given birth before?

"Epidural?" He tapped his fingertips together lightly.

I shook my head. Low breathing in my core. I thought that Amelia might prefer that I have a C-section and be put under so that I'd have no opportunity to bond with the baby.

"Any issues or complications with the prior pregnancy?"

"No."

He looked down at the paperwork in front of him on the desk. "Did you breastfeed?"

Why was that any of his business?

"I hardly think it's relevant." Amelia sniffed. "The baby will have formula just like Natalie did."

"OK." The doctor raised his eyes to meet mine. "OK." He didn't trust me, but so far he wasn't standing in my way.

CHAPTER SIXTEEN

The wheels were set in motion. I was on my way to carrying the Straubs' baby. The embryo transfer was to take place in the middle of May. The hormones and steroids that I took leading up to it were debilitating. I felt sick most of the time, nauseous and bloated, but the physical side effects weren't as taxing as the anxiety—the buzzing undercurrent of fear that it might not work. Amelia would lose faith in me quickly if I wasn't successful. She would move on to another surrogate or birth mother. Her adoration would vanish if I failed her.

I'd had several unexpected visits from Ian since I moved. If he was dropping off plans for Amelia and Fritz, he'd ring my doorbell.

At first I found it intrusive. But after a while I kind of got used to it. We'd have coffee or a drink, depending on what time of day it was. He never stayed for very long. Fortunately, he'd stopped asking about Jasper, but I could still see the question behind his eyes.

In early May he came by late in the day and suggested we go to dinner at a pub in Brooklyn Heights. We sat in a booth and ordered hamburgers, fries, and a bottle of red wine. He told me about the estate he was designing in New Jersey. Then he told me about a pied-à-terre he was designing in Rome. We talked about symmetry, asymmetry, light, shadow, focus points.

The waiter delivered our burgers. CNN was playing on a television behind the bar.

"I have to go to Rome next week," he said. "Will you come with me?"

His invitation was the last thing I was expecting. "No."

"Just for a weekend."

I didn't want to go to Rome. Not with Ian. "I have an obligation."

"Are there rules about Rome?" He tried to laugh.

I looked down at my plate to put ketchup and mustard on my hamburger, then arranged the lettuce and tomato. "I can't."

My "relationship" with Ian, if you could call it that, was supposed to be on a slow track. His request felt like a trick.

"You're trying to live someone else's life," he said, "when your own life could be terrific."

Ian wanted to believe that he understood me better than I understood myself.

In reality, he didn't have a clue. Not a clue.

●   ●   ●

The following day, Eliza greeted Natalie at the front door. My cat was growing used to Natalie's visits. Natalie knelt on the ground next to her. She stroked her behind her ears.

"My mom says she's allergic to cats. She used to say she was allergic to dogs. One day my dad brought Itzhak home. He said he'd return him if she sneezed. And she didn't."

I hadn't told Natalie about Itzhak biting me, and I gathered Amelia hadn't either. I felt it was unnecessary information, especially since the dog's behavior toward me had returned to normal, and I was doing my best to put the incident behind me.

Eliza purred contentedly and licked her paws.

Natalie walked down the hall toward the back of the apartment. "Your apartment has personality already." She picked up a framed photo of Jasper at the beach that I'd placed on one of my end tables. The prior evening, I'd chosen to place three pictures of Jasper in inconspicuous places: my bedside table, an end table, and my desk, as if I didn't want anyone to see them. "That picture was taken at the beach in Venice."

"How often do you talk to him?" she asked.

"Isn't he beautiful?"

"He has black hair." She traced his form in the photo with her finger. "He doesn't look like you."

"We have the same nose." I'd noticed that and been pleased about that trait that I shared with my Jasper.

"Do you miss him?" She traced my form with her finger. She was studying the photo so carefully. Even though I believed in the photo, the same way I believed in my son, I had a few moments of anxiety, wondering if she would detect anything unusual about the picture that would lead her to question its verisimilitude.

I sat on the sofa and leaned back against the cushions. "This morning, I went to the grocery store. Everything I saw reminded me of Jasper." I crossed my legs and adjusted a pillow behind my back.

"When's he coming back to live with you?" She looked around the apartment. I had carefully arranged Jasper's belongings. Not a lot of them—a teddy bear and several children's books had yet to be unpacked. The objects didn't look staged. They looked natural. I had a drawer full of his clothing and a futon for his bed.

"Do you know?" she asked.

I could see Jasper in Venice by the boardwalk. I could see him playing baseball with his father. He had a head of dark curls, roses in his cheeks, and glowing olive skin. I was tempted to tell her that it was a matter of weeks.

The reason he was still in California . . . his father and I had decided that he needed a male role model, a strong man in his life. I felt the loss of Jasper.

"His father has enrolled him in a school there."

Natalie eyed me. "You said he was coming back soon." I heard derision in her voice.

"It's a special school and we've decided it will be best for him."

"What's wrong with you?" She scowled at me.

"I'm looking out for him."

"Does your kid even exist?"

My throat tightened. "Yes. Of course."

"Why aren't you more upset?" Natalie said. "You should be really upset."

In *Who's Afraid of Virginia Woolf?*, there's an imaginary child who dies. It was one of the few plays I'd seen, and I only saw it because years ago I'd dated a second-rate actor who'd performed in an inferior production of it.

"Maybe you feel neglected and you assume that Jasper feels neglected too. But I assure you he doesn't." An image of Jasper locked in a closet played over in my mind. An image of Jasper's nose bleeding and his wrist broken. My little boy. It was my job to protect him. I wouldn't allow any harm to come to Jasper.

"You've abandoned him," she said. Natalie's opinion of me was slipping. I would have to work hard to regain her trust.

I adjusted the pillow behind my back again. "I'm doing what's best for him."

She returned the picture to the end table and stepped away from it, like it was poison. "You're a liar."

"My ex-husband remarried. Jasper has a stepmother and a

father in California." I stood and reached out to take her hand, but she pulled away. "I'm putting his interests first." Tears filled my eyes. I'd always been skilled at crying on cue, when the situation called for it.

"But you're his mom!"

"I send him a letter every day. I FaceTime with him once a week."

"You told me you FaceTime every day."

"It's as often as possible."

In my heart, I knew I was telling Natalie the emotional truth of the situation. I wasn't certain who was responsible for Jasper's injuries. Who was responsible for his scars. Was it me? Was it his stepmother? I forced myself to conjure the image of his stepmother. I used one of my clients, a well-dressed dermatologist, because it was the first one that came to me.

Natalie slumped onto my living room sofa in a despondent fashion. I noticed the chartreuse nail polish on her fingernails, a purposefully ugly color. She picked up my Canon DSLR that was resting on the coffee table and studied it in a distracted manner. Several minutes passed. I remained silent.

Finally she spoke. "It sucks to be young." She removed the lens cap of the camera in her hand. "What are all the buttons and dials?"

She looked through the viewfinder.

"Photography is about light," I said. "Different ways to control the amount of light you want to allow through. Most times you don't have enough light. Occasionally you have too much light."

"How do you give a photo more light?"

"Three camera settings: ISO, aperture, and shutter speed." I pointed to the adjustment for each, respectively.

"Can I take your picture?"

"Look through the viewfinder. Slowly squeeze the shutter until it fires."

She pointed the camera toward me.

"You are beautiful," she said.

It was true that I was beautiful. But I didn't want to be more beautiful than Natalie. Rather, I didn't want her to think I was more beautiful than she was.

She handed the camera back to me and I looked at the photo of myself.

"It's a little dark," I said. "Turn the shutter speed to sixty."

She took the camera. "I went on your website," she said. "I saw the pictures of Lucia in the maternity section."

I experienced a mild burning sensation in my chest. "Did you like them?"

"I didn't know you were in touch with her. I didn't know you took pictures of her."

"Mm-hmm." Yes, I'd taken pictures of Lucia. Of course. I'd taken pictures of most people in my life. I was a photographer, after all.

"Weird that her boyfriend reappeared." She snapped several photographs, then stopped taking photos and looked at me directly. "Don't you think it's weird?"

"You never know what people will do."

Natalie shook her head. She studied my camera and adjusted several of the dials. We played some of the photos back. She had no interest in glamour. She went out of her way to find the moments when I'd divorced myself from my appearance.

"Natalie. I'm amazed by who you are. And astounded by your generosity and your talent."

I opened the door to the patio. It was pleasantly cool outside, a breezy spring afternoon. She followed me out.

"Photography is always better outside," I said. "The sun does the work. Energy is added, not subtracted." Natalie asked me to sit on the chair opposite her and she continued to photograph me. When she played the photos back, I looked over her shoulder to see the images.

"Take pictures of Eliza," I said. "That's one of the most challenging things. Animals keep moving. Same with small children. And they can't help their honesty."

She knelt on the bluestone patio and photographed my cat. Eliza was champagne colored with very dark gray accents on her paws and streaks everywhere, which made for some interesting abstract photos.

For the next two hours, she photographed the patio, the cat, the apartment, my shoes, my face, my sofa. The sun began to set.

"Your parents are going to want you home soon."

"Just a minute."

She was enjoying herself. I went to my camera shelf and looked at my collection. I had two relatively new DSLRs and two mirror-less cameras. I also had an early, but very good, Sony digital, my first camera, that I didn't use anymore.

I handed her the camera, along with its charger and memory card. "You can keep this one and practice."

"What?" Her face expanded with surprise.

"I don't use it."

She was trying not to smile, but I could tell how pleased she was. "It's too big a present. My mom will tell me that I can't have it."

I put my arms around her frame and kissed her warm cheek. "Tell your mom it's a loaner."

Eyes shining, she put the strap around her neck and placed her hands on the Sony in a proprietary manner. I was her mentor now.

•   •   •

On an unseasonably warm afternoon, I was editing on my computer when I heard a dripping sound. I looked in the bedroom and saw a puddle on the floor. Some karmic retribution. I sent Fritz a text and a few minutes later he came down to check it out. It appeared to be a leak from the AC.

While we were waiting for a return call from the HVAC repair company, I offered Fritz a drink. "I was a bartender in a former life." Actually, I'd never worked as a bartender. Over the years, I'd noticed that experimenting with cocktail recipes made alcoholics feel better about themselves, as if consuming an alcoholic drink had more to do with the taste than anything else.

"OK. Surprise me."

I mixed a drink and set it down in front of him on the kitchen counter. "It's called a Silk Panty martini."

Fritz's face colored. He took a sip. His eyes widened, and he took another sip. "You can return to your career as a bartender anytime you want."

I smiled.

He swished his drink in front of him, in a small circle. "Are you having one?" Then he appeared to read my mind. "You're not pregnant yet."

I made myself the same drink, then sat next to him at the counter.

"Here's to Silk Panties." He clinked my glass. "It's delicious, by the way."

I tried to laugh, but the mood had shifted into something harder to manage.

"Natalie's so happy that you've moved in here," he said. "I hope she's not crowding you."

"Never," I said. "And you? Are you happy I'm here?"

He took another sip. "Of course I am." I noticed beads of per-spiration on his forehead.

I was wearing a cream-colored dress with a low V-neck. I ran my fingers down my neck and along the neckline of the dress, lin-gering at the bottom of the V.

Fritz took his glasses off and cleaned them with his T-shirt, a familiar behavior that often seemed to accompany some nervousness on his part. He replaced them on his nose.

Various scenarios ran through my head. Rationally, I understood that sex with Fritz could have negative consequences. Even if Amelia didn't find out, such an action would complicate my position as the Straubs' surrogate. Still, my desire persisted. If I had sex with Fritz, I would be separating Amelia and Fritz from each other, just slightly, so that I would have a more primary position with each of them.

"Is there anything I can do for you, Fritz?" I said.

His cell phone rang. It was Amelia calling.

•   •   •

May 14: The embryo transfer took place at Krasnov's office in the early morning. I was scheduled to return in ten days to find out if I was pregnant.

That afternoon, Ian stopped by. He came into the living room and sat down on the sofa. He had an odd expression on his face.

"I met your son."

I didn't know what he was talking about. I laughed.

"Really," he said. "I met Jasper." He was smiling with his mouth wide open, like a silent laugh. He had a manic look in his eyes.

"What do you mean?" A feeling of nausea made its way from my stomach to my throat.

Ian stood and paced back and forth across the living room.

"My college roommate was in town. He invited me over to his cousin Robert's place for brunch. Robert's son is Jasper. Jasper's mother is Alexis."

My mind raced for a way out of this situation. I was doing my best to control my breath. "It's a funny coincidence," I said, "that the child's name is Jasper. But my son is in California." Long, slow inhalations and exhalations. I needed to appear unfazed by his story.

"You've shown me more than ten pictures of Jasper. I saw one of those pictures in their apartment." He looked around my apartment. On an end table, he spotted a framed photo of Jasper at his birthday party, blowing the candles out on his cake. He picked it up. "I saw the exact same photo on their bookshelf. Same kid, same T-shirt, same cake with a picture of a dog on top. They hired you as their family photographer." He waved the photo in the air. "You know, I memorized Jasper's face because I cared about you, and I imagined, one day, maybe I'd take the kid to ball games. Maybe I'd help him with his homework." He smiled again with the same manic look.

"My son is in California." I kept my voice low and calm.

Ian's smile disappeared and his face turned dark. "For Christ's sake, have you ever told me the truth about anything? Who are you?"

"Shhh." I was worried that the Straubs would overhear him.

He pointed upstairs. "Tell them the truth."

I sat down next to him on the sofa, analyzing the various ways in which I might be able to neutralize the situation.

I took his hand in mine and closed my eyes. "I do have a son." Tears spilled down my face. "His father took him to California when he was six months old, and I haven't seen him since." My whole body shook with heaving sobs. "I don't know if he's safe. I don't know if my little boy is OK. When I met Jasper at his birthday party, he looked like I imagined my son might look. It was comforting to me, just to tell myself that someone was looking after him." I folded onto Ian's shoulder. He pushed me back and stood up.

"Get away. Get away from me." In a moment he was out the door.

●　　●　　●

May 18: six days left.

Natalie arrived at my apartment in blue jeans and a thin almost transparent T-shirt that highlighted her skinniness. It said *Normal people scare me*. It was an indication of low self-esteem. She wore high-heeled wedge sandals. It was essentially the same outfit she'd worn the previous day and the day before that. She was pushing the envelope in her sophistication and maturity and had turned up the volume abruptly. But her personality was still vulnerable.

I consciously chose not to discuss my potential pregnancy,

unless Natalie brought it up—though not a minute passed that I wasn't thinking about it, analyzing every physical sensation in my body, every twinge, every cramp, hoping for clues. I'd been having little conversations with the baby, alone in my apartment, and I believed the baby heard me.

Natalie pulled her Sony out of the camera bag. She turned it over, setting and resetting the dials. "In seventh grade, photography's one of the electives at my school."

I detected a hint of enthusiasm, which was unusual for her these days.

"I'll definitely take photography when I'm in seventh grade."

"What kind of photography subjects interest you the most?"

"People."

In the background, we could hear the peaceful hum of the dryer. I'd never had laundry in my own apartment before.

"There are all the pictures where someone says 'smile' and everyone smiles," Natalie said. "But I want to take pictures of people acting like they really act. When they're sad or angry or scared. Sometimes I look at my mom and I want to take a picture of what she looks like when she's not performing. She's performing most of the time."

Natalie was looking to unmask. It was dangerous to take a photo of someone without their permission, with the intention of catching them unaware and exposing something inside them that they never intended to show to the public. Natalie didn't seem to care.

Later that day I received a text from Ian: *Tell Amelia and Fritz the truth.*

I wrote back: *give me time.*

• • •

May 24: The implantation failed as a result of poor embryo quality. When I learned the news, I felt a heavy weight bearing down on top of me, almost as though I might have trouble staying above-ground. It was Amelia's failure. Not mine. It had nothing to do with my uterus. I was angry with Amelia. But, even so, I worried that she would find a way to blame me.

So I was surprised at her reaction to the news. "Delta, darling, please, please, please . . . Please try again. I know we can do this." She shone all her light on me.

There was no recrimination. No criticism.

"Of course, Amelia."

"I love you," she said.

Even if I'd wanted to, there would have been no way to resist her entreaty.

• • •

I called Ian's mother that evening. We had spoken a few times since she'd moved to Florida. She said the recovery from her hip surgery was slow and painful.

"I'm just pathetic, Delta." Paula laughed. "I still can't drive, not even to the grocery store."

"Tell Ian you need him there to help you." I waited for a response. "Paula?"

She sighed. "OK. OK, fine."

"If you were to fall and no one was with you, Ian would never forgive himself."

CHAPTER SEVENTEEN

I gathered that a second IVF cycle was going to be a financial strain for the Straubs, but they didn't hesitate. We scheduled another embryo transfer for mid-July.

The eight weeks passed as if in slow motion, as did the ten-day wait after IVF.

I didn't talk to the baby this time.

On Day 10, I was pregnant. I belonged to the Straubs. We belonged to one another. If the pregnancy were successful, I saw a joyous future with all of us, Amelia, Fritz, Natalie, and me, raising the child together.

In one single bound, I had catapulted myself into another life, another social stratum. I had power now. I was carrying a baby in my womb, living in the home of artists, in a rarefied neighborhood, and it followed that I had status myself.

I walked to the grocery store nearby, and looked around at the customers and the people who worked there. I practiced looking down on these people and speaking to them with a tone of superiority. I purchased groceries and asked that they be delivered, saying my address loudly and repeating it, so everyone around me could hear where I lived. I walked into a café. The barista did not make my drink correctly. I had the right to complain. My voice mattered. My pregnant body demanded respect.

Some people live their whole life just waiting for the moment when they have the power to scorn others, as opposed to being the object of scorn themselves. Now I could assert my superiority with confidence, knowing that I belonged to a family of means. Fitting in with my clients and their friends had always seemed to be just out of my reach. Now I would seize a place at the table and make sure the rest of the world understood my position.

I was going to partner with Amelia and Fritz as parents. I believed that Amelia was sincere when she talked about my shared participation in the baby's life, but I also knew it was important to make certain. When the time came, I would clarify what my needs were.

I did recognize, without it ever being articulated, that if I didn't succeed in carrying the child, everything would disappear. Like Catherine of Aragon, Anne Boleyn, and women throughout history, my value had all to do with my body, whether I could carry a baby to term. I knew very well that if I lost the pregnancy, I would lose my new apartment, my new neighborhood, my new family. I would lose all of it if I lost the baby. I was paying for all of it with my womb.

Amelia and Fritz were supporting me with low rent, nutritious meals, and health care. I turned down several jobs in order to prioritize my sleep and my health. My income was going to drop and that was perfectly OK. The baby was going to come first.

In weeks four and five, I didn't have any signs or symptoms of the pregnancy. It was a terrifying sensation, as if the baby were a figment of my imagination. But in the sixth week, morning sickness kicked in. My days began and ended with retching. The extreme nausea gave me confidence—tangible evidence of the life inside me.

Amelia was excited, bordering on frantic, busying herself with activities to channel her energy. One Sunday evening in late August, she and I were talking in her kitchen. "I want you to eat as many meals here as you'd like to," she said. "I plan to buy fresh fruit, vegetables, fish and steak, organic yogurt and milk, all the things you really need when you're pregnant." During the lowest points of Amelia's despair, I'd noticed that the Straub refrigerator was often empty. Now, however, Amelia considered the unborn baby's health an acknowledged priority.

She poured us each a glass of seltzer. "It's odd that Ian hasn't returned my calls," she said. "Do you know if anything's wrong?"

"Well . . ." I paused and counted to three.

"What?" She sat down at the counter next to me.

I sipped my seltzer, enjoying the carbonation in my throat, which temporarily relieved my nausea. "He's mentioned a desire for *growth* . . . something like that."

She looked at me like we couldn't be talking about the same person. "He's not happy in his job?"

I shrugged. "I don't want to put words in his mouth."

•　　•　　•

In early September I was seven weeks pregnant and Amelia was soaring. She texted to ask me to babysit and to come upstairs before Natalie arrived home from school, so we could talk. She had returned to the glamorous woman I'd met months earlier. Today she answered the door wearing black pants, a low-cut red silk blouse with no bra, and a very large clunky amethyst necklace. I envied her effortless Katharine Hepburn figure.

I was soaring too, maybe higher than Amelia, but even so, I was aware of Natalie and didn't want her to feel unappreciated, whereas Amelia's attention was fixed solely on "the new baby." In other words, it was fixed on me. Her attention was what I'd been pining for, only, I didn't want it at Natalie's expense. I found myself covering for Amelia at times, distracting Natalie, changing the subject of conversation, when her mother was being particularly insensitive.

At this point, I found it easier to spend time with Natalie *or*

Amelia, as opposed to both of them, so I was pleased for Amelia to invite me upstairs early, before Natalie arrived home. "How I wish I could pour you a glass of wine right now. After the baby is born, we'll have cocktails every day." She held her arms high in the air in a gesture of triumph. I imagined our future with evenings together around the fire and coffee together every morning.

Amelia filled her wineglass and poured me a glass of filtered water.

"Do you mind if I drink in front of you?" she asked solicitously.

"Of course not." I did mind, actually. I found it challenging to watch Amelia drink. Over the last few months, I'd noticed a significant uptick in her drinking, and it hadn't leveled off with the news of my pregnancy. But her body wasn't the sacred vessel. Mine was.

I looked more closely at her amethyst necklace and noticed that the links were soldered together, an indication of twenty-four-karat gold. I breathed in her intense lemon-and-bergamot perfume. It was too much for my heightened sense of smell.

"You know," Amelia said, "Ian's like our family." The subject of Ian had come up a couple of times over the last week, with Amelia using me as a sounding board. She clearly didn't want him to leave the firm, but supporting Ian's ambitions was in line with her self-image.

"I suggested he should talk things through with you," I said, "but he says he can't . . . desert you."

"Desert us?" She laughed weakly and set a plate of green grapes, cheese, and crackers on the kitchen counter.

"You know . . . starting his own firm."

Amelia's eyes widened. I could tell it was an effort for her to maintain an expression of equanimity. "Ohhh." She took a large sip of wine.

"I told him you'd support him."

She hesitated for a split second. "Of course, we would."

"Whether that's clients, referrals, infrastructure," I said. "Because I know how much you care for him."

"Anything . . . of course." Amelia smiled with her mouth, but her eyes betrayed something akin to resentment.

•   •   •

I was twelve weeks pregnant with a confirmed fetal heartbeat. If Dr. Krasnov recognized that I had never carried a baby to term, he hadn't ratted me out thus far. I felt that he and I had reached a truce of sorts. He explained that I'd passed a critical milestone and the likelihood of miscarriage had significantly diminished. Upon hearing his words, a sensation of expansiveness and levity moved throughout my body and filled me completely.

Amelia was standing by in the waiting room at my request. I did take some secret pleasure in these moments, when she was the outsider who was forced to wait for me. I had the critical information before she did.

Afterward, she was invited into the doctor's office and offered a seat next to me. "So far, so good, Mrs. Straub."

The look on her face was like someone who had just finished scaling a mountain.

My power was increasing daily. I was carrying a life inside me. I had an indisputable purpose. My value in other arenas—my professional value, my value to lovers and friends, had never had the same gravity. Not even close. Amelia needed me and it was a life-and-death kind of need. I could feel vibrations of anguish and desire radiating off her.

The doctor shook her hand. "Now Ms. Dawn can continue care with her OB."

Amelia stumbled over her words. "Thank . . . thank you so much."

While waiting for the elevator together, she embraced me. "You're a miracle." I noticed how chapped her lips were and considered offering her some lip gloss, but thought better of it. I remembered the high-end pot of lip gloss on her desk in her home office. I doubted that she'd want to use my brand of lip gloss. Neither would she want my germs.

A sick feeling threatened me, but, just as quickly, it subsided.

•   •   •

Amelia drove me back to Brooklyn in her silver Mercedes SUV and insisted that I join her for lunch at her house. Occasionally I allowed myself to acknowledge why she adored me so much. Of course, it was because of the baby. It wasn't *real love*. Or was it? I understand why some women get pregnant to secure a husband or hold on to the one they have. It's the ultimate power.

I rested on the sofa in the great room, and after a few minutes she brought me a turkey sandwich and a glass of ice water and placed them on the iron coffee table. "I've been thinking," she said. "My dreams are coming true. I want the same for Ian."

"Of course," I said.

"So Fritz and I called him." She sat down next to me. "We told him he should start his own firm." Amelia smiled with what seemed to be considerable effort. "And that we'd support him."

"Wow."

"And that you were his strongest advocate in making it happen." She beamed.

I took a bite of my turkey sandwich and swallowed.

"I guess . . . he was overwhelmed or agitated," she said, "especially anxious regarding his mother's health."

"I'm sure he's grateful." I chewed on a piece of ice in an effort to quell my nausea.

"Well . . . we'll miss him." From her tone of voice, it sounded as though she were speaking of someone from the distant past.

I noticed that I was extremely warm. I removed my sweater so that I was only wearing a tank top. No one would have known that I was pregnant. My stomach was still practically flat. Amelia studied my body. I could tell she was in love with it, in an odd, objectifying way.

There were times when I thought Amelia might view me as being in service to her—as her inferior. Surrogacy isn't entirely dissimilar from prostitution. I have no ethical problem with prostitution. It's a class problem. I'd slept with a guy for money twice, in a hotel room in Florida. He was a loser. So fucking him for money made me into a double loser. Then I left Florida and came to New York.

Amelia probably felt as though she were paying me indirectly—with her love and attention, with the time I spent with Natalie, and with the under-market apartment. But she might not have realized that I no longer needed payment.

She moved down to the end of the sofa next to my feet. She removed my socks and pressed her thumbs into pressure points on the arches of my feet, my heels, and my toes. At first, I was surprised that she would debase herself so. But then it dawned on me that she believed her actions were in service of her child. So there was an element of ego and self-preservation in her behavior. "Some pressure points really support the body's immune system and strengthen it," she said, "allowing the baby to receive all the nutrients and vitamins that it needs."

Her fingers were resting on the faint scar from Itzhak's bite. She didn't seem to notice it.

Natalie appeared in the doorway with her camera in hand and snapped a photo of us. "Is Delta sick?"

"No, I'm fine." I sat up on the sofa.

"Natalie, the baby's healthy so far." Amelia looked from Natalie to me. She clasped my hands. "What a mitzvah."

"*Mitzvah* means 'good deed,'" Natalie explained to me.

"What's your favorite boy's name?" Amelia asked Natalie.

"BoBo." Natalie opened the refrigerator door and looked for a snack.

Amelia frowned. "Sweetheart . . ."

I wanted Amelia to drop the subject. It was obvious that Natalie was not going to engage.

"Do you know if it's a boy?" Natalie opened a kitchen cabinet and rummaged through it.

"A sixth sense," Amelia said. "I like the name Emilio."

"Did you forget about the 'evil eye'?" Natalie asked.

"I'm not naming the baby now," Amelia said. "Just getting ideas."

Natalie pulled out a box of saltine crackers.

"This baby," Amelia said, "will change everything in our lives."

Over the last few weeks, I'd continued to research surrogacy laws in New York and had confirmed what I already understood to be true. If a surrogate changes her mind and wants to keep the baby, the genetic parents don't have a lot of recourse. Even if the Straubs and I'd had a written contract, it would be worthless. That meant I would have the power to make my position in the Straub family permanent. My leaving would not be an option. I planned to bring the subject up in the right way at the right time. I would make sure Amelia understood that I wasn't trying to take anything away from her. Amelia, Fritz, and I would be partners on an exciting journey. We would raise the child together.

Natalie took a bite of a saltine cracker.

"I feel like it's a second chance for our family and my marriage," Amelia said.

"Because your first chance failed?" Natalie licked crumbs from her lips.

Amelia was choosing not to notice her daughter's jealousy. "A baby brings positive energy into a home."

"You're so full of it," Natalie said.

"Shut your mouth."

Natalie closed her fist around a saltine cracker, causing it to crumble in her hand. "Fuck you." She dropped the box of crackers onto the counter and ran out of the room and up the stairs.

I wanted to follow Natalie, but I had a feeling that Amelia wouldn't appreciate it if I did.

Amelia looked up at the ceiling and breathed deeply. "Privilege. It's a double-edged sword. Natalie's surrounded by children who have no clue about the world. I had to work like a dog to get where I am. Natalie thinks my life and Fritz's should revolve around her. News flash. Getting all the attention doesn't make you a stronger person."

Amelia needed to believe what she needed to believe.

•   •   •

Half an hour later I found Natalie reading in her room and suggested she come down to my apartment for a photography lesson.
When she arrived, we bundled up and walked around the block
with our cameras.

"What do you want for your birthday?" I asked.

"It's two months away."

"Let's go to a museum together."

Her eyes brightened. "OK."

"There's a photography exhibition at MoMA that opens in
November. I think you'll like it."

It was mid-October. The weather had turned cold, and the sun
was approaching the horizon. Natalie took out her camera.

"It can be harder late in the day," I said.

She took a picture of a blue jay flying from one tree to another.

"That one will turn out blurry," I said.

"I hope it does," she said. "You can't freeze the bird at one moment in time. I want the photo to say time doesn't stand still. My
mom doesn't realize that. She's too old to have another baby. She's
ancient." I hoped that Natalie refrained from this line of thought
when her mother was around.

We walked almost all the way around the block. "My mom
said I can stay over with you tonight."

"I'm so glad."

Natalie photographed the evergreen magnolia in front of the
Straubs' house. I had to remind myself it was my house too.

"Do you have morning sickness today?" she asked.

"I feel all right." My morning sickness usually died down around 2 P.M. each day.

"Piper told me her mom had morning sickness when she was pregnant with her little brother. She said if you're not nauseous every day, it means the baby isn't healthy."

I found it hard to swallow. "Piper has a lot of information."

She put her hand on my abdomen. "I can feel the baby."

She was right. I'd felt a fluttering sensation over the last few days.

Once inside my apartment, she took off her coat and shoes and left them by the front door, as she'd been trained to do.

I opened a package of chocolate chip cookies, placed several on a plate, and brought them to Natalie. She sat cross-legged on the sofa with the plate in her lap. Slowly and methodically, she took little bites around the edge of a cookie. "You're going to have a baby and then give it away," she said. "I don't get it."

A strong pressure in my sinuses spread to my ears and throat. I felt faint. "Don't worry. I will see the baby." She didn't understand that our lives were going to be overflowing with light and love.

That evening, Natalie and I sat together on the sofa and looked through the photos she had shot on the viewfinder of her camera. She had a strong point of view. For photographers, that was rare. Of course, she lacked skill, but what she already had was almost impossible to teach.

"'If you bring forth what is within you, what you bring forth will save you,'" I said. "'If you do not bring forth what is within you, what you do not bring forth will destroy you.'"

"Hmm?"

"It's something Jesus said about self-expression."

I also had a point of view, but I chose to avoid it most of the time. Were I to embrace it, I would have had to acknowledge other things that I was not interested in acknowledging. People like me created useful stories to paste over other stories. Because the real stories would take you on a deep dive to hell. If you knew for a fact that you'd break into a thousand pieces on your way there, then you might say to yourself, well, Jesus was actually wrong with regard to me.

In my case, I had a structure to my life and my mind, and I wasn't going to trade that in for anarchy and chaos.

Natalie was different than I was. She could stomach her reflection in the mirror, not just once, but over and over, each and every day. She could look at herself and say, *This is the person I am. I have nothing to offer that doesn't come from a place of darkness and ugliness.*

I lay in my bed that night with Natalie in the next room. I rested my hand on my abdomen and felt the faintest movement. The baby was going to provide a pathway out of the grime that had been clinging to me for all these years. I had a window now, and I could see what was possible.

CHAPTER EIGHTEEN

It was Saturday morning. I heard Taylor Swift's "Shake It Off" from the living room. Natalie's iPhone was playing. She didn't see me. Her head was back, her arms in the air, and she was singing and dancing with abandon: *"And the fakers gonna fake, fake, fake, fake, fake . . ."*

Natalie ate a chocolate croissant for breakfast. I made coffee for myself. She perused the apartment, looking at my books, my desk, and in my closet.

I showered and dressed. When I came out of the bedroom, I saw her standing in front of me with her backpack over her shoulders. Her arms were crossed in front of her body and she was staring at the ground, as if she didn't want to meet my eyes. "I need to go upstairs and make a quick phone call." She turned abruptly and left.

Initially she'd said she wanted to stay for the whole morning.

I turned my attention to unloading the dishwasher, which I'd run the night before. I placed all the bowls on one shelf and the plates on a different shelf. When finished with that task, I loaded the washing machine and folded the towels that I'd left in the dryer. I'd purchased expensive Turkish towels when I'd moved. I enjoyed folding them and running my hands over them.

Then I poured myself a cup of coffee and sat on the patio outside my back door. I contemplated the cherry tree, the birds, the sunshine, and found all of it too perfect this morning. I felt certain there was a flaw hidden somewhere.

I heard an incoming text on my phone. It was from Amelia. *We have a problem here. Please come upstairs.*

My stomach dropped. Something bad was about to happen or had already happened.

I wrote back: *Sure. Just a few minutes.*

Natalie had appeared disturbed by something. What had happened to her? The floor underneath my feet was shifting. I needed to know the nature of the problem. I couldn't walk into the Straubs' house defenseless, without the necessary tools.

In the bathroom, I splashed cold water on my face and dried it. Then I applied moisturizer, under-eye concealer, mascara, and lip gloss. I combed through my hair. Finally I was pleased with my reflection in the mirror.

I walked up the stairs, entered the Straubs' front door, and proceeded down the hallway. From across the room, I could see that Amelia, Fritz, and Natalie were all seated around the dining table. The morning sun was shooting in through the skylight from above and through the bifold doors. Amelia's skin looked bright white in the sun. Her lips had disappeared, but her dark eyes were taking up more space than usual in her face. Next to her, Fritz sat expressionless, his eyes flat and dull. Seated across the table, Natalie was looking down, seemingly focused on pointing and flexing her bare feet.

As I approached, I could see that Amelia was holding something in front of her. I took a few steps toward her. It looked to be a thick pile of papers in her hand. I took a few more steps and could now tell it was a stack of photographs. I neared the table, close enough to see the edge of the top photo, and then recognized it. I felt the ground dropping out from underneath me.

It was a graphic photo of me and Fritz in bed together—including a computer-generated image of Fritz's naked groin that I'd photoshopped and fine-tuned until it appeared completely realistic. I'd scrupulously deleted all such photos from my hard drive, but I'd chosen to keep a few of the prints.

I was falling. "Oh God," I said. "That was . . . was so stupid."

"What is this?" Amelia whispered.

Fritz looked up at me, as though he were hoping for a valid explanation.

Amelia flipped to the second photo in the stack. Then the third, fourth, fifth, sixth, seventh, eighth, ninth. She laid them out on the dining table in front of her. They were photos of me and Fritz in different sexual positions. Over the last few months, whenever I'd been bored, I'd gone back to these photos. Sexual experimentation in the photographs had been exciting for me.

I tried to laugh, but it came out sounding like a cackle. "Oh God, see, I had a photo-editing challenge with my colleague. . . ."

"What . . . what the hell?" She held up a photo of me, Fritz, and her in bed together. A ménage à trois.

I felt myself to be in free fall, in a vertical drop. ". . . and we were using a new program, trying to create realistic photos . . . and . . ."

Amelia stood up from her place at the dining table, her face moist and pink and her eyes cloudy. She looked feverish and wild. "Are you fucking Fritz?" she bellowed into the atmosphere.

"No!" Fritz yelled loudly.

"Amelia . . ." I said.

"Yes or no?" she said.

"No!" My mind raced for a way to escape. I looked around the room for possible exits. Itzhak was crouched low in the corner, growling.

"What is it?" Amelia gasped. "Barbie and Ken having sex? Are you so desperate you need to fuck my husband in a picture?"

She fanned the remainder of the photos out like a hand of

cards. Then she placed them back on the table in a stack, and separated them out, one by one. I held my breath. She came to one of herself and me drinking martinis at Buttermilk Channel, then one in which I was very pregnant and we were shopping on Court Street, then one of me cooking in the Straubs' kitchen, and one of her feeding me birthday cake. And next, the photo of Jasper lying asleep in Natalie's room.

"Is this your son?" She looked disoriented.

A pit of nausea in my stomach was making its way to my throat. "Yes," I said quietly.

"When was he here?"

I searched for the correct response to the question. "He was—"

Layers of her confusion seemed to obstruct her speech. "When . . . when . . . was he in the house?"

"I was—"

"Why is he in Natalie's room? Why is he in the photo?"

"It wasn't—"

"Is it really your son?"

"I . . ."

"Who is it?"

She came to another shot of Jasper and his family. My clients.

"It's not your son, is it?"

In addition to a growing panic, a deep anger was threatening to overtake me. I resented Amelia's disrespectful tone.

Her voice blasted through the house. *"DO YOU HAVE A SON?"*

"Jasper is my son." I believed in Jasper. I clung tightly to his image in my head.

Natalie was still looking away, resting her head in her hands.

Amelia came to another group of photos. Lucia. A sharp pain made its way through my skull. It was one of the photoshopped versions and I had drawn a large red X on the photo.

"It's a picture of Lucia," Amelia said. "Why do you have it?"

"I took a few shots of her."

"What does the X mean?"

"It's not—"

"Why do you have it? *WHAT DID YOU DO TO LUCIA?*"

I backed away from her toward the kitchen island.

Fritz stood up. He looked like a wild animal. A speeding train was coming toward me. Head forward like a bull, he ran straight in my direction. He stopped abruptly when he was two feet away and pulled his upper lip back with disgust. "You are some sick pervert."

His words hit me in a bad place. I tried to control myself. I held my voice low. "I'm sorry." I had to say the right thing.

"How dare you use my image?" he growled. "How dare you bring your depravity into our home?"

Natalie looked up. She was watching her father. Her face was pale.

Amelia burst into hysterical sobs. "You should be down on your knees with gratitude to us," she said between her sobs. "Are you mocking us? After all we did for you."

"Did you do something for me?" My breath was catching in my throat. "Remind me."

"You used us." Amelia spoke through clenched teeth.

I was in a tunnel of rage—having difficulty allowing air into my lungs. "I guess that's one way to look at it." In that moment I hated Amelia with every molecule in my body.

"You are *repulsive*," Amelia said.

"Mom," Natalie said. "Enough!"

"It's OK." I tried to make eye contact with Natalie. "I'll leave. As soon as I can get a moving truck."

Amelia took long strides down the hallway toward the front door, grabbing a ring of keys off the hall console table. "You have more shit downstairs. I need to see all of it."

"No." I followed her, but she was fast. In an instant she was out the door, down the front steps. I was behind her. I refused to allow her into my computer, my files, my home. Whatever she thought she was going to see, she was wrong. I caught up to her at the top of the exterior stairs that led down to my garden apartment. I held her arm to prevent her from descending. She wrenched away from me. I ran ahead of her and put my body in front of hers, on the step below her, to block her way.

"Get out of my way," she said.

"It's my private apartment," I said. "You can't enter without notice."

"Bullshit." She pushed me aside.

I stepped back to catch myself, but my foot didn't make contact with the step below me. My feet shuffled to get a hold, but I fell to the stone steps and rolled sideways down the remaining stairs. I landed at the base.

•   •   •

Perhaps this was the way it was meant to end. I felt the cool cement beneath my face. For every action, there is an equal and opposite reaction.

Amelia's blurred face appeared over me, contorted in a sick grimace, and her breath was briefly suspended. Fritz was standing behind her.

"What did I do?" she whispered. "No, no, no, no."

Both of Fritz's lips were pulled back to reveal his gums and teeth. "We need Delta out of here today," he said.

Amelia moaned—a sound from deep inside her. "The baby."

I felt my hip bone and the side of my face against the cement. I felt moisture between my legs. And a viselike sensation around my abdomen.

Amelia knelt by my side. "What did I do?"

"Mom, you pushed Delta?" It was Natalie's voice in the distance.

"No, no, no, no, no." Amelia grabbed Fritz's wrist.

"Calm down," he said.

I was watching both of them, as if in a film—as if I were slightly removed. I noticed the shadows in Amelia's face, hollow spaces that made her look old.

"This baby is my life," Amelia said. "My life."

"I hate you," Natalie hissed from the top of the stairs.

"Go upstairs, Natalie," Amelia said. "Now."

"No." Natalie didn't move.

"Delta, let me help you," Amelia whispered to me.

I felt blood running down my legs. Amelia's gaze landed on my bare foot, which was covered in blood. It had run all the way down my leg.

"No, no, no, no!" she wailed.

A weight on my chest pressed me to the ground.

Up the stairs, I saw Natalie's outline, then her gleaming eyes, her lanky arms, her charm necklace with the clay heart and the zigzagged line down the middle. Fritz led her up to their house. I was left alone with Amelia.

She helped me up. My body was pounding. She helped me inside my apartment. "We need to go to the doctor," she said.

"I think it'll be OK," I said.

"No. No. No." Amelia's eyes were glazed.

I told her I needed to lie down. She insisted I go to the doctor.

•   •   •

Right now I'm the child's mother. And I need to talk to my baby.

I'm the child's mother. Delta Dawn.

And did I hear you say, he was a-meeting you here today,

To take you to his mansion in the sky?

It was my loss. It was my baby.

•   •   •

Amelia drove me to the closest emergency room in downtown Brooklyn. I told her that I would go in by myself. I needed privacy. I'd been asking for privacy when she pushed me down the stairs. This time she didn't dare to object.

Late that night I was released from the hospital. I called Amelia. "I lost the baby."

CHAPTER NINETEEN

Two days later Natalie knocked at the door of my garden apartment and let herself in. I gathered her parents didn't know where she was.

"I'm sorry," I said. "About everything."

I placed a stack of shirts in my suitcase, which was open on my bed. I packed my sweaters, one by one. Then my pants. Dresses. Bras. Underwear.

"It's OK," she said. "I understand."

She seemed composed.

"You're not upset?" I said.

"At least you're choosing your own life."

I shook my head. "I'm not someone to look up to, Natalie."

"I want to go with you," she said.

I thought about the furniture in her room, her desk, her bed. I was overwhelmed trying to picture all her belongings in the moving truck. It wouldn't be big enough for her furniture in addition to mine. "You can't."

An image of Jasper: golden-brown skin in red swim trunks, running on the beach. He was wading in the ocean, the waves splashing up on his thighs, laughter deep in his throat, spilling out into the California air. "I have to find Jasper," I said.

"The three of us could be together." Her voice sounded faint, as if she were out of breath.

I conjured an image of Jasper and Natalie playing together. I could see them laughing and running and swimming. I could see them Rollerblading on the boardwalk. I could hear the waves lapping against the shore. I could smell the salt water and feel the breeze against the back of my neck.

A minute later I was in the room again with Natalie, looking at her slim form in front of me. She didn't draw comfort from images.

"Jasper doesn't exist." As I spoke those words, I felt a blow to my solar plexus, as if someone had punched me with full force. I recovered my breath. "Not actually."

"Then where are you going?" she asked.

"To find him."

Her eyes drifted to my abdomen. I looked down and saw that my hand was clasping my middle in a protective gesture. Natalie was watching me closely. She looked from my hand to my eyes and back again to my hand. "My mom said you lost the baby."

I nodded.

"She says it's her fault."

She approached closer and placed her hand on my stomach, next to mine. "Did you lose the baby?" She locked eyes with me.

I gently removed her hand from my stomach.

Her eyes welled up with tears. I put my arms around her and kissed the crown of her head.

She looked up at me. "I'll miss you, Delta."

Saying goodbye to Natalie was the worst thing I ever had to do.

FIVE YEARS LATER

I hang up his backpack in his cubby. We put his lunch below. Then I hug him and kiss him goodbye. "I love you, boo-boo." After I leave Jasper's classroom, I peer through the small high window in the hallway. He can't see me but I can see him. He's standing by himself. I watch him until he sits on the rug next to a little girl. They start talking. I can't hear what he's saying, but I can see him laugh like he's enjoying her company. Then she pulls out a box of Magna-Tiles. They start by building a tower together.

• • •

I didn't miscarry the baby.

When I was lying in the hospital with needles in my arms, I talked to the baby. I could feel his fear. I told him he was going to be OK. I promised him that I'd never leave him, no matter what. I *promised* him.

●　　●　　●

Over the last few years I've kept track of the Straubs. They didn't have another child. They didn't hire a surrogate or adopt. I also know that Itzhak died, at the age of fourteen. I'm sorry I wasn't there when Natalie lost Itzhak. I wish I could tell her that.

It seems the Straubs never heard from Ian again once he resigned from their firm. I had told them before that he loved Italy. They probably envision him living in Rome. It's an uplifting image and not an unreasonable assumption. I can picture opportunities opening up for him there.

I have the same dream almost every night. Natalie is running toward me, smiling, and I hold out my arms to embrace her. But as she approaches closer, her face changes and I grow frightened of her. Then yesterday I saw her on the street in Venice Beach, but this time it wasn't a dream. She was taller and her face was thinner, but I'm certain it was her. She might be looking for me.

●　　●　　●

I invite Jasper's friend Izzy and Izzy's mom, Maya, to our apartment in Venice for a playdate. They live in a Spanish hacienda–style house on the edge of Santa Monica Canyon, with transporting views of the whitewater ocean, mountains, and canyon, each layer informing the others. I know their house because Jasper and I drive past it on our way to go hiking.

Izzy's dad drops Maya and Izzy off. He smiles and waves from the car, then leaves to pick up groceries. Maya hangs her jean jacket, along with Izzy's, on the hooks in the entryway. She and I chat while the children play Uno. Maya asks about all the framed photos hanging on the wall, opposite the suspended glass cabinet in the kitchen. "They're works of art," she says.

"That's Jasper with his grandparents. They both passed away last year," I explain. "And that's Jasper with his cousins on his fifth birthday." Jasper's green eyes are beaming straight at the camera.

"Oh my God," she says, "you have to take pictures of Izzy's birthday party."

I smile at her. "I would love to."

After Izzy and Maya leave, Jasper and I watch *Mary Poppins* together for the third time. The movie always makes me think of Natalie's carousel. We get to the part where Mary Poppins's friend Bert does a sidewalk chalk drawing of an English countryside. Mary Poppins, Bert, and the children jump into the picture. They land inside the drawing, and the scene comes to life. The picture is real because they want it to be.

ACKNOWLEDGMENTS

Heaven was shining down on me the day I met my literary agent, Stephanie Kip Rostan. Stephanie brought this book to life. Brilliant, kind, with a formidable sense of humor, she is a true partner and friend. Thank you to Stephanie's colleagues at Levine Greenberg Rostan, especially Jim Levine and Daniel Greenberg. And huge thanks to Courtney Paganelli as well.

I am grateful to my dazzling editor, Catherine Richards, for choosing to work with me. With clear eyes and terrific skill, she made this novel infinitely better. Our collaboration continues to be a blessing and a joy. And thank you also to Nettie Finn, for all of her support.

Thank you to Andrew Martin and Kelley Ragland, for believing in this book. To the remarkable Sarah Melnyk, for her excellent ideas and creativity. To Danielle Prielipp, for her enthusiasm. To Paul Hochman. To Chrisinda Lynch, as well as Kaitlin Severini and Justine Gardner. To David Rotstein, for designing a beautiful cover. Thank you to the entire phenomenal team at Minotaur Books and St. Martin's Publishing Group and their fabulous publisher, Jennifer Enderlin, who has been a great champion of this book. I am fortunate to be in their midst.

For her commitment to this book and her excellent notes, I am grateful to Jo Dickinson, my UK editor, and her talented colleagues at Hodder & Stoughton.

I cannot begin to express my gratitude to my magnificent friend Faith Salie. She is the angel who introduced me to Stephanie Kip Rostan.

Because I have the opportunity here and now, thank you, thank you, thank you to the magical Michelle Kroes, who opened doors to a television series, and all of her colleagues at CAA, especially Michelle Weiner and Arian Akbar. Thank you to Sam Esmail, Sarah Matte, Chad Hamilton, Andy Campagna, and Madison Cline for seeing the potential in this story.

I'm deeply indebted to my teacher and friend Helen Schulman for her direction and instruction and for telling me she believed this was a book. Thank you to another teacher and friend, Luis Jaramillo, for his excellent ideas and guidance. To John Freeman and Tiphanie Yanique, both of whom responded with enthusiasm to the first twenty pages.

To three amazing ladies: Dina Lee, KrisAnne Madaus, and Nicole Starczak—all of whom gave me constructive notes, again and again and again.

Thank you to the genius Anika Streitfeld, who taught me more than I can say and whose illuminating notes brought countless moments from my mind to the page.

To Michael Carlisle, for his mentorship and friendship.

I am grateful to my entire family—to all the Carters around the country, as well as the Holbrooks, Heaths, Wiesenthals, Cohens, Schonwalds, Carter-Weidenfelds, and Wellers.

To Ginna Carter, who is always my ally; to Jon Carter, Pamela Carter, Whendy Carter, Ellen Carter, Ali Marsh, Fred Weller, Eve Holbrook, and Claus Sørenson. To Hal Holbrook, who is rooting for me. To Joyce Cohen, a loyal friend. To Arthur Carter and Linda Carter, for their unending love and support.

And to my mother, Dixie Carter, who is with me in spirit.

I am ever so fortunate to have married into the Kempf family—Nancy and Don Kempf, Kathy and Donald Kempf, and Charlie Kempf, who is no longer with us—but especially Nancy Kempf, who treats me like her own daughter and hopes for my success, like she would for her own.

Thank you to Manfred Flynn Kuhnert for many years of education in art and images, story and structure. And for an invaluable friendship.

To Cara Natterson and Sherry Ross for guidance on medical questions. And to Karen Snyder, Larry Golfer, and William Lewis for guidance on photography questions. For helping me in big ways and small ways, directly and indirectly, thank you to Ilsa Brink, Fauzia Burke, Jake Carter, Juan Castillo, Ming Chen, Wah Chen, Ali Clark, Aleksandra Crapanzano, Hayden Goldblatt, Lydia Kris, Dylan Landis, Darya Mastronardi, Lisa Choi Owens, Steve Owens, Mo Rocca, Beowulf Sheehan, Drew Vinton, and Jaime Wolf.

The biggest thank-you of all goes to my husband and best friend, Steve Kempf, who has brought me so much happiness. Without him, I wouldn't have this book. Finally, I am grateful to Eleanor and Henry—the brightest joys of my life. You are everything.